To Nikki

Thanks for our

local author

Best wishes

Larry

Other Fiction by DL Fowler

Lincoln Raw—a biographical novel

Journey into the heart and mind of Abraham Lincoln

Lincoln's Diary—a novel

A young woman's determination to unbury secrets

Ripples

a novel

DL Fowler

Cover by C.A. Feeney

For additional information visit http://dlfowler.com

ISBN   97 8-0-9963805-0-8

Published in the United States by Harbor Hill Publishing

Dedication

To humanity:

How we treat each other matters—the effects will ripple across generations that follow.

Foreword

By A.E. Huppert

Not all wars are fought on foreign soil. Unfortunately, most are fought at home. It's easier to think of a stranger inflicting fear, coercion, and pain upon our children than it is to consider the possibility a family member, close friend, respected adult, or friendly neighbor might harm them. In Ripples, you'll meet two desperate, yet brave, young girls doing their best to survive such atrocities; hoping beyond hope that one day, they will escape. What they can't know is that, even if they escape, the terror will continue, as it has for millions of survivors of Post-Traumatic Stress (PTSD). Far too many children share the aftermath of traumatic experiences, even if the damage was inflicted differently than Amy and Mercedes.

These children and many more adult survivors also share a desire to transcend the evils perpetrated against them - to heal. With mental health, healthcare, and veteran systems broken and ineffective, what should be a natural, organic process of recovery and healing has become a very difficult thing to accomplish. Combine this with ill-informed public opinion and our discomfort over addressing head-on the reality of sexual predators living within our society, and it's no wonder suicide rates for children and adults are skyrocketing.

Is this information new to you?

Gavin DeBecker, is the nation's foremost expert on the prediction and management of violence. He comments about society's tendency to turn away from this harsh reality in his foreword to Predators: Pedophiles, Rapists, & Other Sex Offenders - Who They Are, How They Operate, and How We Can Protect Ourselves and Our Children (Salter, 2003):

"You're so right," they say: "Sexual abuse is an enormous problem, particularly for young teens. Thank God mine aren't there yet."

No, sorry, says reality, the most common age at which sexual abuse begins is three.

"Well sure, if you have homosexuals around small children, there's a risk."

No, sorry, says reality, most sexual abuse is committed by heterosexual males.

"Yeah, but that kind of pervert isn't living in our neighborhood."

Sorry, says reality, but that kind of pervert is living in your neighborhood. The Department of Justice estimates that on average, there is one child molester per square mile in the United States.

"Well, at least the police know who these people are."

Not likely, says reality, since the average child molester victimizes between 50 and 150 children before he is ever arrested (and many more after he is arrested).

"Well, there's nothing you can do about it anyway ... kids are resilient. When bad things happen, they bounce back."

Absolutely not, says reality. Children do not bounce back. They adjust, they conceal, they repress, and sometimes they accept and move on, but they don't bounce back.

Can you begin to embrace the reality of the damage done to tender bodies, minds and spirits? Do you have the compassion to hope that these children, many of whom are now adults, can find a pathway to reclaim the innocence, beauty and strength of a life that was intended for them from the beginning? It seems impossible. However, the drive to survive eventually brings all victims face-to-face with a choice: When the pain of who we are becomes greater than the pain of becoming who we need to be, just one small ounce of willingness to know the truth - about our past, about who we were meant to become, about how we are perpetuating the abuse - is all it takes. Healing begins.

The happy side of the truth? Healing is possible.

I know.

I was one of these children.

Meet me at the end of Ripples, and I'll show you where healing begins.

AE Huppert

Ripples

No man is an island,
Entire of itself,
Every man is a piece of the continent,
A part of the main.
If a clod be washed away by the sea,
Europe is the less.
As well as if a promontory were.
As well as if a manor of thy friend's
Or of thine own were:
Any man's death diminishes me,
Because I am involved in mankind,
And therefore never send to know for whom the bell
tolls;
It tolls for thee.

John Donne (1624)

Chapter One

Amy

Bryce's old chain ... he locked it on my ankle when I was little ... kept me from wandering. The chaparral around us ... full of snakes and coyotes ... other things that kill. Long time ago people got stuck in the snow on a big mountain. Ate each other. Mountains and chaparral aren't all that's creepy. Two summers ago, Bryce said I was fourteen. No one ever told me my age before. That's the first time he touched me under my clothes. Now he makes me take them off.

When I was little, I cried all the time. Had nightmares. Wanted somebody to come take me home. There was another girl, then, but she ran off. Wish she'd taken me. Still have nightmares and cry ... mostly when Bryce touches me.

At least I'm not chained up anymore.

I stub my toe ... drop a stick of firewood. Got it off a dried out Manzanita bush by the side of the gravel road— goes along the edge of the woods ... past the lake ... out to a highway. They don't know I wander so far from the shack.

Kneel to pick up the stick. Next to my foot … the flattest, smoothest stone ever. Set down the whole bundle—twigs snapped off low-hanging pine branches … pieces of sun-bleached scrub and whatnot. Scoop up the rock … tuck it in the palm of my hand.

Rounded edges'll make for a good bounce. Roll it between my thumb and forefinger … eye the lake's smooth surface. Stand … push loose hair behind my ear. Whip a side-arm toss. Four… no five skips. Keep hoping for more.

Rings spread out across the lake … a man's fishing from his shiny dock. He's gotta be bigger than Bryce. He's the only one who lives up here … not counting Bryce and Tess and me. Squint. He's a long way off. Bryce says it's two-hundred yards. Wonder if he's spying on me like I am on him.

How far do ripples go?

Igor and The Witch are names I call Bryce and Tess behind their backs. Don't know how I got those names … always been rattling around in my head. Lots of voices up there. Don't know whose they are. Some sound like ghosts. Others yell … make it so I can't think. Sometimes a small voice screams, "No … no. Don't make me …."

Once, a bunch of screechy voices went off in my head … must have been a hundred of them all at once … I hunched up in the corner by the iron stove. Kept banging my head on the wall … trying to make them stop. Tess saw me… told Bryce. He said, "You're lucky to have a home at all. We tried to give you back to your family. No one wanted you. We could've just put you out to fend for yourself. Who knows what would've happened? You'd probably be dead."

That other girl … she taught me skipping stones … reading … other stuff. She went to school … not me. Bryce said school was a waste … Tess said her girl wasn't going to grow up stupid. The other girl got cake on her birthday. Tess always let me have a piece … even though I am the cause of all her troubles. Bryce would yell at her … say I didn't need no cake. We got candy, too. Bryce didn't know about that. Tess still buys me candy when she takes me to town … we always hurry back so Bryce doesn't get mad.

I like bright red, crinkly candy wrappers—you can look through them. Changes things. I save the wrappers … hide them.

Bryce takes me to town some nights. When I was small I crawled through people's 'doggie doors' and let him in. If no doggie door, the other girl could unlock doors. Now that she's gone, I sneak through windows if they're not locked … hand things out to him. Have to be real quiet.

Bryce says coyotes ate her … or mountain lions. Says there's lots of ways girls can die out there. A prison's not far away where they keep murderers. Sometimes murderers get loose and hole up in the hills. One murderer drove a big truck and snatched girls out on the highway. It's the truth. It was in one of Tess's books. Tess says a truck driver might've got the other girl. Don't like to think about her … get a lump in my throat.

Before the man built his huge cabin, nobody ever came here. Bryce says to stay away from strangers … especially that one. If he ever catches me down at the lake spying … he'll put me back on that rusty old chain. Some nights when Bryce passes out dead drunk … Tess dozes off … can't help myself. I sneak down to the lake and kneel in brush. The man's got lots of lanterns … must have. All those windows … bunch of rooms. You could get lost in a place that big … like in the chaparral. Bryce says the man's cabin is too big … too close … if you're gonna have a palace a couple hundred yards from your front door, might as well move to a city. Tess laughs … tells him it's not like the neighbor can see our shack, with all the trees between us and the lake.

When the cabin was getting built, I'd take extra time gathering firewood, so I could watch. Huge machines dug up dirt … loaded it onto trucks … carried it off somewhere. More trucks with giant barrels came … dumped grey mud where the dirt used to be. The mud got hard … like the granite slab here at the cove where I throw rocks. The man's slab has straight edges … corners. Bryce called it concrete … a foundation. Other trucks came … piled up with boards.

I scrounge for another rock to skip on the lake … the perfect one. If it's flat and smooth, I could get six … maybe seven skips … eight would be the best ever. Bend down to pick up a real good one. An ant crawls up on it. I stomp the thing.

Stupid ant. Damn. *Was* the perfect rock … now it won't do … stained.

Pick up the firewood—stare at the crushed ant. Sorry, little ant. Didn't mean to hurt you. Don't know why ….

Want to search for another rock. No, already gone too long. Better head back or there'll be hell to pay.

When I get back to the shack, I stop … stare. It's tiny … just one window … one door. Tess bitches about its sagging roof. Keeps out the rain … wind … but not the biting cold in winter. Cold isn't all that bites … and there's worse people than Bryce and Tess … family who don't want you … truck drivers who murder. I get the shakes … go inside … arms full of kindling.

Tess gives me the evil eye.

Bryce is sitting at the table. "Took you long enough."

Keep my head down. "Sorry, sir—"

I scoot to a stack of firewood next to the iron stove under the window. Peek back at Bryce. He's watching me. My skin crawls.

"Burnt my hand on that damn stove. Been waiting for you. Need you to rub some honey on it."

"Yes, sir." I drop the load of wood on top of the stack ... hurry over to the cupboard for the honey jar and kneel beside him.

I lather his burn with honey.

He says, "This girl's got a touch like an angel."

Tess grunts.

Bryce strokes my head. "Tonight will be a bath night. You hear? After you finish your chores."

"Yes, sir." I go back to the pile ... straighten it ... grab a broom I made from branches. Start to sweep.

Baths don't make you clean. Sweeping won't be good enough, either. Tess'll finger the seams in the wood floor. Find a spot of dust to bitch about. Bryce'll yell, "No dinner for her." He'll take it back, though. He likes a spunky girl ... a full belly ... fresh, young skin.

Later, Bryce climbs the ladder to my mattress ... breathing heavy when he leans over me. Shut my eyes think of fairy tales. Where do those stories come from? They're stuck up in my head.

He mutters something like, "A good little pet never leaves her master."

I think about ripples spreading across the lake. Does the man on his shiny dock see them, too?

When Bryce leaves ... I don't sleep. His pukey breath stays behind. Take out the candy wrappers ... keep them in a knothole in the wall. You think they're brown ... lantern from the kitchen down below makes them that way. Keep staring at them … they get red … brighter and brighter … redder and redder. Hold up one up to my eye. Makes everything seem … far away … like nothing's real. Tuck the wrappers back in the knothole. Hunch up on the mattress … cry into the stinky pillow so they don't hear me. Want the aching to stop. Never does.

Jacob

Today's fishing was a waste. Not even a nibble. That girl throwing rocks probably scared off the fish—except a couple hundred yards away, the fish wouldn't notice. Besides, she's done it ever since the footings on this place were poured a couple years ago. Some days I limit out, other times just catch a couple, once in a while I get skunked. Same as Wall Street.

Now, the question—Bourbon or beer? Jamesons is another possibility—on the second shelf next to the Bookers and Knob Creek. The top shelf stuff—Macallan 1926, Dalmore 62 Single Hiland Malt, and Glenfiddich 1937—stays untouched except when I want to make the point I can afford anything. Craft brews are more to my liking, anyway. Bourbon County's my favorite. But tonight I can't decide, so it's Irish Death, a foot in each world—dark ale aged with Jameson oak chips. My financial manager, Carl, says I'm a carnivore who lost his appetite for raw meat.

I snatch a bottle of Irish Death, grab my platinum church key, and pop off the top. Tilt the glass, pour, take a sip, and get comfortable on the loveseat facing a floor-to-ceiling, single pane window. Soon I focus on the image reflecting in the window—a sixty-something, bored former-

CEO loitering, as an elegant woman watches, or more correctly, a silver-framed photo of an elegant woman—my wife, Ellen. I'm supposed to be enjoying this place with her. She was still alive when we bought the property at a bargain price from a client—a trust out of San Francisco that was land rich and cash poor. It was the first time in our marriage I asked what she thought. She said I was 'profiteering' off a client's 'misfortune.' I called her a bleeding heart. Told her that's how you get ahead.

This was going to be the place where we could escape the past, cling to the last thing that really mattered—us. But she said it was too late. She withered up and died on me. Everyone else was already gone. My son, Jesse—who was supposed to inherit everything I built—and his wife ended their grief in a murder-suicide. I insisted they'd given up hope of ever finding their little girl Celine, our only grandchild. Ellen and my shrink disagreed. They wanted me to take the blame. Ellen went so far as to say I drove him to it. Jesse's death was the nail in her coffin. About the last thing she said to me was she could live with being married to 'a shell of a husband' who had a tight grip on everything except—his appetite for money, power, beautiful women. But losing her only son and granddaughter was more loneliness than she could bear.

I refuse to believe Celine is gone for good—she was four when she was kidnapped. That's been a dozen years, now. I don't care what experts say, she's got to be alive.

Before I know it, I've finished the full bottle of Irish Death, all the time gazing at the lake. Hoping to see … I don't know what. My eyelids grow heavy ….

A crack of thunder wakes me. The zing of ozone is unmistakable, and I taste smoke. The last thing anyone wants on a hot summer night in a bone-dry wilderness is to smell traces of fire. We had a wet spring and lots of new undergrowth. Now everything has dried out, leaving it a tinderbox waiting for the next lightning strike.

I stumble out to the redwood deck, scan the horizon and sniff. The scent of something burning is faint enough it could be coming from some distance away. With no glow visible from the deck, I head down to the dock. From that vantage, I can pan a full 360 degrees. Across the narrowest part of the lake, a wisp of smoke catches the pale moonlight. Behind the stand of trees along that shore is the only other residence within miles. It's just a shack, hardly habitable from what the surveyors told me.

A larger column of smoke would be something to worry about. No one would have a roaring fire this time of year. Likely, the girl and her family are doing some late night cooking or boiling water for a bath. I can afford propane, but apparently to them it's a luxury they can't. I've never seen the propane truck venture to their side of the lake.

I brush one hand through my hair, little of it as there is, and head to bed, yawning. As I step across the threshold, there's that sound again. Moaning. Plaintive crying. Almost human. Probably just sounds of the night from deep in the woods. I close the door. This would be a good night to get a reprieve from the nightmare that won't let go of me.

Tess

Bryce yanks off the blanket and collapses next to me on the bed. Beer-breath and the smell of semen mixed with sweat send a clear message—he's in that frame of mind. Of course, I already know that from all the banging around he's been doing up there in the loft. When he's done with her I'm always next.

He rolls over and murmurs, "I'm all warmed up ... ready for the kind of lovin' only a real woman can give me."

Don't care if it's a lie. At least he still has an appetite for me. When he started paying attention to the girls a couple years ago, I figured my days were numbered. It's not like it was in the beginning. I had a tight body, perky tits, and flat belly. Not to mention, skin smooth as a baby's ass and no crows feet. Now I have to do whatever it takes to hang onto him. Bryce isn't the most man I've ever had, and he might leave a few marks on me now and then—but they're on the outside. The others hurt me on the inside.

I was shunned by the only family I knew existed, blackballed by a vindictive former boss, scratching for my baby's next meal. I was determined to keep the creep who got me pregnant—then dumped me—from ever being a part of my little girl's life. Mostly though, I was bitter about having no one or no place I belonged to. Still am.

I pull him on top of me, wrap my bare legs around him, brush his scratchy cheek with my lips, lick his ear. When he starts to get hard, I roll him onto his back, sit bare-assed on his stomach, and wriggle out of my shirt.

He smiles. "I like it when you do all the work. Shows me you want it."

I purr back, "I like what you like."

It has nothing to do with *liking*—it's about survival. You'd think he's all about control—has to know what I'm doing all the time, when I'll be back if I step out. Always has to be right, even when he's wrong. The real problem is his fragile ego. Bruise it a little and he goes ballistic. I stay away from that crap. But when I do screw up, I stroke it the best I know how.

I throw back my head and give the performance of my life—blocking out the truth that Teresa Armato has crashed all the way from a University of Chicago degree in economics, six-figure income, and Nob Hill apartment to living off the grid in a rickety shack in the middle of nowhere. A place even its owners couldn't care less about.

Guess I got what I deserved. A dozen years ago I picked a forty-something survivalist/conspiracy nut as my knight in shining armor. He'd never finished high school and was probably at the top of his career ladder—head grounds keeper for an estate that had all but depleted itself, doling out cash to a third generation of drug-addicted trust babies. Okay, I'll admit it ... he was pretty damn hot and so was the sex.

When he's satisfied, he pushes me off and stares at the ceiling. "Now that's why I keep you around."

I pull the blanket over me. "That, and you don't want me turning you in to the law."

His coal black eyes are even darker. "You haven't got the guts to turn me in. I'd hunt you down and kill you. 'Sides, they'd lock you up, too."

I climb back on top and plant a juicy kiss on his mouth, mostly to shut him up. He's right on the last count—being locked up doing twenty-five to life is one of my worst fears, but one day I'll get the chance to prove him wrong about having guts—when he least expects it.

I reach for his joy stick to prime it for another round, but he pushes me off and rolls over. Within a minute he's asleep.

Chapter Two

Amy

Still aching from Bryce ... no sleep. The kitchen window down below lets in light. That's how I know it's morning. Grab fresh clothes ... slip down the ladder. Bryce and Tess asleep. He beds her after he's done with me. Don't know how she can like it when he touches her. When he comes into me ... wish I was dead. Why can't he just fall off the damn ladder one of these times ... break his neck?

I close the door behind me ... nice and easy so it doesn't make noise. Tiptoe through the pine trees between the shack and the water ... pick up pieces of kindling along the way. The mist on the lake ... so thick, hard to see through it. Have to squint to see the man's cabin ... not a single lantern lit ... must be asleep. Peek over my shoulder ... hold my breath ... Bryce might've followed me.

Good ... he's not there.

Take off the sweatshirt I sleep in ... slide into the dark water. Goose bumps crawl over me. I shiver. Bryce says the water's a good place to get away from killer snakes. Says if you see one, get to the water … but don't move too fast. Snakes give me the willies. Slithering … scaly … beady eyes. Bryce's eyes are beady.

Try to rub off the goose bumps. Slide my hands down to my belly and stop. Swallow salty tears. Reach all the way down. Both hands churn … like I'm scrubbing laundry on a washboard. Rub harder… faster. Fingers ache … soreness down there gets worse. Washing won't get rid of Bryce. Never does. Drop to my knees … tears roll down my cheeks … bite my lip … can't let them hear me.

Once I stop crying I get up … wade back to shore … get dressed. But even in fresh clothes … I'm still dirty ….

On the way back, I snap off Manzanita branches … some dead, low hanging limbs. Break 'em down … add 'em to my stack. It'll please Bryce to see chores getting done this early. The firewood'll hide my damp clothes … maybe he won't notice the wet hair. If he does … there'll be hell to pay.

I slip back inside … peek around. Bryce isn't up yet, but Tess snaps at me. "You and me, we're headed to town. Need to pick up some things while Bryce's catching up on his beauty sleep. Better make it snappy. You know how he gets if we're gone too long."

"Yes, ma'am. Will he want breakfast?"

"After all his drinking last night? Don't bother. Just stoke the fire and set up the coffee pot. But be quick. The faster we get going, the sooner we get back."

I shove a log and some sticks into the stove. Puff on the coals until the flames start up. Barely catch my breath before Tess growls, "Don't take all day. I'll be out in the pickup."

Bryce

Damn woman. Wakes me up racing that stupid pickup engine. She makes enough noise she could raise the dead. When's she gonna figure out how to start the thing up right. Shit. It's only 8:20 in the goddamn morning. She and the girl better be back by 9:30. Go straight there. Do their business. Come straight home.

I roll over. Shit. Everything aches, and my gut's doin' flips. Last night's dinner's backin' up into my throat, about to make me puke. If I can't get back to sleep, I'll give her what for when she gets back. Hell, now I gotta piss.

Jump outta bed and run outside to take a leak. When I'm done, I come back in and stumble over to the stove. Pour a mug of coffee. Those whores didn't leave me any damn breakfast? Shit. What'm I gonna do with them good for nothin' bitches?

Turn around and shut my eyes. Fuckin' headache. Damn head's gonna explode.

Snatch a piece of stale bread off the table, guzzle down the coffee, tromp off to bed.

Amy

Bryce says it's less than twenty miles to town ... no reason it should take more than half an hour. The road winds like a snake ... both sides covered with big, bushy trees. Tess calls them live oaks. Thick branches hanging over the road. Not many cars ... but sometimes you get stuck behind a semi. Tess says they low-gear it down the mountain. Hold up traffic.

Like now.

She honks. "What's wrong with him? Thinks he owns the whole road. We just passed a frickin' turn out."

"He … he can't hear—"

"Shut up. Bryce isn't going to be happy if …."

Tess jerks the steering wheel left and presses her right foot all the way down.

God—she's trying to pass it. Wanna scream … *maybe he's a murderer*.

The pickup makes a whiney sound. Tess stares straight ahead … knuckles same color as cold ashes. I peek out the back window at a cloud of white smoke.

Tess gains on the rig … a big black car barrels around the curve below … it's headed straight at us. Can she make it around the truck? My fingers dig into the seat. She tries to make the pickup go faster. I wanna yell … *stop*. But the word gets stuck in my throat. Shove my hand in my pocket. Feel for one of my crinkly red candy wrappers. Not there.

Now, the pickup's nose-to-nose with the rig. I stare up at the trucker. His face is twisted … big round eyes. He can't be a murderer … they don't get scared.

A loud clatter from the semi … wheezing … screeching. The trucker's going slower. The black car … horn's blaring … swerves to the side of the road … kicks up a cloud of dust.

Tess yanks the pickup hard right … cuts in front of the rig … a loud clunk. The pickup jerks … rocks … skids sideways. Tess straightens it out … back in the right lane.

I look out the rear window. The semi's tires are smoking, its trailer's swinging around, stretching all the way across the road, tipping. Shut my eyes … cover my ears. No … it's not real.

Candy wrappers—wish I had one. Bright red, crinkly candy wrapper.

Jacob

I kick off the sheets and sit up. Damn. No fishing this morning. I have to go to town to restock the pantry and fridge. Someone keeps raiding them.

The first thing that went missing was a shotgun I had set out for the excavation crew—in case coyotes started hanging around. I figured one of the guys just helped himself to it.

Next there was some small scale pilfering—food from the outdoor kitchen's mini-fridge. The outdoor kitchen went in just after they poured the cabin's foundation. It was nice to have a place to fix hot meals for the crews. When the world knows you're worth billions, it's smart to throw out a few scraps, give away a little. Otherwise, some wise guy will come along and decide he's justified in helping himself.

Once the cabin was finished, I moved the food inside. The sneaky bastard struck whenever I wasn't around, and it wasn't just food. A few paperbacks disappeared from my library. That's when I ruled out the guys on the construction crew. Whoever it was, they had time on their hands to hang around and watch me.

A padlock on the fridge didn't stop the thief. Of course, that's not the reason for the lock; it was just a test, a kind of game. To be the best you have to beat the best. I had to find out—just how good is this bandit? So, I set out some bait— a crossbow and arrows perched on the top shelf in my office.

Got the contraption as a white elephant gift at a company party—a tasteless joke by a jerk securities trader named Conroy. I eventually canned him; the sleaze-bag couldn't tell the difference between psychological warfare and the physical kind. Even though the gag-gift was expensive, no one dared take it from me on their turn to claim any gift they wanted. Survival rule number one— never challenge the boss. The gift I didn't want became a trophy—a symbol of power.

Within a week of setting out the crossbow and quiver full of arrows in plain sight, the bandit relieved me of the damned things. I stepped up my game by installing deadbolts. He countered by slipping in at night—while I was asleep. I can only imagine how much bigger my war chest would be if my staff had been as bold and resourceful as this bandit.

Anyway, these trips to town have to get done early. Too many people around later in the day.

Just as I settle into the driver's seat of the Jeep Rubicon, my cell phone rings. I glance at the screen—it's the latest private investigator I hired. One of the few calls I'll take. Most go straight to voicemail.

"Talk to me."

"Good morning, Mr. Chandler."

"What's up?"

"Now, don't get excited. I might have a new lead. Of course, it could be a dead-end like all the others. I'm just giving you a heads-up like you've said."

"Okay, but let me manage my own expectations."

"We turned up a report—had gotten buried in a local sheriff's files. Apparently, around the time Celine went missing, there was a suspicious acting couple panhandling for gas money at a truck stop near Yreka—they had two little girls. One fit your granddaughter's description."

The photo of Celine I keep in the dashboard tray stares up at me. "She didn't go missing. She was kidnapped."

"Mr. Chandler, we're doing everything we can. Hopefully, the trail isn't so cold we won't be able to track her down."

"Is that all you have?"

"Oh, there is one more thing. Just got an updated sketch of what she would look like today. Should I send over a copy?"

"I've told you before, I don't want to imprint some artist's rendering on my brain. It could be all wrong. Besides, I don't need drawings. I'll recognize her when I see her. Anything else?"

"You'll know what I know, when I know it."

"Fine ... and, Sam?"

"Yes?"

"Thanks."

"No problem."

The Jeep engine hums for several minutes as I study Celine's picture, pinching it between my thumb and forefinger. A lump forms in my throat as I replay the day she slipped away from me. Before that happened, I'd always been the one in control, dishing out the consequences; never suffered even a twinge of pain or guilt, no matter how much it cost anybody. I slide the picture back into its place and head to town.

Halfway down the mountain, cars are lined up behind the wreckage of a jackknifed semi. It's splayed across the highway, blocking both shoulders. There is only enough clearance on the uphill side to walk along the edge of an embankment that's thick with live oak trees and scrub. Live oaks get so dense you could lose a bicycle in them. As kids, when someone's bike went missing, we'd always check the trees to see if it was hidden up there as a prank.

I park, jump out, and head for two men who are climbing down from atop the tractor that has flipped over on its side.

"Is he okay?" I ask.

One of the men shakes his head.

The force of the tractor slamming onto the pavement must have hammered the driver's head against the doorframe or the pavement, killing him.

Near the downhill end of the trailer, another man's consoling two women. One woman is clutching her forehead. The other is bent over, head buried in both hands, shoulders convulsing.

"Has anyone called for help?" I call out.

The man turns to me. "911 operator said the nearest unit was almost half-hour out when we called it in. They're due any minute."

On the other side of the trailer, a black Yukon is crumpled like an accordion, its hood buried in hemorrhaging cargo. The driver had no choice—it was either crashing into the jackknifed trailer or the trees. The result would have been the same—occupants compacted into the interior. Crimson-stained shards crunch under my feet as I edge closer to get a better look.

I turn, stare downhill—sirens, flashing lights. EMT. Fire engine. Sheriff's cruiser. They're too late, always too late.

I look away. Something's up in the trees ... pink ... a shoe ... a small body tangled in the branches.

Celine's image pops into my head. She's on the ground cowering. Now she's gone. A sharp pain starts behind my ear, arcs to the top my head—again and again—like a short circuit. My breakfast backs up. I bend over and throw up. Everything starts spinning.

Chapter Three

Amy

In town, a building—windows covered with boards ... doors chained and locked. Tess parks the pickup behind it. Doesn't want people to see the truck—not 'registered' ... or something.

Before we get out, she tells me the rules. Stay close. Don't talk to strangers. She says the rules again while we're walking to the store. This time she adds a new one ... keep my mouth shut about passing the truck up on the highway. Must not want anybody to know she was mean ... scared the truck driver.

In the store she buys beer, ice and cigarettes—gets me candy in a red wrapper. Not supposed to tell Bryce I got candy. When she's paying for the stuff a woman comes up behind me. Her little girl says, "Hi. My name's Alexis."

Shuffle my feet.

"What's your name?" she asks.

Tess grabs my arm.

"Mommy, why won't she talk?"

The woman whispers to the kid, but I can hear. "Honey, some children can't talk."

"Mommy, why can't she talk?"

Tess lets go of my arm … digs into her pockets for money.

Wanna say to the little girl it's the rules. You're not supposed to talk to strangers. They can hurt. The woman tells her, "Some children are born that way. But sometimes people get hurt real bad or get very sick and aren't able to talk anymore."

I stare at the girl. My stomach twists in knots. Wanna tell her nothing's wrong with me. "I … I…."

Tess yanks me. "We better get up the hill. Bryce'll be pissed."

Wanna say to Tess, we're out of food. Need to get food. But she'll thump me on the head. So, I keep quiet.

Outside, Tess looks around to be sure no one's watching … pushes me into the alley … pins me against the side of the store … her eyes dark … teeth clenched. "Do I have to watch you every second? You know the rules. What the hell are you doing talking to strangers?" She bites her lip. "You want to go back on that chain? If Bryce hears about this you're going to. You should thank your lucky stars I'm not telling him—not this time, anyway."

We walk to the pickup. I take a lick of my candy, wrap it back up, stuff it in my pocket. Don't know why the woman said something's wrong with me. Why doesn't her girl follow the rules?

Headed back up the mountain, I'm still trying to figure out why the girl broke the rules. Tess stomps down on the brakes. Traffic's stopped.

She turns off the motor. "Hell, all I need is for some cop to come by and see my expired plates. No license—no insurance."

No idea what she's talking about.

Tess grips the steering wheel like she wants to rip it off. "We gotta let Bryce know I'm stuck behind a wreck. Damn trucker turned over his rig, sprawled across the highway."

Is it the truck driver Tess scared? Shut my eyes. Pound on my head ... both hands ... over and over. Don't wanna think about it. Reach in my pocket. Feel the candy in its crinkly, red wrapper. I turn ... look at her.

She stares straight ahead. "If you start hoofing it right now and don't dog it, you can be back up the mountain in maybe three, four hours—just in case I'm stuck down here forever. Tell Bryce there's a wreck and I can't get through. I'll have to go back and get more ice. It'll all be melted if I have to sit here half a day."

My heart jumps. He'll be pissed no matter what. Everything's always my fault.

"If they clear this thing up sooner, I'll pick you up on my way. Remember the rules. Don't talk to anyone. And don't tell Bryce about the damn truck driver. It's the guy's own fault. Didn't pull over when he should've. Blocking traffic— it's just not right. Besides, what kind of a trucker can't keep his rig upright. Sheesh."

A car's honking in my head ... wanna tell it to stop.

I get out of the pickup ... try not to make any noise ... see a big black car up ahead ... smashed into the trailer. A woman's holding her forehead. Another bent over, hands covering her face. A man talking to them.

I walk along the ditch past the black car. Something crunches under my feet. Pieces of glass—dark red, slippery.

Try to keep away from crunching glass ... stay close to the big bushy trees. Hope no one sees me. Sirens blare. Cover my ears.

Something wet drips on my head. I stop. Look up. Maybe a bird crapped. Trees are thick with branches, leaves. Reminds me of ripples covering the lake.

Don't see any birds, but there's a pink shoe up in the tree. A kid ... one leg swung over a branch ... no foot. Watch a drop ... red ... hurts my eyes ... lands near my feet. I yank the candy out of my pocket ... tear off its crinkly red wrapper ... throw the candy away ... hold the wrapper up to my eye ... study the kid in the tree. Could be a girl ... curly hair ... face all bloody—like when Tess guts Bryce's deer, rabbits, and stuff. My stomach gurgles. Throat tightens. Things start spinning. Say to myself ... this isn't real.

In front of me a man stops ... drops to his knees. I peek around the candy wrapper. He's puking. Straightens up. Doesn't see me. He runs uphill, away from the wreck.

I better keep moving. Tess'll make trouble if I'm still here when she comes by. She's a snitch—even makes stuff up. Told me she once had a rich boyfriend ... good job. How'd she wind up with a creep like Bryce? It doesn't matter that she lies ... Bryce believes her. He shouldn't, though.

Above the wreck ... cars headed down the mountain, stopped ... more people hanging around. I walk faster. Someone might try talking to me. One of the cars turns around, comes right at me. I jump out of the way. Tumble into the ditch. Land in a heap.

Roll over ... up on the road a shiny red car—stopped. Dark windows. Can't see inside. Reach in my pocket ... candy wrapper is still there.

The window comes down. I look down. Don't want them to see me.

A man inside says, "Jeez, I'm sorry. Are you all right?"

Maybe if I don't look at him he'll stop seeing me. Wanna shrink as small as an ant.

The car door opens. The man climbs out, stumbles down the ditch. Kneels next to me. "I'm really sorry. Are you hurt?"

Knee hurts bad ... I rub it.

Man reaches for my knee.

Hunch up in a ball.

He backs off ... holds his hands up. "Sorry, I won't hurt you. Sure you're okay?"

I start to get up.

He takes my arm. "Here, let me help you."

Jerk away. Leg hurts worse. Stand on it just the same.

"Honest, I'm just trying to help." He steps back. "Haven't I seen you before?"

Look away.

"Aren't you the kid who lives across the lake from me? You like to skip rocks."

"No."

"Really? I could swear you could be her twin."

I shrug.

"Say, were you in that wreck down there?"

Shake my head.

"Where do you live? I should take you home, to your parents."

"That's okay. I can get home myself."

Can't he stop talking?

"I should get you to your family so they can be sure you're okay."

Knee aches ... wants to fold up under me.

"Please. I won't bite."

Bryce bites.

"It won't be any trouble, really. I've got the time."

People are watching. Somebody might tell on me. Take a step. A sharp pain. Shut my eyes.

He takes my arm. Steadies me. "Here, let me give you a ride."

"No. I'll be okay. Just have to rest a minute."

He nudges me toward his car. "I insist. After all, it's my fault."

No, it's *her* fault.

He opens the car door.

I'll never make it to the shack ... look downhill to see if Tess is coming. I get in.

He climbs in the other side and points to a picture sitting in a tray between us. "I have a granddaughter. I'm not going to hurt you. Just want you to get home safe."

I peek at the picture. A little girl ... happy ... lucky girl. I remember the little girl who didn't have to follow the rules ... the woman who thought something was wrong with me. Think about the girl in the tree. No. She wasn't real. Feel for my candy wrapper. Look back at the little girl's picture. "Is she really yours?"

"Yes, she's really mine, but someone took her. Which is a good reason you shouldn't be out here all by yourself."

Truck drivers snatch girls off the highway. Bet the trucker Tess scared isn't that way.

"By the way," he says, "you haven't told me where you live."

I don't look at him. Point. "Up ahead."

He says, "Mind buckling up?"

Keep staring straight ahead. It's hot in here.

He stops the car. "Sure you're okay?"

"Yes, sir." Cross my arms. Are Bryce's marks showing?

He raises his voice. "You need to buckle up."

My chin quivers. "How does it work?"

"Here." He reaches across me.

My body stiffens. The seat belt clicks. I flinch.

He says, "This is how you undo it when we get you home." He pushes a button on the buckle. The belt clicks again and comes undone.

I take a deep breath.

"Have you walked all the way from town?"

"No."

"How far have you been walking?"

"Not far. Tess had to stop for the wreck. Said, 'get out and walk home.'"

"Tess your mother?"

"No. No mother."

"How about your father?"

Fish in my pocket for the candy wrapper—still there.

"How far up the road do you live?"

"A ways."

"She made you get out and walk the whole way? Who is she anyway—a relative?"

"No family."

He sighs. "I don't have a family, either."

I peek over at him.

"You'll have to let me know when we get near where you live."

No more talking 'til we get to a turnoff ... a little ways before the road to the lake. I point to the side of the road. "Let me off here."

He pulls the car over.

"You sure? I can take you all the way home. I really should talk to someone."

"Knee's fine now." I undo the seatbelt ... fling open the door and jump out. Take a couple steps to show him I'm okay. He smiles and waves goodbye. He's right ... he didn't bite.

I cross the highway and keep watching until the shiny red car disappears. When he's out of sight I limp up to the lake turnoff. As I sneak past the man's cabin I wonder if the girl in his picture has to follow the rules. Once I'm around the bend, I sit on a stump by the road and put my hands over my face.

I still see the big black car ... crushed into the semi's trailer, as if I was standing next to it. Bloody windows ... glass shattered all over the ground ... crunching when I step on it. Blood dripping. The girl up in a tree. My stomach twists in knots ... head spins ... drop to my knees ... puke all over the ground. Lie down and roll on my side ... tuck into a ball ... try not to crap in my pants. Ground's damp, cool ... smells like rotting logs. I look up ... can't see the sky ... trees block the sun. Thank god there's nobody up in those branches.

Close my eyes again ... sleepy ... imagine ripples spreading out across the lake ... taste candy from crinkly red wrappers.

Bryce

Five more minutes gone by. Where the hell are they? Had to get my own damn breakfast. Now it's gonna be lunchtime. Even have to stoke my own fire.

Slam the damn stove hatch, stand and stare out the window. Hour and a half, max. That's all it should take. I grit my teeth, take out my pocket knife, open a can of chili. Set the can on top of the stove and watch it. How the hell long does it take this shit to boil? Jab at it with my knife.

Now, where's the damn bread? I've told them a thousand times, "I gotta have bread with my damn chili."

I stomp over to a box of food and kick it over. Pick it up and empty it on the floor. Hell! Damn bread's on the bottom, smushed. Shit. That bitch knows you don't stack stuff on top of bread. When she gets back, it's gonna get done right.

Need a damn beer. Yank the top off the ice chest—the damn ice is all melted. Two beers left. They better get some ice and beer down in town, or I'm gonna give ....

A long swig does nothin' to calm my nerves. Pace back and forth. Stop at the window each time I pass it. Hate staring out a damn window, waiting for women to come home—useless whores, every one of them. Make a fist and punch the palm of my other hand. They's gonna be sorry.

I plop down in a chair, take another swig. Slam my hand on the table. Damn can's empty. When I head over for the other beer I stop to look out the window. Won't let myself do it this time. Not gonna look out that damn window again. Hope they drive the damn pickup into a ravine and bake to death in the hot sun. And when they do, I ain't goin' looking for them.

Amy

I bolt up—crawl backwards. Bryce's bony hands all over me. I look around ... he's not here.

Don't know how long I've been out. My stomach knots up again. If Bryce sees me sitting here by the side of the road, he'll be on the warpath. I get up … follow a narrow trail down to the cove … my favorite place for skipping stones. Go there because it can't be seen from the shack … lots of smooth, flat stones.

At the cove, I splash water on my face, dry off with my shirt. My knee's stopped hurting. My first stone toss is a dud. Plops straight to the bottom. The next one, three skips. Third try's a charm—eight skips. I pump my fists and spin around. Have to bite down on my lip to keep from squealing. Eight rings of tiny waves head out across the lake. Best ever.

Uh oh. The man's standing on his shiny dock, staring through binoculars—straight at me. I drop to the ground … crawl for cover. Please don't make a ruckus. Bryce'll hear.

Haven't gone far … I freeze. Can't breathe. Snake— black and tan, wagging its tongue. The deadly kind Bryce always warns about. Coiled on the granite slab.

Wanna run. Can't move. Can't get to the water. The snake rattles its tail faster, louder. Jerks its head from side to side … tongue licking the air. Bryce says snakes can taste fear. Will bite if you're afraid. Hope its bite won't hurt as much as Bryce's.

Tires crunch out on the gravel road. Oh my god! Tess is already back. Bryce is gonna kill me for sure. She skids to a stop. My heart pounding … can feel it in my ears. How does she know I'm here? Please … go away … don't spook the snake … it'll bite.

She's crashing through brush. Start to close my eyes … can't. Brace for snake's bite. It drops its head … unwinds … it's running away.

I leap up, spin around, scramble for the water. Turn, run hard along the shore ... stumble into the brush ... catch my breath ... wait.

Jacob

There she is, skipping rocks. I'd bet good money it's the same girl. I grab my 20X binoculars.

Damn. It is her—same girl I almost ran over with my Jeep. Why'd she lie, and why is she down on the ground crawling? And what the hell is that? A small brown pile on a sun-bleached granite slab. God, is that a rattler? Shit, it is. I jump in the Jeep. Probably won't get there before the snake strikes, but I *will* keep her from dying. I reach under the driver's seat for the first aid kit. It's there. I punch the gas hard after turning out of my drive onto the gravel road.

Just around a bend I spot a game trail leading to the water. Slam on the brakes. I grab a shovel from back of the Jeep and storm through the brush, hoping to God I'm not too late and I'm at the right spot. With those binoculars, I'm sure what I saw was a Northern Pacific Rattler coiled up and ready to strike. Their venom can kill you.

At the water, I stop dead, looking in every direction. No girl. No snake. But there's the granite slab—this has to be the place. I examine the spot where the snake had been.

Celine's image pops into my head. She's on the ground cowering. Now she's gone. A pain stabs at the base of my skull and arcs to the top of my head. I drop the shovel and tumble to my knees. Sweat oozes from every pore. It's happening again. I groan—please, no .... Everything goes black.

Amy

I peek through the bushes ... duck back down. Too quiet. Makes no sense. Tess should be hollering her head off. She came crashing through the brush. Where'd she go? Maybe the road? That's it. She snuck out to the road to wait for me. There's gotta be a way out of this.

I know. I'll crawl along the shore without making much noise. Cut back to the road without being seen. Walk up to the shack just like I was supposed to. If Tess asks how come she didn't see me on the highway, I'll say ... must've been peeing in the woods when she came past.

There's a low moan. I stop and listen. It's coming from the cove. I crouch down. God, did the rattler get her? Wait ... that's not Tess. Moaning's too low. Not Bryce either. He makes a whistling sound when he snores. I sneak up closer, keeping my head down. After a couple minutes, the moans stop. Tiny hairs on my arms and neck stand up. It's a trap.

I peek over the brush. A man's lying on his side in the cove. Can't see the face, but he's bigger than Bryce. And his clothes ... same as the man in the shiny red car.

It's the neighbor. There's a shovel on the ground next to him. Did Bryce sneak down here and knock him out? Is he still around? No, wait. That's not Bryce's old shovel. Gotta be the man's. Bryce wouldn't hide. He'd stomp around, cussing. Yelling.

I keep low ... on hands and knees ... creep through the brush to the man's side. Study him. His chest rises and falls, but only a little. He's breathing. Have to leave him here. Too heavy to carry. He'll wake up and be all right—I hope.

I start to pick up the shovel. No. He might need it to help him get back to his car.

Oh … the car. Must've been him who skidded to a stop on the gravel road … thought it was Tess. It wasn't. His car is out there in plain sight. If Tess sees it when she gets back, she'll snitch, and that's trouble. Bryce can't know the neighbor's been this close.

I sneak out to the road … the motor's running. Gotta get the car back to his cabin. Peek around … start to open the driver's door … there's a noise in the trees. I hold my breath, spin around, scan the woods.

Is it Bryce?

A gust rustles some branches. I let out my breath. Not Bryce.

I pull open the door and jump in. Gotta think this over. Tess moves this stick thing to get going. I pull the stick all the way back. Whoa, the car jerks. Hold my breath and slide my right foot onto a long pedal. Press down easy. The car starts rolling. Grip the wheel real tight, turn it hard to the left, and press down easy with my right foot. My shoulders are all knotted up, knuckles ache.

When I park in front of the man's cabin, the knots in my shoulders go away. I stare at the picture of the little girl. It's sitting in a tray … begs me to pick it up. I hold it … touch her cheek with my finger. I know that face. What would it be like to be happy like her? Tears trickle down my cheeks.

I wipe my eyes and put the picture back in the tray … climb out of the car and close the door. After taking a deep breath, I gawk at the cabin. A voice in my head says, "Go inside." Another screams, "Don't go." I cover my ears 'til they go away. The last voice says "Go."

I walk onto the deck and peek through a big window. That bed is huge, and this room could swallow up Bryce's whole shack. Check out all his stuff. Only kings in fairytales have that much. 'Course, I've never seen a real fairytale king. Scrunch up my nose. No lanterns. He must have electricity like they do in town.

I'm about to turn and head back to the shack ... hear tires kicking up rocks out on the road. Must be Tess driving like a bat out of hell. I take off into the woods ... follow the trail along the lake. Gotta beat her back. Run hard as I know how.

When I burst into the shack ... can barely catch my breath ... Tess is trembling ... telling Bryce about getting stuck behind the wreck. Talks about cops ... she thought she'd get pulled over ... expired plates. No license ... no registration ... they'd have taken her to jail.

He yells, "I send you out on a simple errand and you make a mess of things. What the hell's wrong with you?"

Tess slaps her forehead. "How was I to know some eighteen-wheeler was going to turn his truck over and block the highway?"

Bryce turns to me. "And what's with you? Where you been all this time?"

If he catches me lying, no telling what he'll do—I lie anyway ... wanna keep him from going after the neighbor. Cringe as I say Tess probably didn't see me out on the highway 'cause I was peeing in the woods.

He yells, "You're a damned liar."

I hunch up. Whimper. Wish I was a tiny flea ... could hide anywhere. Not an ant. Ants get stomped on.

"Damn it!" he shouts. "I've got half a mind to ...."

I blurt out, "A woman made me get in her car ... thought something bad was going to happen to me if I was out on the highway all alone. She said, 'If you don't get in I'll call the police.' I couldn't say no. Got in her car. Made her drop me at the turnoff before the lake. Didn't want her to come all the way here. After that ... hung out in the woods."

Bryce crushes an empty beer can with one hand. Takes off his belt ... yanks down my pants ... pulls them all the way off ... shoves me across a wooden chair ... face first ... ass up. I peek. He whips the belt around over his head ... eyes black ... cold. I gulp ... the buckle dangling at the loose end. My body tenses up. I think, candy wrappers ... crinkly, red candy wrappers ... I love cinnamon candy.

When he's done thrashing me, I curl up on the chair ... gasp for breath ... gawk at my naked ass. My heart stops. Candy wrappers! How did those candy wrappers get all over me? I reach for one—bright red ... crinkly. But it's not a candy wrapper ... it's damp. My leg stings when I touch it.

Bryce isn't done with me. He chases me up the ladder.

Wanna kick him when he yells, "Climb faster." But don't. Would just make him madder. Wish he'd fall off ... hit his head on the floor ... die.

Up in the loft he pushes me down on the mattress. Lays on top of me. Presses his face against my neck. Wanna puke.

He says, "Better drive my seed all the way in."

I whimper. Count ripples ... candy wrappers ... nothing works.

He shoves it in me. Yanks it back out. Pounds it in again .... again ... again. Grunting and wheezing. He whispers, "Yeah, cry like a baby. That's right. A baby's what you need to keep you where you belong." He gets up and sneers. "Starting tonight, I'm doubling your chores. Every inch of this place will be spotless before you go to sleep. And if you're not finished before daylight, you can just skip sleeping until you learn to work faster."

I curl into a ball ... his slime dribbles out.

He stumbles down the ladder ... leaves me on the mattress, sobbing. Soon as his feet hit the floor below, he starts chewing out Tess. "You shouldn't have let her go off on her own. Next, she'll get the idea she's free to wander off anywhere she pleases."

Poke at the places where Bryce's buckle made welts on my leg. They burn ... ooze tiny beads of blood. The marks are bigger than the swelling he usually leaves behind. I crawl to the knothole in the wall ... my candy wrappers. Pull one out and look through it at the sores on my leg. Smooth the wrapper over the worst of them.

When he finishes yelling at Tess, he stomps over to the ladder ... shrieks, "Get your sorry ass down here and get to work. Now."

I get up ... hide the blood-stained candy wrapper. What doesn't ache or sting is sore in other ways. I stumble to the ladder and hurry down. As my foot touches the floor below I see Tess, with her shirt unbuttoned, leading Bryce to their room. He looks back at me like he's king of the world. Points to the stove. "You can start by shining that thing so good I can shave with it."

Don't know how Tess stands his touching ... even likes him doing it.

Jacob

How the hell did I get here ... on the wrong side of the lake, staring up at the stars? Last thing I remember, I stopped at a bad accident to see if anyone needed help. I check my arms, legs, ribs. Nothing seems broken. Crank my neck. Just sore and stiff from lying on the hard ground. There is a tender spot on top of my head ... when I touch it, a sharp pain shoots through my skull ... don't feel any blood. Search for my cell phone; it's nowhere around.

Good thing there's a decent moon out. Makes walking back to the cabin along the gravel road a bit easier. Everything seems fine, but that changes when I turn down my drive. The Jeep. Why would I have parked like that? I open the driver's door, and my cell phone's in plain sight. I pick it up and punch the first name on my favorites list— Carl, my advisor for more than twenty years, and probably my only friend. While the phone's ringing I study Celine's picture; it's been moved.

"Jake, what's up?"

"Sorry to call so late."

"It's only ten. Since when is that late for you?"

"Carl, I think it happened again."

"You blacked out?"

"Maybe that, too. But I think I had another episode, like the time I went to view that little girl's body the police thought was Celine. The docs called it a cataleptic seizure."

"Are you in a safe place now?"

Why isn't Celine's picture in the tray where it belongs?

"Jake, you still with me?"

"I'm home—but this time I was out for hours and can't remember a thing that happened beforehand, except the accident—"

"Accident? Are you okay?"

"I'm fine. I wasn't in it. There was a jackknifed semi stretched across the highway, an SUV accordioned into the trailer. Something snapped in me as I was checking out the SUV. My mind's a total blank after that, until I wake up across the lake from my cabin, looking up at the stars."

"Sure you're okay?" Carl asks.

I'm not sure about anything at this point.

"Jake."

I open my mouth but nothing comes out.

"Damn it, Jake. Answer me."

I force a reply. "Carl ... I'm okay. Just a little worried."

"You pay me for advice, but here's some for free. It might be a good idea for you to get down off the mountain and spend a few days with Sandy and me. We have plenty of room."

"No. I'm fine."

"Okay, but you told me if you ever had another blackout, I should make you lock up your booze. Remember, doctors say it can make the seizures worse."

"I don't need a damn babysitter."

"No one says you do. Just want to make sure you're taking care of yourself. Why don't you try to get some rest? I'll call you tomorrow around noon. Okay?"

"Sure." I hang up and return Celine's to the tray.

As I climb out of the Jeep, the moaning that keeps me awake some nights is back. I'm beginning to think it's human. I try to hone in on the sound. Wish I could figure out where it's coming from, but it blends with the chorus of other noises. As though the whole forest is feeling its pain.

Back inside the cabin, I open a bottle of tempranillo before locking away the rest of my booze. I bury the key in a drawer under some dishtowels and grin. Okay, Carl. Does that count as locking up the stuff?

I pour a full glass, take a sip, and let the wine soothe my throat. After wandering into my library—wine glass in one hand, the nearly full bottle of wine in the other—I sit at my desk and peruse a stack of papers.

Amy

Halfway through the night … can't get the neighbor out of my head. Is he okay …? God! He could be dead.

I prop the broom against the wall and tiptoe over to Bryce and Tess's room. Listen. Bryce is snoring the way he does when he's conked out cold. Not a peep from Tess. I bite my lip. Creep over to the front door. Hold the latch with both hands … pinch down slowly … press against the door … open it just a crack. Stop … peek over my shoulder … listen for Bryce or Tess. Nothing. Hold my breath as I slip outside and close the door with barely a sound.

Down at the cove … I sigh. The man is gone … but his shovel! Oh no, he left it. If Bryce finds it here, that'll be trouble. Why can't the man just stay on his side of the lake? Leave us alone.

I pick up the shovel and carry it back to the shack. Hide it where I'm sure Bryce won't look. Slip back inside and scurry around … try to be quiet … but the stove hatch, still hot … clangs when I set it down. Tiptoe to their bedroom door. Listen. Still sleeping.

Go back and polish the stove 'til my fingers ache … burn my hand a couple times… still doesn't shine. Get down on my hands and knees … use an old toothbrush on seams in the floor. Keep listening for any peep out of Bryce or Tess. Wipe down the walls with soapy water … standing on a chair to reach the highest parts … even scrubbing the ceilings as much as I can. Most of it I do twice, just to be sure.

By morning I'm too tired to keep going. Hunch up in a corner and close my eyes. Can't get the little girl's picture out of my mind. Bet nobody touches her like Bryce touches me. Reach in my pocket for a crinkly red candy wrapper. Nothing. I stuffed it back in the knothole when Bryce called me down. Start to cry and can't stop. The tears just spill out.

The bedroom door creaks open. My eyes are swollen, achy. Tess walks to the kitchen ... runs her hand over the table ... studies the stove. "You lazy bitch. What have you been doing all night?"

I stare at the floor. Answering will make matters worse.

"Think your ass is dragging now? It'll be hell when you're eight months pregnant."

Tess leans in close ... her breath sour.

"I got chewed out because of you. Can't believe you were too damned lazy to hike up a little hill. Some gratitude. Bryce and I are probably the only reason you're alive. But don't worry. You're going to pay for this."

Bryce stumbles out of their bedroom. Plunks his butt down at the table. "What the hell do I have to do? *Ask* for my damn coffee?"

I rush over and set a cup in front of him and pour.

"Am I gonna get breakfast?"

I hurry back to the stove and load up a plate.

Tess says, "I found her napping when I got up this morning. Not even half her work done."

Set the plate in front of him. Wanna say she's lying. Wasn't napping. Chores done. But he won't care. Everything's always my fault.

Bryce balls up his fist. It flies off the table—catches my jaw. My head snaps back ... pain shoots through my teeth ... neck. Land in Tess's arms ... she shoves me to the floor. "Don't plan on me having your back, you little bitch."

Shut my eyes tight. Not gonna let them see tears.

Chapter Four

Jacob

Dawn's broken. Haven't seen the girl for a week—about the time of my 'episode.' How often in the past two years has she missed showing up? Hope she's all right.

Time for my morning ritual—walk down to the dock, bait a hook and cast my line in the water. Ripples spread over the lake toward the opposite shore. Like a stock tip—the first ring is your insiders getting a heads-up, next it's a select group of Wall Street traders, and so forth. When Main Street finally gets the word, it's old news.

My throat tightens. A scene from my nightmare comes at me out of the blue. Celine is standing in plain view next to her kidnapper. They're too far away for me to get a good look at his face. My cell rings. I glance down at the screen. Celine screams. I look up. She's gone.

I reel in line. A tug. My rod bows. The girl's picking up kindling on the other shore. I set down my rod and grab the binoculars, dial her into focus—want to be sure she's okay.

Tires crunch on the gravel drive. I glance over. Carl's black BMW. I look back across the lake, the girl's not there. I check my line, it's gone slack.

Carl steps out of the car. His idea of mountain-casual is starched pin-stripe shirt, creased trousers, and Italian loafers—sans coat and tie. He's also wearing a smirk as he walks up onto the deck. "You look like you've lost your last friend. Except, I know you don't have any."

"Good morning to you, too. Just skip the psychoanalysis and tell me how the depositions went."

"Nice to see there's still some of the old Jacob Chandler left in you."

"The depositions?"

"Just as your lawyers expected. The other side is shoring up their defense with witnesses to prove what an irrational bastard you turned into."

"Can I get you something to drink?"

"Isn't it a bit early?"

"I'm talking about coffee here. What ... you think I've gone over the edge?" I raise an eyebrow.

"No. I've always known you're nuts. CEO's have to be." Carl flashes a smug grin. "Make mine black."

I frown just to let him know I'm not into his humor at the moment. "I know. We're all just a hair's breadth away from being serial killers."

"That's what the docs say at that famous mental hospital in England."

I step toward the French doors that open into the kitchen. "Come on inside."

Carl follows. "Their defense is that you ran a tight ship and kept everything on an even keel. Then the domestic violence allegations against Conroy surfaced, and you went psycho. You didn't give the system a chance to do its job. That spooked everyone."

"They're reaching." I draw two espresso shots into Carl's cup.

"We hope the judge sees it that way. They say you broke your own HR policies and started bullying Conroy. He spiraled into depression. Committed suicide. They're even trying to get their hands on your son's suicide note to prove a pattern of abusive behavior. Office gossip is that Jesse took his own life because of the emotional scars you inflicted on him, especially after Celine's kidnapping. If they're successful, the board will press for a finding that your conduct puts the wrongful death judgment outside the indemnity clause of your employment contract."

"I never mistreated my son." I scrunch up my nose. "Two shots enough?"

"That may be, but everybody your lawyers deposed in your defense had a colorful anecdote that shores up the other side's case."

"If I was such a liability, why was the board pissed when I quit?"

"They were angry. Your abrupt exit made them worry. How many other screw-ups might come to light?"

"Okay, so give me the high and low points."

"Their most damaging witness is your old admin, Madison. She recalls you hiring a private detective to spy on Jesse, and she claims you said something to the effect that there's no punishment harsh enough for guys like Conroy, and that '... we should line them all up and push them off a cliff somewhere ....'"

I choke on my coffee. "She invented that."

"That means a jury will have to choose who to believe."

"So, what's the good news?"

Carl grins. "Conroy was doing her ... big time."

"Who? Madison?"

He sighs. "Yeah, the poor girl thought he was going to dump his wife and marry her. Give her the life she always dreamed of."

"Bastard."

"Of course, the jury will have a tough time buying her testimony once they hear about the affair."

I fidget with my cup. "Can I confess something, Carl?"

"Confess? How can a person confess if he doesn't have a conscience?"

I gaze out over the lake. "If I'd had the chance to push Conroy off a cliff, I might have done it."

Carl sits back and studies me. "You're not serious? I thought the thing that separates guys like you from other psychopaths is that you don't get your hands dirty."

"Relax. Conroy spared me the trouble. He's not a problem I have to worry about anymore. Besides, I'm a bit more connected to my softer side nowadays."

Carl runs his fingers through his hair—too thick and black for guys our age. "Yeah, but losing this lawsuit could cost a lot. Hell, just trying the case is going to eat into the puny returns we're squeezing out of this sluggish economy."

"Money isn't as big a deal to me as it used to be."

Carl holds out his hands, palms up. "Have you been abducted by aliens? Money has always been at the top of your list—ahead of your family, friends ...."

"I don't have any friends, remember."

"My point exactly. Friends require trust. The only thing people trust you to do is to use them until they have nothing left to give."

"Friends or no friends, my troops were always pretty loyal ... and there were plenty of them around when I needed them."

He sits back in his chair. "Not because they liked you ... because they knew hanging onto your coattails was safer than being on the opposing team."

"Ellen never felt that way."

"Ellen wrote you off years ago. She would have divorced you half-a-dozen times if she wasn't afraid you'd find a way to make her life even more miserable than it was. When you weren't around to hear, she'd call you 'a shell of a husband and father.'"

"So what you're saying is that I'm a colossal ass."

"That's about the size of it. But since Celine went missing you've been all over the map. One minute you're the old Jacob Chandler, the next you're somebody else. Maybe it's time you let her go and start living again. Whether or not you want to acknowledge it, you don't have that many years left."

"She didn't go missing. She was taken. And, who knows what kind of hell she's been through?"

"I get it, Jake. It haunts you. But you're letting whoever took her make you a victim, too. Just like ...."

I look out over the lake—again. "Do you know how many victims there are out there? I mean, people's lives that have been ruined by some low-life?"

He pinches the bridge of his nose. "Are you talking about the corporate world, or life in general?"

"Don't get cute. I'm serious." I point to the other shore. "Take the girl who lives across that lake."

Carl searches the shoreline. "What girl?"

"She's not there now, but she was when you drove up."

I shake my head. "Something's not right. I mean, why is she over there every day tossing rocks in the lake when other kids her age go to school?"

"Maybe she's home-schooled."

"Why isn't her mother teaching her something? The girl's just loitering, wasting time."

"Hey, teenagers go off by themselves and sulk. You just weren't around enough when your kid was going through that stage."

My chest tightens.

"Besides, why do you give a rip? She's not your responsibility."

"I just worry …."

"You aren't going soft are you? Guys like you aren't supposed to worry about people."

"The thing that scares me—"

"*You* being scared scares *me*. Pretending to be afraid to get the upper hand on someone is one thing, but actually being afraid—it's not you."

"Things are changing inside here …" I tap my chest "… that I don't get. Know what I mean?"

"How old is she?"

"I don't know. It's hard to tell. She could be fifteen, maybe sixteen."

He leans back in his chair. "Jake, do you see what's going on here?"

"What do you mean?"

"Are you sure you aren't trying to turn this girl into Celine?"

"There's something I haven't told anyone about the day Celine was kidnapped."

He shifts forward in his seat. "What do you mean?"

"Just that … let's say I …." I choke back tears.

"Christ, Jake. Are you okay?" He grips my wrist. "You don't need to go there. Let's just stay focused."

"Sorry, I didn't mean to …."

"About the girl over there. Be careful sticking your nose into your neighbor's business. You could set yourself up for another expensive lawsuit. It wouldn't take much of a lawyer to put her parents onto the scent of your billions."

"Yeah, you're looking out for my welfare … and your fat fee."

"I've never seen you like this."

"By the way, speaking of people getting into my pockets, I'm tired of these detective agencies and their dead ends. If this one doesn't come up with something solid soon, I'm going to take things into my own hands. I should have done that in the first place. Celine would be home now, safe."

Chapter Five

Jacob

Used to be I wouldn't hit the sack until 2:00 or so. Then up at 5:00. Anymore, 2:00 is when my bladder wakes me. My nightly ritual includes peeking out the sliding glass door to see if I can catch the bandit in the act. I've been leaving out small stuff in the unlocked Jeep as bait.

Tonight, nature's call is early—1:30. When I glance outside, the Jeep's interior light is on, and someone's bobbing around in the driver's seat. I duck to the floor and crawl over to the bed. My loaded $25,000 Beretta SO5 shotgun is propped next to the nightstand. I keep it there on the off chance something like this might happen.

I click off the safety, scoot to the wall next to the sliding-glass door, and stand. It doesn't take much to goose open the slider a few inches—doesn't make a sound, thanks to the silent track system. A muffled clunk outside tells me he just closed the Jeep door. I crane my neck and peek outside. A small figure crouches near the rear wheel.

I coax open the door wide enough to slip through. Thank God for quality hardware. The silhouette next to the Jeep, backlit by moonlight, stays put. One light-footed step at a time, I move onto the deck and over to the steps. No loose planks. Made sure of that, micromanaging every turn of each screw while the deck was being built.

Just as I draw the butt of the shotgun to my shoulder, the perp jerks around. I lower my weapon. It's too dark to be sure, but something says this is the girl from across the lake. Before I calculate my next move, the figure bolts for the woods. My bare feet and 60-plus-year-old legs are no match for someone that quick. Besides, if it's her, I know where she lives. I gaze out over the lake for a few minutes before retreating to my bedroom to slip on a pair of jeans and boots. I trade the shotgun for a flashlight. I don't plan to confront her. Just checking things out.

A few feet into the woods I find a game trail that leads along the lake. A quarter mile farther, the trail forks. One branch veers away from the lake, the other seems to continue on around to where the girl lives.

Memories flood into my mind, sending my pulse into overdrive—a dozen years ago out by the coast—trudging through woods near a reservoir—hoping to find Celine. Search parties marching twenty abreast, calling out her name. Beams from flashlights glancing off trees and brush in the midnight forest. Glaring lights from emergency vehicles lining the roadside. My heart calms as the images dim.

The trail peters out at the edge of a small clearing. I switch off the flashlight and wipe grimy sweat off my brow. A few yards away sits the rustic shack where I suspect the girl lives—a pickup parked beside it. A thick stand of trees screens the shack from the lake. Off to the left, behind the shack, an old firebreak cuts into the forest. Around front, the gravel road angles off to the highway, and a dull light, likely from a lantern, filters out of a window next to what appears to be the only door. I edge up to the corner of the window and peek in.

A man's standing with his back to the window in the middle of a small kitchen, his wiry frame partially eclipsing a smaller figure—a girl. She's cowering. The man raises a leather strap over his head. I slam my flashlight into the window, sending shards of glass rattling across the kitchen floor. I shout through the broken window. "Don't lay a hand on her!"

The man jerks around and leers at me.

I lunge toward the door, reaching for the latch, but he's too quick. The door flies open, and he's standing there, still clenching the leather strap. "What the fuck?"

I tighten my grip on the flashlight. "You touch that girl and you'll have me to answer to."

"She's none of your business," he shouts back.

"I'm making it my business."

"*You* don't call the shots around here and, you're trespassing. I can get your ass thrown in jail."

"Okay. Call the sheriff. He'll probably be glad to stick his nose into what's going on here."

"Nothing's going on here that anyone needs to go ballistic over."

I point towards the girl. "Then you won't mind if we have a little chat."

"I said she's none of your business."

"Fine. I'll have CPS up here first thing tomorrow, and they'll make it *their* business."

"If you want what's best, you'll butt out. Now beat it!"

"You've got no idea who you're dealing with."

"Hell, candy asses like you are just a bunch of talk."

"You think so? Tomorrow morning I'm coming back with the sheriff." I nod at the girl. "And if she has the slightest bruise, your ass is going to jail ... which is where you'll want it to stay. Because once you get out, it will belong to me."

He peeks over his shoulder at the girl. "Get yourself to bed. I'm done with you for tonight."

She scurries out of sight. I grit my teeth and mutter, "You're done with her for good."

"I said beat it. And you owe me for the damned broken window." He steps inside the shack and slams the door.

I glare at the closed door for a moment before reaching for my wallet. I yank out a couple Ben Franklins, step over to the window, and toss them in. "This should take care of your damned window."

On my way back to the cabin, I keep wishing I'd brought my Beretta. If I had, that girl would be on her way home with me right now.

Amy

Tess weaves the pickup back and forth through the middle of the firebreak ... trying to dodge ruts ... plowing over saplings almost as tall as the hood. It's dark. No headlights. The clock on the dash says 3:00. She wanted to wait 'til daylight, but Bryce told her to go now. The neighbor's threatening to call the police. Police put people in jail.

She glances at me, curled up against the pickup door. "This is no holiday we're on. You understand?"

I scrunch into a tighter ball, trying to get as far away from her as I can.

Tess squints. "We'd better stay out of sight awhile. Just in case that busy-body neighbor tries to make a federal case out of last night's misunderstanding."

The pickup bounces into a deep rut, banging my head against the door handle.

"Damn," she says. "Can't see where I'm driving for all this brush. Good thing it's not much farther."

Another rut ... we bounce again.

After a few minutes, Tess points. "Looks like somebody's up."

I raise up and peer through the windshield at a light in the distance.

When she pulls up to the ranch house, a man's standing on the porch, about Bryce's size, aiming a shotgun at us.

Tess cuts the pickup's engine and sticks her head out the window. "Easy Eric. Just me, Tess."

"Good thing I recognized the truck." He's got a deeper voice than Bryce. Just as skinny, though. "'Bout time you came around. What's it been—a couple years? Thought I'd never see you again."

Tess gets out of the pickup. "Yeah, way too long."

"So, did you finally get rid of the bastard?"

"I wish," she says.

He props the shotgun against the doorpost. "I'm always here ...."

"It's not that easy."

"I'd do anything for you."

"You've already done plenty. That was huge, what you did for my girl. Wish I could show you ...."

"Just dump him."

"Yeah … he's got his claws too deep into me. Anyway, he'd kill us both." Tess stuffs her hands in her pockets. "Say, have you seen any sign of her since you let her get away?"

I sit straight up inside the pickup. Is she still alive?

"Sorry," he says. "But the honest truth is I didn't let her go. She busted out on her own."

"I thought you were going to take her to the bus station … give her some cash to get away."

"When Bryce came around to collect her she was gone. I wasn't gonna tell him we let her escape." He folds his arms across his chest. "And you never came around asking."

Tess turns and kicks the dirt. "Damn you."

"It's not like I didn't try to find her. I drove up and down the damn highway several times, searching. But she must have holed up in the woods, figuring the highway wasn't a safe place."

She glares at him.

"And I searched all through these woods. All I found was a hut a couple miles from here, but I guess it's abandoned. A few months after she ran off, my sister's boy was helping out around the ranch. He said he'd seen a crusty old man living there. Doubt she'd have trusted a crazy buzzard like that—after what Bryce done to her. My guess is if she didn't catch a ride out on the highway, she couldn't have survived the first winter on her own."

I slink down in the seat. Bryce is right. She got eaten by coyotes or murdered by a truck driver.

Tess points to me. "Eric, we got a situation here. The girl and I have to lay low for a while."

Eric grunts. "Thought I'd be the last person he'd trust after the other girl got away on my watch."

Tess shrugs. "As if he trusts anybody."

"So what's the emergency?"

"This time I'll be doing the babysitting. All we need is a place to hang out. Bryce'll hike over here when the smoke clears and let us know it's safe to go back. I figure it'll take about a week."

"There's an empty stall in the barn for the girl. You can have the couch."

Tess tucks her hair behind her ear. "What about sticking us in your spare room so I can keep a closer eye on ...." She grins. "You know, things?"

Eric shakes his head. "My sister's boy stays with me now. She took off a little over a year ago to follow her boyfriend up to Portland. Didn't want a stringy 16-year-old tagging along."

Tess yanks me out of the pickup. "Do you have some chain and a couple of padlocks? The old man gave me orders."

"You must have a wild one."

Tess frowns. "You can say that. She's the reason my life is in the dumper. But I'll keep her on a short leash while we're here ... she won't cause any trouble."

Eric nods toward the barn. "You'll find what you need in the tack shop. I'll get some blankets while you get her settled."

Tess shoves me. I step barefoot on a patch of tiny burrs ... start hopping.

She laughs—shoves me again. "Dance, girl."

I hop around, driving the stickers into the soles of my feet.

"Keep moving." She pushes again.

When she opens the barn door, horses snort. Paw the ground. A big brown one bucks against its stall.

I fall to my knees.

Tess kicks me … I crawl all the way to the end of the barn. She herds me into an empty stall and stands over me, hands on her hips. "This is your home for the time being. Get used to it."

I keep my eyes down.

She walks away.

I don't peek up … even when she comes back.

A chain rattles on the stall's gatepost … again when Tess loops it around my neck. The padlock snaps shut. I flinch.

She pats my head. "Just relax. You won't be going anywhere 'til I say so."

I choke back tears, she turns and walks away. I pick at the stickers in my feet.

When the barn door clunks shut, I reach into my pocket. Nothing there. Bryce chased us off so fast … left my candy wrappers behind.

Tears rush out and stream down my face.

Sunlight comes through tiny cracks in the sides of the barn. My eyes are gummy. Got a headache, sore neck. The chain rattles when I move.

The barn door creaks … I freeze. A boy talks to the horses in a soft voice, calling each by name. When he stops at the bay across from me, all I can see is his red curly hair and his back. Tall and skinny. I hold my breath, hope he doesn't see me. He turns to walk away.

I let out my breath and hug my knees. The chain clanks. No … forgot the damn chain. He stops … turns … comes into the stall … kneels next to me.

RJ

"What the f—?" A girl ... chain padlocked around her neck. I reach for the lock.

She jerks away.

"Who the hell did this?"

She buries her face in her hands.

I grip the padlock. "Did Uncle ... did he do this to you?"

She shakes her head.

"I'm not going to hurt you. I can help. Just tell me what's going on. How'd you get here?"

She starts crying.

"What's your name?" I say.

She mumbles.

"Tell me your name ... please."

She murmurs, "Amy."

"Hi, Amy. I've got no idea what's going on, but whatever it is, it's gotta get fixed."

"No, leave me be. You'll just make things worse."

"Just give me a chance to figure things out."

I storm out of the barn, over to the ranch house, and throw open the back door. A woman's at the kitchen sink, wearing one of Uncle Eric's shirts. My cheeks start to burn. What the hell? Half her damn ass is showing.

She spins around and glares. I stare back, my whole face is on fire.

Uncle Eric says, "RJ, meet Tess. She dropped in last night needing a place to lay low for a couple of days."

Tess sticks out her hand.

After we shake, she turns to Uncle Eric. "Need to teach this boy how to shake hands like a man. That was about the wimpiest ever."

"Tess has a situation, and we're helping her out."

"Yeah, I noticed." I glance toward the barn.

The woman scowls. "Not as innocent as she looks. She's like one of those unbroken horses people bring here for your Uncle Eric to tame. Nothing but trouble. Lucky she's treated as well as she is."

"I can give up my room for a few nights. Don't mind the barn." I glare at Tess. "Long as I'm not chained down."

With a scowl, Uncle Eric says, "Boy, this is parent business. You best stay out of it."

"Fine. I'm just saying. She can have the couch—it seems to be free."

Tess rolls her eyes.

He folds his arms across his chest. "That's none of your business, either."

"Whatever. I've got horses to feed."

"Then get to it. And stay away from the girl."

"Can I at least take her something to eat? She's probably hungry."

Tess struts over to the table and scrapes the leftovers from their breakfast onto a plate. "Sure. But don't talk to her."

"Yes, ma'am." I snatch the plate out of her hand.

My stomach knots up when Uncle Eric calls after me. "And, boy. Give the stallion a ride when you're done feeding him. He needs some exercise."

"Yes, sir," I mutter.

Once out the door, I hustle over to the barn, yank open the wide wooden door, shut it behind me, and stomp to the farthest stall. Amy cowers when I set the plate of scraps down next to her.

"Sorry, Amy. It's the best I could do."

She whispers, "Thanks."

"Met the bitch. She's a piece of work."

"You mean the witch?"

"Huh?"

"Witch … Wicked Witch."

"Oh. Right."

She picks at the food.

I kneel next to her. "I have an idea how we can pull this off."

"Pull what off?"

I glance over my shoulder and whisper, "Get you out of here."

She jerks back. "No."

"What do you mean, no?"

"Bryce needs me. Tess needs me."

"I'm not arguing. I'll take care of everything. Trust me."

She covers her ears. "Stop. Can't run away. No place to go. Girls die out there."

"I'll be back … with help. Do what I say and everything will be fine."

She sniffles, shaking her head.

The barn door creaks open. I hustle to the opposite stall and catch a glimpse of Amy still cowering.

Tess yells at me as she marches toward Amy's stall. "Thought I told you to stay away from her."

"I was only giving her food."

She peers in at Amy. "That should have taken only a couple of seconds. What were you doing, spoon-feeding her?"

"No, ma'am. Just trying to get her to eat."

Tess looks me over. "It's not your problem if she starves to death. You got that?"

"Yes, ma'am."

"It's RJ, right?"

"Yes, ma'am."

She keeps her eyes locked on mine. "Don't let the little bitch fool you. She's big trouble."

Bryce

Making my own breakfast is bad enough. But getting my own wood, starting the damn fire? Women ... fuck. I dump my plate and fork in the wash tub. Look around. Better get rid of any sign of the girl, just in case that nosey neighbor makes good on his threats.

I climb up the ladder, drop the damn mattress through the opening to the floor below. Same drill with all of the little bitch's stuff. What the hell does she need with three sets of clothes? Better get rid of that bar of soap, toothpaste, toothbrush—everything.

I drag the mattress into my bedroom and stack mine on top of it. Grab a hammer and crowbar, along with her shit, and head outside to check for a loose panel of siding. If I remember, there's a loose seam near the corner around the side. Planned on fixing it one of these days. Yeah. There it is. Hell. Worse than I thought. Don't even need the crowbar ... pull back the siding by hand. A shovel falls out from between two studs ... nearly smacks me in the forehead.

Damn. How'd this get here? Shit ... looks new. I squint at the trees between me and the lake. Is that damn neighbor up to something? Wouldn't put it past him, not after last night. He better not come around looking for it. Finders, keepers. 'Sides, I could use a new shovel. Old one's rusted ... blade'll snap off one of these times.

Stuff the girl's clothes and whatnot into the empty space between the studs and tack the plywood siding back into place. I laugh. Guess I finally got around to fixing it.

Back inside, I check the place one more time to be sure there's no sign of the girl. Damn. They better not figure out Tess lives here, either. I'm alone. Keep to myself. If I wanted company, I'd move to a city. Not responsible for anybody but me. Never bothered the fella across the lake. No idea why he has it in for me.

Gather up Tess's stuff and hide it with the girl's things.

Chapter Six

Jacob

Twenty minutes on a wood bench waiting in the sheriff's substation has me strung tighter than piano wire. Now, seated across the desk from a uniformed bureaucrat, I scrunch up my brow as he finishes his standard spiel.

"Sheriff, I appreciate your situation. But a child's safety—maybe her life—is at stake."

He combs his fingers through his slick, black hair. "It's Deputy Sheriff Baker, Mr. Chandler." I'm sure he used a level to straighten that name tag on his starched uniform.

I clench my teeth. Reminds me of those stockbrokers who spend half the day preening in front of the mirror. Resting on their laurels. Everything's about making an impression. Give me a hungry, young buck any day.

He goes on. "And as I said, we'll check out your complaint. We have procedures to make sure these things are handled properly."

"This is about a child's welfare."

"I understand that. Now if you'll just relax, I'll write up a report and get a copy over to Child Protective Services."

"So you're willing to take personal responsibility if something goes terribly wrong in the meantime?"

Baker pulls back his broad shoulders. "My job *is* taking personal responsibility—24/7."

I lean forward and plant both hands on his desk. "Believe me. If that girl ends up hurt or—heaven forbid— dead, everyone's going to pin the blame on you—from the grandma in line at the grocery store to the governor. In fact, the president's going to hear about it during our next round of golf." I lean back and fold my arms across my chest. "The first hole we chat about the wife and kids—his. I don't have any left. On the second fairway we cover the economy. Things like abused kids and bureaucratic bungling get handled before we sink our putts on the third green."

Baker stands. His full 6'2" frame looms over the desk. "Listen. This isn't Wall Street and it's certainly not the Oval Office. You're not going to get any special treatment by coming in here, throwing your weight around, and making threats. We handle every matter that comes to us with the same professionalism and diligence."

I sit up straight. "It's not a threat unless she's in danger. He was getting ready to use a belt on her."

He sits down and types something into his computer. "Did you see him hit her?"

"No. When I saw him raise the belt, I smashed his window with my flashlight. Busted it trying to get his attention."

"Sounds like your neighbor should be the one filing a complaint."

"He's abusing the girl, and I'm trying some help."

He makes another entry in the computer. "See any marks—bruises or the like?"

"Didn't get close enough."

He looks up from the computer screen. "Mr. Chandler, give me something to work with here."

"How about the fact the girl should be in school?"

"That's not imminent danger, but we'll check it out. I have to tell you, though, I've never heard of this fellow or the girl, and I know who lives in my part of the county. The only girl up your way belongs to some single gal. Don't have their exact address on file, but they show up in town now and then. There's never been a need to check in on them."

I bang on his desk. "I hear sounds every night."

"Mr. Chandler, you need to calm down. What kind of sounds?"

"Whimpering, moaning, like someone in pain."

"Could be coyotes or owls ..."

"That's what I thought, but they sound human."

"Human?"

"Yeah, maybe a kid crying."

"Every night?"

"Pretty much."

"You say he was going to take a belt to her. How can you be sure?"

"He was holding it up about this high ...." I raise my fist up above ear level. "She was cowering."

He types again.

"Deputy Baker, I'm sorry I came across like a jerk—but this girl has me worried. It's not like I go around trying to save the world. My granddaughter was kidnapped a few years ago ... we never got her back. I don't want to see any kid go through what my Celine ...."

Deputy Baker picks up the handset on his desk phone and punches the intercom button. "Grimes, what time am I supposed to be over up to Central to see the Sheriff?"

He stares up at me as he waits for a reply.

"Got it. I'm going to run a quick errand—a little out of the way, but I'll have time if I head out now."

Baker hangs up, stands, and plucks his hat off the rack behind his desk. "Okay, Mr. Chandler. I'll follow you up to your place. You can point the way from there. I'll let you know what I find."

"Thanks."

"Don't get too worked up. You still haven't given me a whole lot to work with."

After turning off the highway, I pull the Jeep to the side of the gravel road and wave the sheriff's cruiser straight ahead. Once Baker passes, I turn down my drive and spot Carl standing on the redwood deck, frowning.

I step out of the Jeep. "What are you doing here?"

"If the sheriff just blew past here, I'm a too late. Came to talk some sense into you about this thing with your neighbor."

"It's not a *thing* with my neighbor. It's a kid's life...."

"Got your voicemail. God, Jake. What's gotten into you?"

"What's that supposed to mean?"

"Since when do you let stuff like this get under your skin? What is it with you and this girl?"

"It would get to anyone ... anyone who's human."

"You? Human? For God's sake .... Okay, you weren't yourself right after Celine. Who wouldn't come apart? But that wasn't the real Jacob Chandler. The real Jacob Chandler only *pretends* to feel things. And then only to get the edge on somebody."

"Maybe I've stuffed my feelings down deep so nobody could use them against me."

"I thought your shrink called you a hardcore narcissist … incapable of real feelings. You just put on a show to exploit other people's weak spots."

"Yeah, the same *doctor* that can't get to the bottom of these holes in my memory? The best she can come up with was some psycho-babble about me suppressing guilt over Jesse's suicide. Said for me to 'heal,' I have to accept responsibility for the emotional damage I inflict on others. She made it sound like *I'm* the head case."

"What damage did you do to Jesse that a thousand other CEOs haven't done to their sons?"

"Supposedly, I caused Jesse to have PTSD, and that's why he killed his wife and himself. Hell. Jesse moped around half his damned life. Guess, I didn't have to call him a wuss, though. After all, he was my son."

"He laid into you pretty good in his suicide note."

"Yeah. A few weeks before it happened, I came down on *him* pretty hard over his production. Told him I was tired of my top producers moaning about nepotism."

"You told him to take his client list elsewhere and get a taste of the real world."

"He made me mad, said losing Celine was all my fault."

"But how does this memory thing have anything to do with Jesse—that was, what four, five years ago? You were getting things under control—until this girl thing."

I grip the deck rail. "Damn it, Carl. I'm not going to stand by and watch another girl go through what Celine …."

"This girl isn't Celine. And whoever she is, she's none of your business."

"I don't know what's going on. It's like something's caged up inside me, bouncing around, wanting to break out and run amok."

"Get a hold of yourself, Jake. You've taken your eye off the ball. You need to get back on track."

"I care about this girl." I stare out across the lake. "How—how do people do it, Carl?"

"Do what?"

"Deal with feelings."

The blood drains from Carl's face. He must be as freaked out by me talking about feelings as I am. I brush past him into the kitchen. "I'll pour some coffee—settle those jangled nerves of yours."

"Mine are fine, but you need something to *numb* yours."

I grin. "Locked the stuff up. Your advice, remember?"

Bryce

Car tires crunch outside. Jump to my feet. Hurry to the window and look out. Hell, the damn bastard actually went and called the law on me. I scan the room again just to be sure nothing's out for anybody to see. Once I'm sure everything's put away out of sight, I step out on the stoop to greet him. Best if I let him think visitors get my attention. People don't come around—ever.

"Hello," he says. "I'm Deputy Sheriff Baker. I'm just stopping by because we got a call from your neighbor."

"Is there a problem, officer?"

"Do you have any form of ID?"

"Sorry, sir. Don't drive. Don't hardly go out. Never had a need to identify myself."

He's smiling. That's a good sign.

"Name's Bryce, though."

"Bryce, your neighbor said something about a girl. He claims you threatened to hit her with a leather strap."

"Haven't got a clue what he's talking about, sir. No one here but me. Don't really like being around folks, especially women and kids. Try to keep to myself."

"Do you mind if I come in and take a look around?"

"Sure, if you think you need to. Ain't got nothing to hide."

He nods. "Thanks. This should just take a minute."

The cop steps past me and stops a few feet inside. I stop behind him.

"Just live here by yourself, you say?"

"That's right, sir. Don't need company."

He glances back at me as he points to the bedroom. "Mind if I take a peek over there?"

"Be my guest."

He walks across and peeks into the bedroom, turns and studies the ladder. "What's up there?"

"Just an empty loft. Not much use for it. I'm no hoarder."

"Yeah, I can see that. May I, anyway?"

"Of course."

He goes up the ladder, looks around, and comes back down.

Before he asks, I say, "Wanna see what's around back?"

"No thanks, I've seen all I need. Sorry to bother you."

The deputy heads outside, starts to open his car door and turns back. "Ever seen a girl hanging around?"

"No, sir. But I don't get out much."

"Ever had any kind of run-in with your neighbor?"

"Just the one time when he came over and tried to get me to sell my property. Told him no, but he got pretty insistent. When I held my ground he got downright angry. Made some threats."

"What kind of threats?"

"Said he'd make life miserable 'til I changed my mind."

"Did he ever follow through on his threats?"

"I try not to let stuff bother me. He almost ran me over once when I was walking down the road here. Drove over to my place a time or two—knocked on the door. Blasted his horn. Banged on the window over there with his flashlight— broke it, trying to get me to come out and talk. Didn't want to have nothing to do with him. Just sat at my table and had myself a beer."

"If anything like that happens again, come down to the station and file a complaint."

"Should I be worried about this guy?"

"He seems to like throwing his weight around. Bullying people he thinks don't have the backbone to stand up to him. I just don't want him to get the idea he can move into these parts and shove good folks around."

He waves as he gets into the police cruiser. "Thanks. You've been very helpful."

Jacob

When I bring out our coffee, Carl starts to say something, but he's distracted by the sheriff's cruiser turning down the drive. I strain to see if the girl's riding in the back seat. She isn't.

"He's back so soon? Was hardly gone long enough to step out of his cruiser and say hello to the creep."

The deputy is grim-faced as he walks up the steps to the deck, shaking his head.

"What's the story?" I ask.

"Was just about to ask you the same."

Carl extends his hand. "Carl Samuels. Jake's friend and business associate."

The deputy shakes Carl's hand. "Deputy Sheriff Baker."

Baker looks back at me. "There's no girl living there. Just an old buzzard named Bryce."

"Just how hard did you search the place?"

"There's not that much to search. And he was cooperative, which is more than I can say about you."

"Great. He's probably hidden her away somewhere."

"He tells me you've been harassing him, trying to get him to move out."

"That's ridiculous. He doesn't even own the place. It belongs to the trust I bought my place from. Everything beyond the lake belongs to the trust. He's probably a squatter. If I wanted him gone, I'd just contact the trustee."

Baker folds his arms across his chest. "Or, maybe he has their permission ...."

Carl looks down.

"So tell me about this late night visit to your neighbor. Why'd you go over there in the first place?"

"My bladder woke me up—on the way to the john I spotted the girl crouched next to my Jeep. She's probably the one who's been breaking in, stealing stuff."

"Someone's been breaking in?"

"Ever since I moved in. Actually, before that—while my place was going up."

"You ever report this?"

I look away. "No. It was nothing to get worked up about."

"But now you're saying it is a big deal. That you went traipsing through the woods to your neighbor's place in the middle of the night. Smashed his window with a flashlight. He says you threatened him."

"I didn't threaten him. I told him I wasn't going to stand for him abusing that girl."

"Mr. Chandler, as I've said, there's no sign of any girl. And your story has some holes in it. At least your neighbor's version makes sense."

I step toward the deputy. "A girl's life could be at stake."

Carl cuts between us and clutches my arm. "Deputy, my friend here has been through hell the past few years. Let's just step back and see if I can't get him some help. In the meantime, I'll keep him in tow."

"See that you do. And for the record Mr. Chandler, it wouldn't matter if you played golf with God. You're not moving into my county, throwing your weight around. Next time you haul me up here without solid evidence of a crime, I'll stick you with felony filing a false police report. For the last time, there's no girl."

Carl hands the deputy his business card. "Good day, deputy. Maybe if you give me a call, I can help clear up some things." As the sheriff heads back to his car, Carl nudges me toward the French doors to kitchen.

I stop in the doorway and spin around, meeting Carl eye-to-eye. "Me, harassing that bastard? That's a crock. If this sheriff doesn't do his job, I'm gonna ...."

"Just get a hold of yourself before you ...."

"What? Do something *stupid*?"

RJ

Mercedes' hideout is a couple miles from Uncle Eric's ranch, tucked back in the trees at the bottom of the ridge. The hut overlooks a clearing about half the size of a soccer field. Beyond the clearing it's chaparral and another large meadow. Of course, Mercedes hates the word "hideout." She calls it home. Been on her own for more than two years. The old bastard she escaped from has probably given her up for dead.

I slide off the stallion and unsaddle him at the usual spot in the woods, a quarter-mile from her place, half-way up the ridge. I slap his hindquarter to send him on—that's her heads up I'm coming. When she sees him, the plan is she'll sneak up near the top of the ridge and perch in a cluster of live oak to watch and see if anybody's following me. After she caws like a crow I drop down and go inside where I sit and wait.

Inside, the place smells like rotting wood. I pick up a book from a box in the corner. Today, it's by some dude named Stephen King. Already been through all the hunting magazines and issues of *Guns and Ammo*. No idea where she gets this stuff.

It's taking a long time for her to come down off the ridge. The wait gives me butterflies. I put down the book and start fiddling with the pocket knife Uncle Eric gave me. Even taught me how to keep it sharp. Tote it around in my back pocket. It has a bunch of cool gadgets —one's a church key. He says a guy should always carry a church key —never know when you'll come across a bottle of beer that's screaming to be opened—or a can of beans. I know Uncle Eric isn't the greatest role model, but if you never knew

your old man, and your mom pretty much abandoned you
…. Maybe that's why my face burns when I lie to him about
this place. Told him an old coot lives here. Mercedes swore
me to secrecy.

Finally she sees fit to join me, and the gutted rabbit
she's carrying by the ears explains what kept her—dinner.
She drops the critter in a bucket she uses for cleaning up,
and hangs the crossbow and quiver on a nail in a wall stud.
No wall board or insulation—just plywood siding outside,
nailed to studs. The place gets bitter cold in winter, but she
finds ways to manage.

She offers me something to eat—most of her stuff, she
scavenges from a fancy cabin a few miles away.

I put away the knife and pick up the King book.

She sits cross-legged next to me on the plywood floor—
it's rotting through in a few places. With her dark curls
hanging down over one eye, she's kinda sexy. Sometimes I
wish I could let myself ….

"Missed you," she says, glancing at me sideways.

"He's had me doing chores, round the clock. No time
off for good behavior. Anyway, I need your help."

She snatches the book out of my hand. Her eyes turn
almost black. "Yeah, and I could use some help around here
fixing the place up."

"Things seem fine to me. What are you talking about?"

"Like, there's a leak in the roof." Mercedes points
overhead with the book.

Dust floats in a streak of light coming through a crack.
"Okay, okay. I'll fix it. But since when are you so helpless?"

She hugs the book. "Since you've been so scarce." She
lays her hand on my knee. Her fingers are slender, but
strong.

I pull away. Not gonna let her go there. Seen enough of how my old lady treats guys. *Use 'em 'n lose 'em*—that's her motto.

"So what kind of help do you need?"

"A woman showed up at the ranch house last night with a girl about our age."

"I don't give boy-girl advice." She turns away.

"Whoa, don't jump to conclusions."

She gives me the kind of look Xena—Warrior Princess has when she draws her sword on a band of evil dudes.

"Say, what's the name of that old bag you lived with?" I reach for the book.

She hides the book behind her back. "Tess. Why?"

"Didn't you say something about another girl?"

"Yeah, about a year or two younger than me. Didn't have a chance to tell her I was running away. She was back at the shack, I was at your uncle's ranch. Besides, I wasn't even sure I could fend for myself out here."

"It's them."

She scrunches up her nose. "Who's *them*?"

"The woman who showed up last night. Name's Tess. And she brought a girl—keeps her chained up in the barn."

"That sadistic bitch." Mercedes grabs both my hands. "Do you know the girl's name?"

"Amy."

She springs to her knees. "Damn. That's her."

"We've gotta help her."

"Was there a man with them?"

"No. My uncle's doing the old bitch. She was wearing his shirt this morning, and I don't think she had on anything else." My cheeks burn. I used to hear my mom humping a different guy practically every night I lived with her.

Mercedes stands and sidles up to me with a frisky smile. "You're putting thoughts in my head talking about that stuff." She cups the back of my head and kisses me.

I jerk away. "I'd better get back. My uncle will kill me if I'm gone too long."

"Yeah. Whatever. It's always about you."

"No way. I came to get your help rescuing that girl."

"What, so you can get into her pants?"

"Jeez, not everything's about sex."

"Don't tell me you haven't thought about it."

"I swear—I—"

"You swear what? You only think about me? Is that what you wanna say? Hmph."

"No girl's going to make a fool out of me. I've seen enough of that shit."

Mercedes grabs my face and kisses me again. Her mouth half open.

I push back. "Why do you always have to make things so complicated?"

Mercedes turns away. "So, what is it you wanna do ... exactly?"

"I was thinking we could help her escape sometime when Uncle Eric and the bitch are screwing."

"You said we?"

"I could keep lookout in the house while you sneak into the barn and get her out of those chains."

She twists a loose curl hanging beside her cheek. "Wouldn't be hard. But what'll we do with her once she's free? It's not like she could make it on her own. That's why I didn't go back for her. She would've been dead weight."

"She could stay here ...."

Mercedes rolls her eyes.

"Just for a couple days—'til I get her into town. Maybe someone could help her find her folks."

"But when Tess finds she's gone, she's gonna come hunting for her. No way I want people snooping around here. They'd spoil everything."

"Okay. I'll make it look like she took off on the mare and headed down to town. I can ride the old nag along the dirt shoulder for a ways. Leave tracks."

"Guess it's the least I can do—after leaving her behind."

"Yeah. We better do it tonight. Tess said something about her old man coming to get them in a few days—after the coast is clear."

"Just as soon get it over with. Never planned on going back there. Not after ...." The pain in her eyes reminds me of the stories she tells about being a prisoner at Uncle Eric's place. Still can't believe that's true. Uncle Eric wouldn't do stuff like that. Just the same, I say, "I understand."

"It's tonight, then."

"Great. My room is next to Uncle Eric's. I'll signal you with my flashlight when I hear them getting it on. Then you can sneak down to the barn."

"That'll work ... as long as Bryce doesn't show up. He can get nasty ... and violent. He'd kill them both if he caught 'em at it."

"That Tess woman is pretty nuts, too."

"Only because Bryce bullies her. And she's got a thing against Amy for some reason."

"Don't know. The girl seems pretty nice. She's really afraid of the old witch."

"This sure as the hell better not be about springing her just so the two of you can hook up. I'm not about to start being anybody's damned matchmaker."

"I told you ...."

"I heard what you said."

I watch her walk over to a box in the corner and pull out a pair of black shoes, black pants and black hoodie. "So we're on for tonight, right?" I ask.

"Yeah, I've got stuff to do."

"See you tonight, then."

"Sure, tonight." Mercedes looks at me, her eyes misty. "Must've been a lot worse for her after I split."

Mercedes

After RJ leaves, I dig out my lock picking tools and practice on several different types of padlocks. Bryce taught me how to use them before I was ten. He made me help him rob folks in town. He'd sit in the pickup until I signaled the coast was clear. That way, he could take off if I got caught. He claimed the cops would go easy on a 10-year-old girl. I wonder if Amy inherited the job once I bailed.

Chapter Seven

Jacob

It's been dark for an hour and a half. Longer, if you count from when the first stars were visible on the horizon. I walk over to the fridge—for the twelfth time—open it, and stare at the six bottles of Irish Death. A pint has as much alcohol as a double shot of eighty proof whiskey.

Robert Dugoni's legal thrillers always keep me glued to the page, but tonight, not even his latest bestseller holds my attention. Not his fault I can't concentrate. I find myself out on the deck staring across the lake, waiting for that sound. Can't shake the image of that girl cowering under the bastard's belt.

I storm into the cabin for my Beretta twelve-gauge, but it's not by the nightstand where I keep it. I retrace my steps for the past few hours, but there are too many holes in my memory. Then it hits me—must have left it in the underground bunker when I checked the expiration dates on medical supplies earlier in the day. Back in my office, I activate the hidden doorways into the bunker. After turning on the lights, I stand at the top of a half-flight of stairs and scan the 'safe room'—a row of file cabinets near the back, shelves and glass-front storage cabinets on the walls. In the middle of the tiled floor, my Beretta is laying on an 8-foot long table. I pick up the gun, grab my night-vision goggles, and return to my Irish Death.

Nearly an hour later, I crouch in the shadows near the neighbor's shack, shotgun locked and loaded, with a clear line-of-sight through the front window. If the girl is in there, hopefully, I'll see her.

I let Celine down a dozen years ago. That sucked the life out of Ellen and our son. For this girl, maybe I can get it right. My jaw tightens. Deputy Baker probably never stepped inside the place when he "checked things out." It was easier for him to buy the story about me harassing my neighbor into selling his property cheap. No doubt the bastard is still gloating over how he conned the law.

A half-hour later, there's no sign of her or anyone else. I plunk down at the base of a large tree and lean back against the trunk. Another uneventful half-hour passes before someone appears in the window. I scramble to my feet to get a better view. My legs wobble—the left one stinging from a thousand pin pricks.

Before my legs are steady, the neighbor opens the front door and shuffles down the steps, cradling a shotgun in his arms. Without hesitating, he walks around to the back of the shack and follows the firebreak that cuts through the woods.

After a couple of minutes, I sneak up to the window and peek in. Appears that nobody else is home. My heart races as I turn the knob, check over my shoulder, and push the door open a crack. I listen for any sounds ... then step across the threshold.

There isn't much to the place. A living area, wood stove, washstand with a bucket and towels, and one bedroom with two mattresses—one on top of the other—a dresser and some boxes. No sign of a girl here. A ladder leads to a loft. I climb up and glance around. The space is hardly bigger than a closet, completely bare. Hell of a place for a kid. The bastard's treating her like an animal. But, where is she?

I climb down the ladder, slip out the door, and steal around back, stopping short a few yards from the firebreak. I click off the safety and step lightly, my eyes darting right and left, half-expecting the neighbor to pop out from behind cover. After a few steps, I kneel to study the grass— it's been mashed down. Probably the pickup I saw parked here the other night. After I threatened to report the bastard for child abuse, he must have driven her back into the woods to hide her from CPS. That's why Baker didn't find any trace of her. I prop the Beretta on my shoulder, and follow the tire tracks.

Bryce

Sheriff said the neighbor's some big shot banker. Must think he runs the whole damn country. Maybe so, but it sure didn't take much for me to get the law on my side. Guess most folks find it easy to root for the little guy when some rich jerk tries to horn in on what doesn't belong to him. Bet Tess'll be surprised to see me so soon. Not expecting me for another couple of days—or longer. Just hope this Eric clown hasn't blown it again and lost another one of my girls.

I pat the stock on my twelve-gauge. If he has, it'll be his last screw up. Something snaps behind me. I'm being followed. I crouch and peer into the shadows all around me. Stay still ... keep my eyes peeled for a couple minutes.

Nothing. Guess it was my imagination ... either that or a deer. Sneaky bastards. Ya hear 'em, and the next second they're gone. I get up and head to Eric's place, listening for sounds that don't belong.

Jacob

Almost an hour later, the firebreak opens up into a decent sized pasture—pretty well grazed from what I can little tell in the pale moonlight. At the end of the pasture there's a ranch house—a couple of lights on—also a barn and corral. Someone's walking up onto the porch, toting a shotgun. Must be the bastard I've been following.

I sneak up to some woods at the base of a ridge that borders the ranch to find a good vantage point—someplace where I can watch the front and back of the house as well as the barn. The pickup parked out back is the one from my neighbor's shack. He must have left it here when he brought the girl. Didn't want the sheriff to trace his license plate. Probably has a criminal history he's hiding.

Mercedes

Never thought anything could get me back here again. Just seeing the ranch house down below makes my skin crawl. There's just one light on inside. The moon is little more than a sliver. I rub dirt on my forehead and cheeks. Should do the trick. That, and the black hoody, pants and shoes. Even if

Tess and her fella come outside for some fresh air, they won't see me. Not even RJ could pick me out of the shadows, and he knows I'm out here.

The mental picture of Tess and RJ's uncle going at it—grunting and moaning on a squeaky bed frame—turns my stomach. Back when I escaped from under Bryce's thumb, I made up my mind that from then on sex was going to be on my terms. Of course, it's not as if I've been able to prove my theory yet. RJ's the only prospect I have, and he won't let me get close. And I'm not doing this for *him*. I owe it to Amy. I was a bitch to leave her behind with that bastard. We were like sisters. She'd never have done that to me. About time I did the right thing by her.

Finally. Three blinks from RJ's flashlight. Coming, Amy. I slip down to the barn where one side of the double door is propped open, waiting for me—just like RJ promised. Heavy wooden door. It creaks as I pull it out wide enough to pass through. As I slide inside, a chain rattles at the far end. I move quickly past the stalls, toward the far end of the barn. Step lightly so I don't startle her, hoping I don't have to raise her from a dead sleep—that wouldn't be good.

A blast of gunfire sends me darting into the open stall where RJ said I'd find her. She's cowering—hands covering her head. I reach for the padlock hanging from the chain on her neck and fumble for my lock-picking tools.

She jerks away, whimpering.

"Shh... it's me—Mercedes. We're getting you out of here."

Amy lurches back. "No. Mercedes is dead."

"I'm not dead."

Amy peeks up.

"See, it's me."

"Can't be. You got eaten by coyotes or .... Bryce said so."

I stick the pick in the padlock. "Almost. But I've got a place. An old hut a couple miles from here. It's safe."

She pulls away. "Can't leave."

Another loud kapow shakes the barn. I flinch. The horses paw the ground, snorting. I look at her. "What do you mean?" The pick slips out of my fingers.

"Just can't."

I fumble for the pick on the stable floor. "Once I pick this lock, you can go anywhere you want."

"No."

I find the homemade pick and start working it around inside the keyhole.

A third shotgun blast sends the horses bucking against their stall gates. That one was right outside the barn door. I keep my head down, maneuvering the pick until the lock springs open. I jerk Amy to her feet and drag her toward the rear door of the barn. "You can't stay here. We gotta go."

After a few steps, Amy drops to one knee and grabs her right foot.

"Damn. You're not wearing shoes."

She shakes her head.

I scan the barn ... gnawing on my lower lip. The horses ... snorting and squealing. Reminds me of when I met RJ. His horse had thrown him. He was lying on the ground half conscious. Right then I swore I'd never climb up on one of those beasts.

An angry voice roars from just outside the barn door. A fourth blast sends the horses into full panic.

I kick off my shoes. "Here. Put these on."

Amy hesitates.

I glare at her. "Do it."

As soon as Amy's feet are in the shoes, I yank her up and pull her through the back doorway and scour the area for someplace to hide. When the next shotgun blast rattles the barn, our only hope is to outrun the bastard. I shove Amy toward the woods and we race uphill.

Jacob

The first clap of gunfire stuns me as I crouch at the edge of the woods, watching the backside of the ranch house. A second blast sets the world around me spinning. My heart is still in my throat a few moments later when two people explode out the backdoor—one a few seconds ahead of the other. The first one activates motion sensor floodlights. He's a lanky, redhead kid who limps for cover behind the pickup. The second guy is the creep from across the lake. He swaggers out toward the barn, waving a shotgun and yelling. I rattle my brain—what's going down? Is the girl inside the house, shot dead or dying? Should I slip into the house to save her? Or rush the man headed for the barn?

Two more explosions from the creep's shotgun rip the night, and a couple of small figures catapult from behind the barn. A girl screams. Another loud boom. The redhead kid behind the pickup takes off for the woods to my right, dragging one leg.

Screams fill my head. Echoes of Celine sobbing years ago when she reached out for help. My head throbs—a rapid fire string of stabbing pains arcs from behind my ear to the top of my head. A wave of nausea hits me. My lips quiver. I tuck my head between my knees. *Celine—cell phone—she's gone.* I collapse.

Mercedes

My chest aches as I sit cross-legged on the floor of the hut cleaning sores on my feet. That finishes the night's ration of drinking water. The chest pains aren't from sprinting through the woods, halfway up the ridge, with Amy in tow—jerking her to her feet every time she stumbled. I'm still shaking from those shotgun blasts back at the ranch. Can hear them ringing in my ears. He probably killed RJ—my only friend in the world. That would make Amy hate me more than ever, and I wouldn't blame her.

Since leaving his shack, I've tried to forget everything about him, but his voice won't go away. It makes my skin crawl. Somehow my skin remembers things my mind wants to forget. Bryce had to be the one who sprayed the barn with buckshot as we escaped out the back door. And it was probably that damned shotgun I swiped from the men building the cabin across the lake. Bryce laid off me for a few weeks after I gave it to him.

He must've lost our trail after chasing us through the woods for about a quarter-mile. That's when I pushed Amy across a rockslide and up the side of the ridge. After the rocks, there was the fall-down from recent windstorms. My feet got all cut up. We hid behind boulders and watched him fume when he lost us. He had no idea which way we'd gone.

God. It must have been terrible for Amy. Look at her, curled up in the corner, asleep. Sleep's probably the only relief she gets from the torture of remembering the two years I left her behind. I wipe a tear from my cheek and dip a hand in a jar of honey I swiped from the fancy cabin on the lake. Honey's supposed to help the cuts heal, keep them from getting infected—at least that's what Bryce always said.

Amy used to nurse everybody. Started when she was little. Her touch was like being brushed with a feather. When she patched us up, you could see her eyes reflecting your pain. She worked on Bryce with the same tender care.

When my feet are all lathered up, I wrap them in strips torn from a ragged T-shirt and dig out a pair of one-size-too-large running shoes from a box in the corner. Even with the honey, I wince when I pull the shoes onto my raw, swollen feet. They sting worse when I stand. Each step sends the throbbing deeper into my bones. To discourage Amy from taking off if she wakes up before I get back, I slip off the shoes she's wearing and hide them.

Pain or no pain, this has to get done. The nightmare's not over 'til someone takes out Bryce.

On my way to the lake, an owl screeches. I shudder. It reminds me of Tess's shrill voice and how bitchy she always was to Amy. The night shadows play tricks on me, too. I see Bryce lurking behind every tree. That confirms my mission. It all ends tonight.

I detour down to Eric's ranch. After escaping that place, I swore I'd never go back, but getting a second chance to save Amy changed my tune. When I was a prisoner there I didn't spend my nights in the barn, like Amy. Eric kept me locked in a bedroom, the window nailed shut. One day he hauled me into the kitchen to scrub the floors, walls, stove, sink—left me all alone. Only, he forgot to padlock the doors. When he rode off on the stallion, I bolted.

The only reason I went back earlier tonight was to set Amy free. The only reason I'm back again is that I need to fetch some serious firepower. My crossbow will be too clean, too quiet when I face off against Bryce. His death has to be as savage as he is. I remember a gun rack over the fireplace in Eric's living room—two shotguns and a hunting rifle.

At the edge of the meadow, I kneel. The haze around the ranch house reminds me of a graveyard where Bryce took me once to see the headstone of a girl my age—proof, he said, of what could happen if I disobeyed. The air that night at the graveyard was misty, just like now. Quiet. Not a light anywhere. I grit my teeth and limp down to the house. The closer I get, the faster my heart pounds. Where's RJ? I hope to God he made it out alive.

To be sure no one's guarding the place, I circle to the front of the house—no motion lights there—and creep up onto the porch. The curtains are drawn shut, except for a small opening at one edge of the window. I peek in. Don't see any signs of life, there. I sneak along the side of the house, checking each window as I head for the kitchen around back. The drapes in Uncle Eric's bedroom are closed. I listen for a minute. Not a sound.

What must be RJ's window is wide open. Only piles of clothes and stuff on the floor this side of the bed. The knots in my shoulders unwind for a second. There's a chance he's alive. But then, he could be lying dead on the other side. When I get around back, I move slowly around the corner until the lights come on, then dart back to the side of the house and wait for someone to come out. After a couple of minutes, nobody appears. I ease up to the back door.

I turn on a light inside the kitchen as I step through the backdoor. This is where I made the choice to run. There were lots of times I thought about Amy. Knew I should've gone back to the shack and set her free. Guess that's part of the reason I've hung around for two years, trying to get up the nerve. Should have done it a long time ago.

I rummage through the kitchen, making mental notes of supplies we can come back for. In one of the drawers I find some shells for a twelve-gauge. Stuff several in my pocket, go straight to the living room, and take one of the shotguns off the rack.

I glance down the hallway at three doors. They kept me locked up in the first room. Must be RJ's, now. How ironic. But, what if? I take a deep breath and inch toward the doorway. A chill runs up my spine. Is he in there? In a pool of blood? Dead? There's only one way to know. I swallow hard and peek in. No RJ. I lean into the door jamb. Dizzy.

When everything stops spinning, I move to the bathroom, flip on the light. It's clear.

I step back into the hall and stare at the open doorway to Uncle Eric's bedroom. Did RJ try to be a hero? Stop Bryce from killing the only one in his family who gave a shit about him? I have to know.

As I cross the threshold into the bedroom, I fight back the urge to puke. My knees wobble. I drop to the floor. Uncle Eric's stiff, naked body and mangled face are too much to take. I shut my eyes and try to replace the gruesome sight with any other picture I can imagine. I remind myself of the other times I've had to suck it up to survive.

Slowly, I get back on my feet and step around Uncle Eric's corpse to check out the bathroom on the other side of the bed. No sign of RJ. My body goes limp. I drop to my knees next to the toilet and let the vomit rush out. When I'm done retching, tears roll down my cheeks. There's still hope RJ's alive.

RJ

Before all hell broke loose at the ranch, I heard footsteps coming down the hallway and ducked behind my bed. The footsteps didn't stop at my room—the intruder didn't check there, kept going. I let out the breath I'd been holding onto. When someone started yelling from Uncle Eric's room, I knew things were getting ugly. I slipped out into the hall and made a mad dash for the kitchen. I'd only taken a couple steps when a shotgun blast roared in my ears.

My heart stopped. I froze. Tess shrieked from Uncle Eric's bedroom. A split second later the intruder yelled, "Come back here." I bolted. Just as I got to the end of the hall a second blast was deafening. A spray of buckshot ripped my leg. I dove into the kitchen. Fear must have blocked the pain. I sprang back to my feet—knew I had to get the hell out of there, or I'd be dead. As I lunged toward the backdoor, I snatched up Uncle Eric's shotgun that was propped against the wall. Outside, I took cover behind the bitch's pickup. The man followed me out, but headed for the barn, firing his shotgun a couple more times. The first chance I got, I made for the woods, dragging my leg.

After stumbling through chaparral for what seems like half the night, every step aggravating the pain, no light to speak of, I finally reach a cabin at the lake. It's bigger, fancier by a lot more, than what Mercedes described when she opened up to me—told me about the hell the bastard put her through. Maybe the creep won the lottery and rebuilt the place after she ran away. I crouch in the brush near the deck, trying to get up enough courage to limp up to the door. I'm Uncle Eric's only real family. It's up to me to even the score.

A man comes out of the cabin. My heart races. He's bigger than Mercedes said. What this monster did to her must have really messed up her head. It's no wonder. My mind is a train wreck after just one night of his terror. Can't imagine what it's like for Mercedes. She suffered through it most of her life.

My throat is dry. Uncle Eric—dead. Sweat stings my eyes. The fuzzy figure on the deck stands motionless. I tell myself to walk away. I'm not inside some video game. There's no restart button. No extra lives or special powers to put a player back in the game. It's a good thing this guy's just a blur.

Bryce deserves to die for what he's done. Not only for murdering Uncle Eric, but for terrorizing Mercedes. Maybe putting an end to the bastard will give her a second chance. I brace myself and anchor the butt of Uncle Eric's shotgun in the hollow of my shoulder. My arms tremble. I take a deep breath and hold it. Close my eyes and squeeze the trigger.

Click.

Damn. Forgot to load it.

The bastard darts back inside ... no doubt going for his gun.

I bolt, ignoring my throbbing leg as I race through the underbrush into the woods.

Tess

All the way back to the shack from Eric's ranch, Bryce keeps reminding me how he spared my life and how he wasn't going to let anybody leave him ever again ... not like *she* always did. He was going to "take back what belongs" to him.

That's when it clicked. He hasn't been helping me out these years. It never was about saving me and my baby from the streets, helping me settle a score. By *she* he meant his mother. He kidnapped me to be the mother he wanted but never had. And ransoming Amy was just how he planned to get his hooks into me. It's all been about the little boy who stared out the window all those nights, wondering whether his mother'd come home, whether she'd been behind the wheel drunk and wrapped her car around a tree somewhere, left him alone.

When we get to the shack, he tells me to clean up. He takes off in the pickup to get rid of my bloody clothes—bury them somewhere away from here so no one can find them. While I'm washing blood off my face I stare in the mirror. I've taken his shit far too long. I'm done. I walk over and grab his shotgun. Load it and wait for him to get back.

Don't have to wait long before he pulls up and parks the pickup. His footsteps on the other side of the door raise the hairs on the back of my neck. I watch the door latch as it begins to turn, bring the butt of the shotgun to my shoulder, and draw a deep breath. The door swings open. The concussion from the blast sends me stumbling backwards. Everything goes dark.

Mercedes

I reach the lake and duck down in the underbrush about ten yards from Bryce's shack. The whole nightmare floods into my head. Bruises ... sore all over ... him pounding his prick inside me, grinding his clammy chest into my back, his stale beer-breath filling my nostrils. Amy whimpering in the corner—knowing she'd be next. I've woken up night after night since I left this place—sweaty, achy, shaking. No matter what it costs me … I have to make him pay.

In a matter of minutes, the pickup comes rumbling up the gravel road. My heart turns as hard and cold as granite. Bryce slides out of the driver's seat and grabs a shovel from the back—swaggers up to the door. I stand, quivering—my face and neck dripping. I bring the butt of the shotgun to my shoulder and step lightly toward him, aiming at his head. He deserves this. Amy deserves this. Hell, I deserve this.

Sweat trickles into my eyes, blurring my vision. He's not human. He's a monster. A life form that shouldn't exist.

The door opens.

Boom.

I stagger back. Jerk the trigger. Another boom pounds my ears. My head snaps back, eyes shut tight. When I open them, Bryce is lying in a heap in the empty doorway. Flames flickering inside the shack. Someone's lying on the floor. I gasp for breath, my heart throbbing in my ears as I clutch the shotgun in both hands.

Tess

Flames are spreading over the floor. I can make out pieces of a broken lantern in the middle of the flames. I get up. Head aches like hell. Must've banged it against something when the shotgun's recoil kicked me on my ass. I stumble toward the open doorway. Bryce lies across the threshold, lifeless. Blood pooling around his head. I start to puke. Hold it in. Gotta get out of here.

The pickup door is still open. I slide in behind the wheel and crank the engine. As I barrel down the gravel road, I swallow back acid that's pushing up into my throat. There's been way too much blood. Everywhere I look I see red, like I'm wearing blood splattered glasses—the seat, the windshield, the road, my white blouse, my hands. I try to rub it away as I drive over the gravel road past the lake. It won't come off, doesn't even smear. It's unreal. I don't bother checking for traffic as I careen out onto the highway. Somehow, somewhere I'll outrun this horror.

Deputy Sheriff Baker

We find Jacob Chandler staring at smoke billowing up into the night sky—flames shooting out of his neighbor's shack. He's drenched in sweat, emergency vehicle lights pulsing all around him. I shine my flashlight on the bloodied blade of the shovel resting at his feet and ask, "Is that yours?"

He stares blankly.

"Mr. Chandler, is that your shovel?"

"Uh … sorry. What?"

I pick up the shovel with my latex-gloved hand. "Is this is your shovel?"

Chandler looks around. "Where are we?"

I signal the EMT who's been hovering nearby.

The EMT takes out a pocket flashlight, examines Chandler's eyes, and asks, "Sir, are you feeling okay?"

"Yeah … just a bit groggy. What's going on here?"

The EMT points to the back of the paramedic truck and steadies him as they walk. "You'd better take a seat."

After Chandler sits down at the back of the emergency vehicle, he looks at the EMT. "Can someone tell me what's going on here? Is my place gone?"

"No, Mr. Chandler. This is your neighbor's place."

"Is the girl okay?"

"There *is* no girl. We've been over that."

He stares at the burning shack. "She's not in there?"

"No girl."

"You're sure?"

"As I said, she doesn't exist. Now, I'm going to ask you one more time. Is that your shovel?"

"I don't know. Could be. I have one that's similar. Are my initials on the handle?"

"You're JC ...?"

"Yeah, why?"

I point to the initials etched on the handle. "What happened here tonight?"

"Not sure."

"How'd this blood get on your shovel?"

"No idea. Guess I was trying to put out the fire."

"With blood?"

"I said, I don't remember. I don't even know how I got here. Suppose I wanted to help ... when I saw the fire."

"It's my impression your neighbor didn't want you coming around."

"I wouldn't just let the place burn down. For sure I wouldn't let the girl get hurt." He looks around. "The pickup's gone. He must have taken her somewhere."

"Your neighbor doesn't own a pickup, and he doesn't have a driver's license. I checked him out after my last visit up here."

Chandler wobbles and lists to one side.

I catch him before he tumbles off the back of the paramedic truck. "Mr. Chandler, these folks are going to give you a ride down to the hospital. One of our deputies will go along to keep you company."

"Are you sure that's necessary?"

"Positive."

As the EMT helps Chandler climb into the emergency vehicle, I nod to the deputy who was holding the shovel. "We'd better tag and bag that thing."

Chapter Eight

RJ

My eyes ache, and sunlight poking through the tree canopy doesn't help. I put up my hand to block the glare. My throbbing leg reminds me of last night's chaos.

After the shotgun misfired at the lake, I panicked and scrambled off, hobbling through trees and scrub toward Mercedes' hut. Didn't make it far. My knees buckled, and I landed on the shotgun wound, driving buckshot deeper into my flesh. Pain was too much. The cool ground brought on the shivers. My forehead burned with fever. I must've passed out. I kind of recall headlights racing past, but I could've imagined it.

I shake the cobwebs out of my head and push up off the ground, standing on my good leg. Bite down on my lower lip and shift some weight to the wounded leg, but it collapses underneath me. I land hard and every pellet buried in my leg stings twice as bad.

What a klutz. Lost the damn shotgun at some point during the night. Now I can't even use it as a crutch. Coulda, woulda, shoulda. If only I'd remembered to load the damn thing. I clench my teeth and prop up on my good knee so I can scan the area nearby. Just out of reach, there's a branch lying on the ground. Probably knocked down during a wind storm. Just the right size for a cane. I pull myself along the ground until I'm close enough to grab it.

After hobbling for nearly a mile, I recognize the terrain. My heart beats faster, this time it's from more than exhaustion. Uncle Eric's ranch is around the next bend in the trail, just out of view. Can't bear to relive that nightmare right now, so I detour higher up into the woods and trudge ahead.

Later, I'm on the ridge overlooking Mercedes' hut. I lower myself to the ground and stretch out my throbbing leg. My throat tightens. Did the girls make it back? God, Mercedes could be dead. Then who'd I have left? Can't imagine my mom would want me even if I found her. I let out a loud caw then wait for Mercedes' to give me the all clear.

Mercedes

My nerves are still jangled from last night when a familiar 'caw' sends my heart into my throat. He's alive?

I rush over to the door, swallow hard and, return his signal.

Amy joins me at the doorway. "What's going on?" she asks.

"RJ."

"He's alive?"

"It's our signal. He's the only one who knows it."

Amy searches the ridge. "Where is he?"

"It'll take a few minutes." I point to a stand of pines. "He should come from over there."

The first sight of him takes my breath away. He's hobbling, supporting himself on a long branch, stumbling, almost dropping to one knee.

Amy grabs my arm. "Does he need help?"

I know how this is going down. He'll have the hots for her in no time. She's a regular healing angel. Always patched up Bryce when he got hurt. If it'd been me, I would have made sure the damn wound got infected bad enough to kill him.

"You mean like he helped us?"

"That's not fair."

"Of course he needs help. He's a boy." I start out the door. "You coming?"

We race up the ridge and I get to him well ahead of Amy. He collapses in my arms. I stiffen at the sight of his bloody leg.

"He's been shot," I murmur to Amy as she comes up behind me.

She doesn't hesitate taking charge, easing him out of my grasp, and cradling him in her own arms. "He's burning up with fever," she says calmly, looking up at me as she strokes his hair. Her eyes take on his pain. His body relaxes.

When we get him into the hut, we lay him on the pine-needle mattress in the corner, and Amy starts barking orders. "Quick, I need bandage stuff. And boil some water."

I'm already under her spell, the one she casts over everybody when her healing powers take over. "Clean rags," I mutter as I scan the room.

"Hurry," Amy scolds, rushing to the wash basin to scrub her hands.

I wander over to a corner of the hut and dig through a box. I pull out several towels swiped from the man's cabin at the lake. "Here." I toss them at Amy.

Amy scowls. "Boiling water?"

"Right. I'm on it. It'll take a few minutes." I stoke the fire in the little cast iron stove, grab the water pail, and head down to a spring I discovered not far from the hut. A horrible thought burrows into my brain like a worm. *I saved her, now she's going to steal my only friend.*

Amy

I rip open RJ's pant leg and start picking out buckshot with my fingernails. When Mercedes comes back with the water, I keep my head down and ask her for a knife. Out of the corner of my eye, I watch her set the water pail on top of the stove. She opens the stove door and sticks a knife inside, into the flames. When she's done sterilizing it, she brings it to me.

I stay focused on RJ's wound. "Thanks. How's that water?"

"It'll take a few more minutes to boil."

I poke deeper into his leg with the knife. RJ flinches. A towel soaks up blood oozing from his wound. Mercedes watches.

After I've fished out what I hope is the last of the pellets, Mercedes kneels next to me with a jar of honey. She says, "Ever used it on anything this bad?"

"Yeah, Bryce."

"Of course, Bryce."

Deputy Sheriff Baker

Outside the interview room where Carl Samuels is waiting, I study the ME report on the victim from last night's fire. After that, I check the list of weapons we collected at Chandler's place early this morning. A handgun and shotgun are registered to Carl Samuels. A shotgun recovered from the fire looks to have enough damage that ballistics won't be conclusive.

I step into the room and greet Samuels. "Can I get you coffee?"

"No thanks. I filled up this morning before I left the city."

"I appreciate you offering to come in and help shed some light on your friend. By the way, have you spoken to him lately?"

"Spoke with him by phone yesterday after lunch. Why?"

"Nothing in particular. Just wondered how close you two are."

"We've known each other for almost forty years. As his career advanced, I've enjoyed similar success."

"I've known my ex-wife for a few years, but that doesn't make us close."

He grins.

I haven't gotten to the tough questions. Wonder if he's ever given a straight answer in his life.

"Help me understand your relationship with Mr. Chandler. That way I'll know how you can help us."

"I run what we refer to as a family office. He's our largest client."

"So, you have a business relationship."

"We like to think it's a good bit more than business, but money is a big part of it. All of our clients have networths over a billion dollars."

"That must mean Mr. Chandler is worth—"

Samuels grins. "That's confidential."

"I see. So I'd have to have a subpoena."

He shifts in his chair. "Are you driving a something, Deputy?"

"Sorry. I guess I was trying to make a joke. Lighten up the conversation, since you seem to be a bit guarded."

"An occupational hazard, I guess. Clients expect us to be discreet."

"I understand. Maybe you can tell me what you thought I ought to know about your friend, Mr. Chandler. He is a friend, right?"

"We like to think all of our clients are friends."

"I'm sure you do." I cross my arms and wait. As the rule goes, the next one to talk winds up caving.

It doesn't take Samuels long. "Yes we're friends."

"You called him yesterday. Is that something you do regularly?"

"Jake's been through a lot over the past dozen years."

"But you do check up on him?"

"It's his memory."

"Is he suffering from dementia?"

"No. The doctors aren't sure what causes it. He just has these episodes when he forgets blocks of time. So, if he sounds a little sketchy when you ask him for details, he's not trying to be evasive. He genuinely can't remember."

"Has he ever gotten violent during those episodes?"

"No. Never."

"How often do you check on him?"

"Most every day."

"But you live where?"

"South of the city."

"By city, you mean San Francisco?"

"Yes."

"You don't actually see him every day?"

"No. He spends most of his time alone. But, I've never seen ... excuse me, Deputy, but is something wrong?"

"Mr. Samuels, do you hunt?"

"Do I hunt? What does that have to do with anything?"

"It's just a question. Yes or no. Do you hunt?"

"Haven't for years."

"Do you recall leaving a weapon, specifically a shotgun, in Mr. Chandler's possession?"

"Ah ... a few years ago I gave him a shotgun as a gift."

"Why wasn't the transfer recorded?"

"I don't know. I suppose it was a detail we overlooked."

"That little detail happens to be a law."

"You're right. I'll check into it. Whoever was responsible will be dealt with."

"You and Mr. Chandler were responsible."

"But in the scheme of things?"

"Yes. Speaking of the scheme of things, how many guns did you give him?"

"Only one that I can recall."

"Last night we found Mr. Chandler standing in front of his neighbor's place as it was burning to the ground. His shovel was on the ground next to him."

"So he was trying to put out the fire."

"You might think so, but the shovel blade was covered with blood, and the fire crew pulled out a charred body. This morning, the ME tells us that the decedent was shot in the face at close range with a shotgun, then the face was bashed in with Mr. Chandler's shovel. The only finger prints on the handle belong to Chandler."

The blood drains from his face. "Where's Jake now?"

"He's at the hospital, under observation. He was pretty disoriented when we found him."

He stands. "I'd better get over there to check on him."

"You can see him later at the county jail. He'll be under arrest as soon as he wakes up. I checked gun registration records, and Mr. Chandler owns several weapons, including a pricey Beretta shotgun. When we searched his residence for weapons early this morning, we couldn't find the Beretta. However, we were able to make out the serial number on the shotgun we recovered from the fire. It was registered in your name."

He tugs at his starched collar and says, "There's got to be a logical explanation."

"Yes. I can think of one very logical one."

"You're making a big mistake, here."

Jacob

A plastic band cuts into my wrist. When I start to sit up, a strap digs into my chest. "What the ...." I fall back.

A chair slides on the floor somewhere near me.

"Take it easy, Mr. Chandler." The words rumble around like I'm in an echo chamber.

"What's going on?" I groan.

I turn my head and study a uniformed man walking like he's in a slow motion video.

"Keep your voice down." His mouth is out of sync with his voice. "No need to get excited. We brought you in last night so the doctors could check you out. They gave you something to help you sleep."

I lift up my hand to show him that it's tied to the bed rail. It drops to my side. "What's this for?"

"Sir, you've been placed under arrest. Deputy Sheriff Baker will be here in a moment to explain."

I shake the cobwebs out of my head. "Arrest? For what?"

The deputy pulls out a laminated card and reads aloud. When he finishes, he asks, "Do you understand your rights as I've explained them?"

I shrug.

Baker appears in the doorway. His voice is sharp and clear. "Mr. Chandler, the deputy asked you a question."

"Yes. I understand. Now can someone tell me what's going on?"

"Are you waiving your rights to counsel?"

"Of course not."

"Do you want to call an attorney?"

I look out the window. Everything is in focus now. "Yes."

"Mr. Chandler. We found an adult male body inside the shack that burned last night. We haven't identified it yet, but we believe it's your neighbor. And the shovel we found at the scene was covered with blood—matches the decedent's type. Your initials are engraved on the handle."

"Give me my phone."

Chapter Nine

Jacob

Behind me is a concrete wall, institutional beige. I sit in a metal folding chair, staring at Carl's grim face in the monitor. I take the handset off the wall. "Do I have a good lawyer?"

"Yeah. How are you doing?"

"How would you expect?"

"Just keep positive. Your arraignment's tomorrow. I've got the funds all set. If the judge grants bail, you'll be out of here before dinner time."

"How the hell do people do it?"

"Do what?"

Though I try to restrain myself, my voice raises an octave. "*If* the judge sets bail. How do people put up with someone else controlling their lives? When I got here, the duty sergeant took my fingerprints, they gave me an orange jumpsuit, and a guard led me to a cell with a cot. Every move I make is based on a schedule somebody else decides works for them. I eat whatever slop they feel like serving, where I'm told, when I'm told. That's what gnaws at me—they do the telling, I do the doing. If this isn't rock bottom, then everything from here must be a flat out free fall."

"Just hang in there. It'll be over soon."

"Sure—and what if I don't get bail? What if I'm convicted? That's a minimum of twenty-five years."

"That's why we've hired the best defense attorney in the state. He'll have you out of here like you were Houdini."

"You know Carl, until Celine slipped out of my hands, there was never a day that I wasn't in full control—not just of myself, but everyone around me. I thought the low point of my life was hearing them say Jesse had taken his own life. But the bleeding didn't stop—Ellen died, then the board fired me from my own firm."

I draw a deep breath and exhale. "I started from scratch—my first client was a 27-seven year-old gal who'd just won a $300,000 personal injury judgment. From there I built it to the largest investment firm in the country. I put San Francisco's financial district on the map, single handedly. How do people put up with someone else controlling their lives?"

Carl sits back. "Fear."

"What do you mean ... fear?"

"Fear is why folks let other people control their lives. It's easier to accept failure if they can blame somebody else when they come up short. Someone bigger, stronger, smarter, more successful, richer. If that doesn't work they pick on the schleps below them. Complain their employees are lazy, taxes are high, government's too intrusive, suppliers are cheating, people are stupid, whatever. They're afraid of taking responsibility for their own screw ups. Fear is why they let others have control."

I stare at the screen for a long time. Finally, I say, "Yeah, I'm afraid. Maybe the system isn't going to work this time."

Carl clears his throat. "Let's not over think this, okay? Just keep your eye on the ball. Act sane and sound, confident you're innocent. Don't give the judge any signals to doubt you. Keep focused and I'll buy you a fat juicy steak for dinner tomorrow night."

"And an expensive wine to wash it down."

He smiles. "You've got it."

I've been waiting nearly a week for that steak dinner, but my arraignment keeps getting postponed. So much for a speedy trial. At least when I go to court I get to wear a suit and tie. For today's appearance the color's heather-blue—supposed to give the impression I'm honest, trustworthy.

Roger Dugan, my criminal attorney, stands tall—dressed in a dapper tan suit, pale blue tie—shoulders pulled back. "Your Honor, the defense requests bail." Even a hundred miles from home, the courtroom is his turf.

The assistant district attorney, Kate Chang, jumps to her feet. "The State objects, Your Honor. The defendant stands accused of a capital crime. He is single with no ties to the community and has considerable means, so that bail would not be a deterrent. We consider him a flight risk."

Dugan counters. "Your Honor, the defendant has experienced a series of tragedies, leaving him without family. That's true; however, the event that instigated those unfortunate circumstances was the abduction of his 4-year-old granddaughter over a dozen years ago. Since then, he has devoted his life to finding her and would certainly not jeopardize his chances of continuing that search."

The prosecutor shakes her head. "Your Honor, the State will present DNA evidence at trial showing Jacob Chandler's granddaughter has been present in the residence where the crimes occurred, giving the defendant sufficient motive."

I jump to my feet.

Dugan grabs my shoulder and pulls me down. "We beg the Court's indulgence, Your Honor."

I wipe away a tear.

Judge Edwards looks at Chang. "You may continue."

The prosecutor clears her throat. "We will argue the defendant believed the decedent was involved in his granddaughter's disappearance and that he willfully committed the act of murder out of vengeance. We contend the defendant poses a risk to society as he recklessly continues to hunt down whomever else he believes was responsible for his granddaughter's disappearance."

Dugan rises. "May I, Your Honor?"

Judge Edwards nods.

"First of all, the State has yet to identify the deceased, and they have no forensic evidence connecting a murder weapon to the defendant. They only presume the body is that of to my client's neighbor, and that Mr. Chandler's shovel and a weapon possibly owned by him were involved in the alleged crimes. Their theories regarding motive and means are without foundation. In fact, not once since his granddaughter went missing over twelve years ago has Mr. Chandler shown any indication he would resort to violence against anyone. And, why would a disciplined and successful executive like my client kill someone who might have knowledge of her whereabouts? For the entire time she has been missing, my client has employed licensed private investigators to search for her, and he continues to do so to this day. Furthermore, the State can't have it both ways. On the one hand they argue Mr. Chandler doesn't have ties to the community, but they also speculate his granddaughter is in the vicinity."

The judge toys with his pen, then signs the bail order. "Agreed, Mr. Dugan. The State seems to be stretching its points about Mr. Chandler's threat to society and risk of flight. Bail is set at two million dollars."

When Judge Edwards raps his gavel, I grab Dugan's arm. "Hey, what's this about my granddaughter?"

"I'm hearing it for the first time. Have you been holding back something? Because if you are …."

"Are they saying Celine was the girl that bastard was going to assault with his belt?"

"That's the first thing I'm going to check out. So you're telling me you had no clue?"

"There's no way that girl is Celine. They don't look a bit alike. But if Celine was there at some point, where is she now? Hell, if only that bastard were here to tell us."

Dugan shakes his head. "He's not."

"Maybe, the girl can tell us something."

Dugan heads out of the courtroom into the corridor without a word. Carl and I follow. Out in the hallway, Dugan looks at me and says, "We'll drop you at your cabin on our way back to the city. Sit tight until you hear from me. In the meantime, Carl can keep you company."

I squeeze Dugan's arm. "If she's in the area, we've got to find her."

Dugan's eyes widen. "Sit tight and let me take care of things."

Chapter Ten

Amy

RJ's fever broke after three days. A week later, his cheeks have color. Now, he's eating soup. Me, spooning it to him. Mercedes watches from another corner of the hut, sour-faced.

I rub his knee. "How's your leg?"

He smiles. "Let's test it out."

Mercedes rolls her eyes. "Finally. The freeloading comes to an end."

"You're sounding like Bryce," I mutter.

"Whatever," she sneers.

RJ stands, keeping his weight on the good leg. "And fighting's not going to get us anywhere."

Mercedes crosses her arms. "Let's get something clear. This is my place. Don't wear out your welcome."

I get up, eyeing Mercedes. "She's right, RJ. We have to make her happy. It's her way or the highway."

She steps up to me, her fists clenched.

RJ hobbles between us. "We have to work together, at least 'til we know …."

Mercedes looks at him. "Know what?"

I finish his thought. "If Bryce is coming."

Mercedes mutters, "Bryce isn't coming after us."

My shoulders tighten. "You don't know that."

"I know what's real and what's not. If you're going to survive, that's something you'll have to learn, too. Bryce isn't coming after us—so I don't want to hear any more about him."

I look at RJ, hoping he understands. He shrugs.

Mercedes plants her hands on her hips. "I'm not feeding and fetching water for all of us. You two need to start carrying your weight."

RJ limps over to the bucket. "I'm on it. I need some fresh air, anyway."

I stand beside him. "Me, too."

Mercedes holds up a hand. "It's a one person job."

"I've got it, Amy," says RJ. "But if I'm not back in a few minutes, my leg's probably given out."

Mercedes sneers. "If you fall, crawl back. We aren't carrying you from here on."

RJ shakes his head and limps outside.

Mercedes turns to me. "You aren't going to skate by playing the maid. Everyone cleans up after themselves. I've had to get along on my own for two years."

"Okay. What do you need done?"

"Do you wanna eat? It's everybody's job to put food on the table."

"How?"

Mercedes rubs her forehead. "Nobody taught me. I had to figure it out to stay alive."

"You had the guts to run away."

"You're right. I couldn't afford any dead weight then, and I still can't. Surviving means making hard choices. Sometimes those choices put you on the same level as animals."

I look down. "I've got no shoes."

"You've been holed up here for days eating through food I've scavenged, and you don't make the effort to notice what's right under your nose." Mercedes points to boxes in the corner. "This is the last time I'm bailing you out. After this, it's sink or swim—save your own hide."

I walk over to the boxes. Dig through them and pull out a pair of sneakers. "Why didn't you say so before?"

Mercedes shrugs.

RJ stumbles into the hut with a full bucket. "The leg's holding. I think I'll live."

I cinch up the shoelaces. "Good thing. If you die, she'll make you dig your own grave."

Mercedes furrows her brow. "We need to make a trip back to the ranch house. I scoped it out the other night. There's plenty there to keep us going for a while." She takes the crossbow down from its peg.

RJ and I smile at each other.

Mercedes glares. "You two coming?"

Mercedes

I gag on the stench as soon as we open the back door to Uncle Eric's ranch house. By the time we get to his bedroom, the odor sticks to me like grime, caking in my throat and burning my eyes. His bloated corpse is lying in a disgusting pool of slime that still oozes from rotted patches of skin. A swarm of flies buzzes around him. RJ recoils at the sight of maggots eating away at the dark purple crater where a face used to be. He retches. Amy presses her face against his back and shuts her eyes.

"Let's get out of here," I mutter as I step back into the hallway, skirting past RJ and Amy. Halfway down the hall, I call over my shoulder. "I said let's go."

When they join me in the kitchen where I'm rummaging through the pantry, I tell them, "We might as well take as much of this as we can carry. It's not like he has any use for it."

RJ chokes back tears. "We need to bury him. I can't leave him like that for who-knows-what to pick apart. I'm sure I can find a couple shovels in the barn."

I stuff cans and boxes of food from the cupboards into a couple of garbage bags and point to the fridge. "Amy can help me empty that."

Amy moves over next to RJ. "I'll help him dig."

"Do whatever you want, but I'm not carrying all this back to the hut by myself."

RJ starts for the back door and stops short. "Let's just move in here. The place has everything we need."

I toss a box of mac-and-cheese into a plastic sack. "My place is safer. Too easy for people to find us here."

RJ scratches his head. "What's wrong with people finding us?"

I shake my head. "I'm not staying under somebody else's roof—ever again—especially this place."

Amy tugs RJ's sleeve. "Come on RJ."

I point to the hallway. "The last thing we need is for someone to find us here with a corpse. They'll think we killed him. We'll spend the rest of our lives in jail."

Amy pulls RJ out the door.

I call after them. "We don't have time for loafing ... or socializing."

While they dig, I collect and sort everything in the house we might be able to use. Stuff we'll need right away—perishable food and the like—goes into garbage bags we can hang over the horses' backs. Other things go into boxes I find stacked in a closet that I empty. We can come back and get the boxes later.

When that's done, I walk back to the bedroom. This time the stench stops me cold at the doorway. Stomach acid works its way up into my throat. It seems worse than earlier.

I turn away and take a deep breath before rushing into the room. I jerk the sheets off the bed and fling them next to Uncle Eric's body. When I bend down to start wrapping him, he seems to stare at me with eyes bulging out of his mangled face. I start to heave. Tiny stars swirl in front of me. I dart back into the hall. My skin tingles. I bend over and gasp for breath.

A moment later, I charge back into the bedroom, kneel in the pool of slime, fight the urge to puke, throw a sheet over him. But in my head I still see maggots, holes where buckshot tore into his skin—skin that makes the world's worst case of blackheads look good. I turn the body to wrap it in bedding ... flesh comes off the bone ... I drop the foul mess ... it falls in my lap ... I stare at the slime covering the palms of my hand, my fingertips. I retch all over poor Uncle Eric's stomach. I try to take deep breaths ... get control of myself, but the stench I've tried to block out of my mind fills my lungs, my mouth, my nose. I bolt out of the room.

Out in the hall, I pull my shirt over my face, hoping to block out the foul, putrid smell. Breathe slowly. Figure out how to handle all this. We have to clean up this mess. What if someone finds it? Worse, what if they somehow connect it to us? Prison's not an option for me. I'd rather die.

I rush back into the room, telling myself this isn't real. Just like when I skinned my first rabbit. This is survival. I kneel again on the carpet next to Uncle Eric. He's just sleeping. It's not slime … just mud. No. It's not really him or anyone else. It's a roasted pig. I've read about what they call luaus. When they're done right, the meat pulls right off the bone—the same as small game. I tell myself that's how it's supposed to be … stretch out the bedding next to my him, roll him over, tuck the bedding around him, roll him again until the bedding is all used up.

When the roasted pig is secure in his wrapping, I stagger into the hall, again gasping for air. I hope it's enough to stop the oozing and keep us from making a mess as we carry him outside.

In the kitchen, I find RJ and Amy standing at the backdoor, whispering. "What took you so long?" I ask.

RJ looks over at me. "We wanted to bury him deep enough that nothing could dig him up."

Amy nods. "We found a couple picks to loosen the ground and two shovels so we could dig at the same time; otherwise, we'd still be at it."

I point to the hallway. "I've wrapped him up to make him easier to carry. Come on, give me a hand."

Instead of the grotesque sight of Uncle Eric's corpse, a near-formless bundle lies just inside the bedroom door. The putrid odor still hangs in the room, the carpet still gives away the room's gruesome secret. Each of us grabs a handful of blanket and lifts on my count of three. Amy's corner drags as we waddle through the door.

"Keep it off the ground," I insist. "The slime's leaking through."

Amy chokes back nausea as she wrestles with her corner. She loses her grip several times, leaving smudges along the hallway and kitchen floor.

Once the body is buried, I lead the others back inside. "This damn mess in the hallway is a dead giveaway. Anybody who stumbles in here will figure out in no time what's gone on." I scrunch up my nose. "Let's get it cleaned up."

"Wait," RJ holds up a hand. "We have something we wanna say." He looks at Amy. She nods.

"What is it?" I fold my arms across my chest.

RJ pulls back his shoulders. "We're okay with staying at your place as long as you promise to stop bullying us."

"I'm not bullying. I'm just taking charge. Neither of you knows how to survive out here on your own."

Amy glares. "We just wanna have a say."

I study her, taken off guard by her boldness. "And if I don't agree to stop ... bullying?"

"Then Amy and I stay here, and you leave all that stuff behind. It's my stuff now that Uncle Eric's ... dead."

I stare at RJ, waiting for him to blink. He doesn't.

Finally, I break the standoff. "Everyone carries their own weight and I'll be fine."

He nods. "I've fed and saddled two horses. Figure we might as well use them. I put the rest out to pasture."

My jaw drops. "You expect me to climb on one of those things?"

He shrugs. Amy snickers.

Someone bangs on the front door. We all look to the hallway.

The banging is joined by a raspy voice. "Anybody home?"

RJ's eyes widen as he whispers, "It's old man Miller. He lives down the road."

"Does he know you?"

"Yeah. He stops by sometimes. Last time, he chewed my ass real good about us neglecting the horses."

I nod toward the hallway. "Go see what he wants. And get rid of him."

Miller bangs on the front door and calls out again.

"Just a minute," RJ shouts.

Amy and I follow RJ down the hall and hold back as he turns the corner a few feet from the front door. When RJ steps out on the porch, Miller demands to see Uncle Eric about those "damned horses and that god-awful stench" he's smelled the last couple times he's dropped by.

"He's out riding," RJ tells him. "I can have him come by your place when he gets back."

"And what about that smell? You didn't let one of those sick horses die, did you?"

"No, sir. We had a stillborn colt. I just got around to burying it. It had been laying out behind the house."

"You and your damned uncle belong in jail for the way you treat those animals. I'm done talking about. It's animal cruelty." Miller's voice cracks.

"Mr. Miller, I swear I'm taking ...."

"You aren't doing squat."

"I've been sick."

"That's no damn excuse. I've come by here for the past three days. And every time, those poor horses were shut up in filthy stalls full of piss and dung. They'd have starved if I hadn't thrown them some hay."

"But, Mr. Miller ...."

"Keep your whining for the sheriff. I expect they'll be here real soon."

"You called them?"

"You betcha, I did. So you best saddle up and go find that worthless uncle of yours. I'll just wait here 'til they come."

RJ hobbles around the corner and stops short in front of us. His face is ash-white. He whispers, "Did you hear that? He called the sheriff. We gotta get out of here or our asses are going to jail."

Amy's face goes white. "They'll hang us."

I grab her by the shoulders. "Get a grip. This is not time for hysterics. Out to the barn. Now."

The three of us hurry into the kitchen, take the loaded garbage bags, slip out the back door, and rush into the barn. Once we've tied the bags onto the mare, I grab RJ's arm. "You ride your horse hard, that way." I point out past the side of the house. "While the old man's keeping his eye on you, we'll lead the mare out the back way and up into the woods. You can circle back around and meet us once you're out of his sight."

"Can't you just meet me back at the hut?"

I gulp. "I'm not climbing up on that thing."

He looks at Amy. "Do you know how to ride?"

She shakes her head.

"Can't believe it," he mutters.

Deputy Sheriff Baker

Old man Miller stands on the front porch. "About time."

"What's that odor?" I ask.

"The boy said something about a stillborn colt rotting out back."

"Is the boy around?"

Miller points toward the pasture. "Sent him after his uncle about half-hour ago. The boy said he was out for a ride."

"Let's go check the horses. They still in the barn?"

"Saw some of them out in the pasture when I got here. Guess the boy finally got around to doing some of his chores. Damned kids these days."

I smirk as I round the corner of the house toward the barn. Miller follows, recounting what he'd witnessed of the horses' neglect over the last several days. About halfway between the ranch house and the barn I stop and stare back at the steps to the kitchen. Miller tracks my line of sight and asks, "What is it, Sheriff?"

Without a word, I walk back to the ranch house, scanning a path along the ground where something heavy appears to have been dragged. At the back steps I put on a latex glove, dab my finger on a wet spot, and sniff. "Shit!"

"What is it?"

"Not sure. How long did he say the colt's carcass had been laying out here?"

"Didn't say. But obviously long enough to rot."

I hold up a hand. "Don't touch anything."

I walk follow the trail of soft dirt, stopping now and then to crouch and get a closer view. At several points I poke my latex-gloved finger into splotches of slime. After about twenty feet, I stop where a patch of ground has been dug up—about six feet long and a couple feet wide. I press the 'Talk' button on the radio Velcroed to my shoulder. "This is Deputy Sheriff Baker. I need a team with their forensic kits up here at Eric Lamb's ranch. And ... better alert the coroner. I think we've got another body."

I stand and walk back to Miller. "This whole area's a crime scene. Why don't we go back to the front porch and have a little chat about your neighbor?"

On the front porch, Miller rants about Eric Lamb and their disputes over his neglected horses. Miller acknowledges he never felt threatened by his neighbor—a mild-tempered sort. Yes, he heard gunfire occasionally, a lot of it a few nights ago, but figured someone was knocking down a pack of coyotes. He didn't know about any enemies his neighbor might have and hardly ever saw visitors coming or going. A boy, his nephew, had been staying with him the past couple of years. The boy was lazy like most, but polite, respectful. Never noticed any anger problems.

After a half-hour of getting no leads from Miller, my backup unit comes barreling up the long dirt drive from the road, raising a cloud of dust. I send the old man home.

As the two deputies step out of their vehicle, I ask, "You guys got the warrant?"

"Right here." Deputy Grimes waves a folded paper at me.

"Grimes, you start around back. I think there's a body buried off one corner of the house, about twenty feet from the back porch. Thompson, you join me inside."

Thompson and I cover our mouths and noses as we enter through the front door, into the bare-bones living room. A gun rack over the fireplace has one empty slot. Nothing else catches our attention until we come to the hallway—a spray of buckshot and traces of blood spatter on the wall at the entrance to the kitchen. I nod down the hallway in the direction of the bedrooms. "Let's see what we find back here. Watch your step. That mess on the floor is evidence."

The stench hangs like a thick fog as we move down the hallway. The first bedroom is small. A couple of rock band posters pinned up on one wall, dirty clothes scattered on the floor, bed unmade. "The neighbor mentioned a boy," I say to Thompson. "This must be his room. Let's check out the other one."

The second bedroom is larger. I choke on the odor, burns my lungs. Flies swarm all around. The bed's been stripped. Blood splatters on one wall and a large stain on the carpet where a body must have bled out, and the corpse likely lay decomposing for several days. Could have been a couple weeks, and by the looks of things, the body was recently moved. "Dead colt, my ass," I mutter.

I scan the floor for casings. None evident. "Whoever did this knew to pick up after himself. The kid looks to be too much of a slob to be so thorough. Could have been him, but I doubt it."

Thompson nods.

I wave my hand around the room. "You get some pictures while I go out back and check with Grimes."

Down the hallway toward the kitchen, I sidestep the smudges, not wanting to contaminate any evidence. I glance around the kitchen and jot a note. Someone appears to have been packing or unpacking, but didn't finish. Either a typical teenage boy, or a looter who got interrupted.

I pause on the back steps and assess Grimes's progress. A dozen plaster casts in the ground around the grave indicate footprints left behind. He's started excavating what figures to be a grave, about six inches deep so far. He's being deliberate.

"Need a hand?" I ask.

Grimes hands me a field shovel. "Be my guest."

"Wanna take bets on how deep he is?"

Grimes grins. "Isn't betting against the law?"

I scoop up a bit of loose dirt.

A foot down, I blot my brow with a handkerchief. "We've got to hit him soon."

Grimes takes over. Close to eighteen inches, he wipes his forehead. "Guess we can't call this one a shallow grave."

After about six more inches, with beads of sweat dripping from his face, Grimes holds up one hand. "I've got something."

I grab a paintbrush from the forensic kit and start sweeping away loose dirt.

"Looks like an arm, Boss."

I nod. "Here, you finish. I'll call in the cavalry."

Within an hour, the coroner is processing Eric Lamb's body and a half-dozen reserve deputies are casing the scene for traces of evidence.

Carl

The French doors leading into Jacob's kitchen are wide open. I peek in—no Jacob. A moment later, he slides open the door to his bedroom a few feet away. "Carl, I'm over here."

Inside the bedroom an array of survival gear and a backpack are laid out on the bed. Propped up next to his nightstand is his Beretta SO5.

"What's this about?" I ask.

Jacob stuffs things into the pack. "I'm going to find the girl."

"And the shotgun—what's that for?"

He smirks. "Who knows? I might come across a bear or something."

"Didn't the sheriff confiscate your firearms?"

"They must've missed the bunker. I found it down there when I grabbed the rest of this stuff. Not the only time I've misplaced it lately."

"Don't take this wrong—but I have to ask. Did you?"

"Did I what?"

"You know. Shoot your neighbor."

He drops his pack on the bed. "Honestly, Carl—I wish I could remember. I don't know how I got there—or the shovel either. I went to his shack earlier that night. Followed him for a couple miles along a firebreak to a ranch house. Someone started shooting inside the place. A couple of people came running out. Then everything goes blank until I'm standing in front of my neighbor's shack watching it burn—and Baker starts asking questions."

"So, you don't have an alibi."

"No."

"Look, let's say the girl's real. You're not just imagining things. How do you know she's still out there? She could be anywhere by now."

Jacob throws the pack over one shoulder and rests the barrel of his twelve-gauge on the other. "I'm doing this, whether you like it or not." He starts toward the sliding-glass door.

I step in front of him. "Have you lost your mind?"

"I'm not about to do anything stupid. I'm just looking for a lost girl."

I let him pass. "Got your cell phone?"

"Of course."

"Keep me posted."

"Sure."

Once he's gone, I wander into the kitchen and stop next to the marble-topped island. The man I've known for over forty years is more of a mystery now than the day we met. I turn and look down the hallway toward Jacob's library. The door's open. That means I have Jacob's tacit approval, right?

Okay, no expectation of privacy here. I pick up a stack and start perusing. In typical Jacob Chandler style, his desk is covered with neatly arranged stacks of files and papers. There are scores of pages of pleadings, depositions, affidavits, court transcripts and the like about the wrongful death claim filed by his former employee's family. After thumbing through the stack, I lay the documents aside and sort through a similar pile—a set of correspondence having to do with the indemnity case against his old firm.

On top of the third heap is a 9x12 envelope with a detective agency's return address. Inside there's a half-dozen page report about Celine's abduction. I sit behind the desk and study the document. Page three stops me cold. I read the middle paragraph a second time. I squint and read it a third time to be sure I'm getting it straight.

I feel around in the envelope and come up with a DVD, load it into Jacob's computer. The images popping up raise more questions than they answer. The first photo shows Jacob's son, Jesse, embracing a woman, a brunette—not Celine's mother. In another shot, the same woman is holding a child—no more than a year old, but it doesn't appear to be Celine. Why did Jake have a private detective following Jesse? And the woman. Was Jesse having an affair? Is this woman connected to Celine's kidnapping? Something about the woman rings a bell.

As I lean back in the chair to process what I've seen, footsteps echo down in the hallway. I press the eject button, stuff both the DVD and the report back into the envelope, and bury them at the bottom of the pile. I grab a sheet from the top of the pile and pretend to be reading.

Deputy Sheriff Baker walks in the room. "We knocked. Nobody answered, but the door was open."

"Can I help you?"

"We're here for Chandler."

"He's not in. Is there something I can do?"

"When are you expecting Mr. Chandler back?"

"I'm not sure."

"He didn't say anything before he left?"

"Not about when he planned to be back."

"Oh, what did he say?"

"Nothing much."

"Don't stonewall me, Samuels."

"I'm not stonewalling."

"There's a deputy on his way with an arrest warrant—and a warrant to search this place."

"You've already searched the place once and arrested him, as well. He's free on bail."

"Bail's been revoked. We're looking for anything that connects him to the murders, not just weapons. We have another body."

"Another body? You can't possibly think ...."

"Mr. Samuels, it takes more than thinking to get an arrest warrant. And I'm sure by the time we finish searching here we'll have a few more loose ends tied down."

I gesture toward the door. "You'd better step outside while you wait for your warrant."

"And maybe you should join me."

"Sure. Mind if I use the bathroom, first?"

"As long as you make it quick."

"After you," I offer.

Baker stops in the doorway and turns toward me. "Oh, and one more thing."

"Yes?"

"Don't do anything we might consider obstruction."

"I wouldn't think of it."

I cross the hall to the bathroom and watch Deputy Baker take his time walking to the kitchen and out onto the deck. My gut tells me those Jesse pictures could lead to trouble, especially if Baker gets his hands on the suicide note. Add Jesse's accusations of emotional abuse to the Conroy mess, and there's no telling what a DA's imagination could make of it. Taking down a high profile guy like Jake could make a prosecutor's career.

I wait long enough to be sure Baker is out of view before darting back across the hall into Jacob's library. I grab the envelope from the bottom of the stack and tuck it into the back of my pants, concealing it with the tail of my sports jacket. Before joining the deputy, I return to the bathroom, flush the toilet and wash my hands.

When I step onto the deck, Deputy Baker scratches his head. "You know, it seems odd that your boss—I'm right, he is your boss?"

"Client."

"It seems odd Mr. Chandler would go somewhere without taking his vehicle ..." Baker points to Jacob's Jeep "... and not give you any idea where he was going."

"I'm his business advisor, not his mother."

"It doesn't matter what you are. Obstruction of justice means not being straight with us while we're investigating a crime." He stares hard. "It's a felony that gets you hard time."

I grimace.

"So one more time, Mr. Samuels. Where's Chandler?"

Jacob's had more than half-an-hour head start. It would take hours for Baker to put together a search party. Besides, maybe telling the truth would create enough of a distraction to insure I can get away with the envelope I stuck in my pants.

I look out at the lake. "Hunting."

"For what? Nothing's in season, and we've impounded his firearms."

"The girl."

"Damn. Where?"

I point. "Somewhere out there."

Baker wheels around and yells into the radio strapped on his shoulder. "I need a search party up here right now. And get the nearest K-9 unit you can find."

Jacob

I click 'Answer' on my cell phone. "Hi, Carl. You're not talking me out of this, so don't even try."

"That's not why I'm calling."

"Sounds like you're driving."

"Yeah. On my way back to the city."

"So why are you calling?"

"You need to be straight with me. Is there anything you haven't told me that your attorney needs to know?"

"There's nothing I know for sure that he hasn't been told."

"That's not my question."

I don't reply.

"Jake, why did you have a private detective following Jesse?"

"I'm not answering any more questions."

Carl pauses. "How are your survival skills?"

"What's that supposed to mean?"

"Deputy Baker is organizing a search party, including a K-9 unit. He's setting up a command post at your cabin."

"So, he's decided the girl's for real. Of course, he didn't have a choice after that DNA report."

"That's not it. Your bail's been revoked. They found another body and he thinks you did it."

"Who? Where?"

"A man. They didn't say who he was. Shot in the face and chest with a shotgun."

"Where did this happen?"

"There's a dead-end road that angles back from the highway a half mile or so below the turnoff to your place. Leads to a couple of ranches."

"I think I know where you're talking about. I can get to it on foot from here."

"No. Better not show up there. It's a crime scene and there might be cops all over the place."

"You've got a point."

Carl pauses again. "How do you know about this place? Seems like it's a bit out of the way."

"Remember the ranch house I told you about?"

"From the night your neighbor was shot up. You followed him there, and heard gunshots inside the place."

"Yeah. I think it's the same place."

"Jake, things aren't good."

"I know. Any chance they've tapped our phones?"

"How would I know?"

"Just in case, we'd better sign off. And Carl …."

"Yeah?"

"Don't call me. If the police get a hold of your phone records and see you've been calling me it could mean serious trouble for you. Think of Sandy and your family. The kids and grandkids."

"Jake …"

"Yeah?"

"Never mind …."

I check the cell phone display to be sure we're still connected, then put the phone back to my ear. "You still there?"

"Yeah." More silence. Then Carl continues, "I was thinking. Are you sure you don't want to rethink this whole thing? Turn yourself in."

"Not a chance. I'm going to find her. I know she's out there. Only now, I can't perch myself somewhere and wait for her to wander by. I have to keep moving or those dogs will find me."

"Okay—but don't you think it would be a good idea to call your attorney and clue him in?"

"I suppose you're right. But, you make the call. I'll be turning off my phone so its signal can't be tracked."

"Jake, you will call if you really need help, right?"

"Don't worry. I can take care of myself."

I tap "End Call," and sit down to rummage through my pack. I recall a cranky old neighbor from back when Ellen and I were first married. The neighbor lined the border of her yard with ammonia to keep dogs from peeing and crapping on her grass. Would have round-filed that memory, but my first big M&A deal involved a clever product that took the sting out of insect-bites. Its active ingredient was ammonia packaged in small pencil-sized vials so you could smear a couple drops directly on a bite.

Who would have guessed? The same stuff that keeps dogs from peeing also stops insect-bites from itching. I dig through my backpack.

Voila. Four vials. Too bad I left the rest in my desk at home. Back when I handled the merger, folks thought I was a genius when I handed out samples at cocktail parties and barbeques.

I throw on my pack and start hiking.

Chapter Eleven

Mercedes

I stare across the meadow at the two of them, RJ sitting behind her on the stallion, his hands on hers while she holds the reins. If that girl lets him make a move on her, I swear she'll wish she was dealing with Bryce. That boy's not teaching her squat.

I watch over my shoulder as I walk into the hut. A bit later when the two come through the door—him laughing, her smiling, which she never does—I pretend not to notice. But my back is tighter than a bowstring as I work on the rabbit I bagged for dinner.

RJ asks how 'we' can help.

I wheel around. "So you've decided to give riding lessons. When do I get my turn?"

RJ shrugs. "Sorry, I thought you didn't like horses."

"Life's not about what we like. It's about surviving."

"I know. I just thought—"

"Yeah. You just thought about what you wanted."

"Honest. I just thought you didn't want to."

"I tore my feet up running through the woods because I couldn't ride a damn horse. And I did it to save her ass." I point my knife at Amy. "Next time, it'll be my ass I worry about. And, my feet."

RJ rolls his eyes.

"I'm not blind. I can see what's going on here. You're just trying to get into her pants."

"Please."

"Don't 'please' me."

Amy steps in front of RJ. "I'm the one who should be pissed, not you."

RJ and I stare at her. Where'd this Amy come from? Her? Pissed?

"What are you staring at? I'm the one who got left behind for two years of hell. And, if you didn't want me around, why'd you risk your neck rescuing me?"

RJ shoots me a stupid grin. I search my brain for a snarky reply. Instead I blurt out, "It's the last time I'm saying this. Pull your weight or you don't eat." I stab the rabbit carcass with my knife.

He sighs. "Tomorrow morning, first thing, I'll teach you how to ride."

Amy picks up the water bucket and heads for the door. RJ follows. She stops and holds up a hand. "I can handle this."

When Amy is out of earshot, RJ turns to me. "What's gotten into you?"

"Me? I'm not the one playing the hero so I can sleep with her."

"I thought you were the one who knows what's real and what's not."

"I know what I saw out there."

"Oh, I get it. You're jealous."

"What are you talking about?"

"I didn't know you were into girls. It didn't even occur to me that you guys were ... you know... that you two had something going before you ran away."

"Shut up—jerk."

"Hey, if you want her she's yours." RJ throws up his hands.

My jaw drops.

His eyes grow wide. "I mean, did you run off because you got into some kind of fight?"

"No, you freak. I ran away because I was being raped. Every other night he had one or the other of us. Sometimes both." I start to cry.

RJ holds out his hands. "I'm sorry."

"Don't touch me." I fold my arms across my chest. "I'll decide when I wanna be touched."

RJ looks away.

I glare at him. "Make yourself useful and get us some firewood."

After taking a couple steps toward the door, he turns back. "My mom brought a different guy home almost every night—most were druggies or drunks. Listening to them carrying on turned my stomach. Actually made me throw up a few times." He shuffles his feet. "There are times I want you to touch me. But when you get close, all I can think is— my mother's a whore and I don't even know who my father was."

"Join the club. Bryce brought Amy to us when she was about four. Said he 'found' her. Never could tell with him. Anyway, her folks never bothered to come after her."

"Maybe she was lucky."

"Lucky? Bryce treated her like garbage. Always made her feel like something he kept around just to be used. Nothing could be worse than Bryce." My voice goes hoarse. "That monster. Anybody who gives him a face full of buckshot ... they deserve a medal."

RJ's eyes are misty. He clears his throat. "What about you?"

"Damn bastard. He called me 'special.'" I almost choke on the words. "But here's what's real—that bitch Tess never lifted a finger to stop him, even though she said she was my mother. At least I know Bryce wasn't my father. She said the louse who knocked her up was a worse loser than him."

"Jeez. And I thought my old lady was bad news."

"No big deal. Not sure I believe her. She's such a liar."

"Why would she lie about shit like that?"

I shrug. "Lying's in her blood."

RJ stuffs his hands in his pockets. "You know ... we can make it. We just have to pull together." He nods toward the door. "I'll get some firewood. You okay?"

"Go. I'm fine. But thanks for asking."

As soon as he's outside, RJ's shouts, "Mercedes! Get out here."

I rush to the door. "What?"

"It's Amy. She's taken off."

"She's what? Why would she ...?"

The water bucket Amy was taking to the stream is lying on its side a few feet from the door. I look around for signs of her. She's nowhere in sight.

RJ points to the tree where he'd tied the horses. "The mare and her saddle are gone."

I scan the horizon. Nothing.

He bolts for the stallion. "I'm going after her. She could get herself in real trouble."

"Wait. I'm coming with you. Let me get the crossbow." I head back inside.

He calls after me. "You'll have to teach me how to use that ... so I can start pulling my weight."

When I come back out of the hut, RJ has just finished cinching the saddle. He turns and his mouth gapes. He's eyeing the two shotguns I'm balancing on my shoulders. "Where the hell did you ...?"

"Picked up this one at your uncle's place, and found this one in the woods a few nights ago." I hand him the one from the woods. "You know how to use it?"

He studies me as he reaches for it. "Yeah. But it works best with ammo."

I pull some shells out of a side pocket of my quiver. "You mean these?"

RJ grins. "Where did ...?"

"Your uncle's."

Amy

I drop the reins and stroke the mare's neck, let her graze on the tall grass. I take a deep breath, deeper than I've ever breathed before. Taste the fresh air. Never thought I'd control anything, let alone an animal this big. RJ's riding lessons have opened my eyes. I do have power. I'm free.

I grit my teeth. But, I'm not going to trade one set of bullies for another. Back at the hut, when I threw the bucket on the ground and saddled the mare the way RJ taught me, freedom was the only thing on my mind. Now that I've had a taste, all I know is I want more.

I look up at the horizon. Somewhere out there is a new start. With storm clouds gathering on our left, that somewhere must be to the right. I take the reins and nudge the 'old girl' to 'giddy up.'

The mare snorts and jerks her head. A bear cub scampers into the meadow ahead of us. The horse rears back. The mare's front legs land hard and she bolts to the right, breaking into a gallop. I lose my grip on the reins. My arms and legs flail. I tumble to the hard ground. Pain shoots through my elbow, shoulder, neck.

I try to sit up ... fall back. Raindrops splat on my face. I shiver, chilly and tingly all over. My arms sink to my sides. I start floating ... like a feather in the wind. It's dark now.

RJ

The first half mile out from the hut—Mercedes and me riding double on the stallion—we have an easy time following Amy. The afternoon sun at our backs highlights hoof prints in a thin layer of dusty topsoil. But as heavy black clouds sweep in from the east and fill the sky, shadows make our job tougher. Mercedes' keen eyes aren't good enough.

She leans forward into me and tightens her grip on the saddle horn, digging her elbows into my sides. "Those clouds don't look friendly," she mutters.

I spur the stallion forward. After a few yards, I rein him in and lean down to study the ground. A large raindrop splatters on the back of my neck. I wipe it away and nudge the animal to the left. "Hope this storm holds off. It'll be impossible to track her if it rains too hard."

Mercedes shifts her weight on the back of the saddle. "Thunderstorms freak me out."

"It's just like fireworks ... the Fourth of July."

"Maybe to you. But you don't see Bryce in every flash of lightning."

Her body stiffens against my back as I prod the horse forward.

As the sun disappears into the black sky, solitary raindrops grow into solid sheets of water. The hard-packed ground turns to mud. I shiver at the quick drop in temperature, and no amount of shaking can unglue my shirt and jeans from my skin.

Mercedes clutches me tighter around the waist, burrowing her face into my wet back. She winces at every clap of thunder. When lightning strikes so close it's just a white light all around us, I turn the stallion into a nearby stand of trees for shelter. "There's no use," I shout over the rain.

As our feet hit the ground, Mercedes throws her arms around me and nests her body against my chest. She's trembling. I cup the back of her head and draw her close, pressing my cheek into her wet, musty hair.

"I'm sorry," she whispers into my shoulder. "All this is my fault."

I pull back and clutch her face, forcing her to look at me. "Why?"

"It was my tantrum. She didn't want to make either of us mad. She'll do anything to keep the peace."

I let go of her. "How's taking blame going to fix anything?"

"I figured if she thought I was jealous, she'd back off like she always does."

"And do what?"

"I don't know. I didn't expect her to run away."

"She did. So think about it. Is there any special place? Somewhere she'd go? "

"Back to Tess and …."

"Even after—?"

"Maybe she thought it was her only choice. Or that … he … he and Tess might go easy on her if she came back with her tail between her legs. She always does whatever … whatever keeps them happy."

"Jeez. She's one messed up chick."

"Yeah, aren't we all ….."

"If she's going back to him, she's headed the wrong way."

"She's probably lost. Can't imagine she knows her way around well enough to make it back to them. Bryce never let her wander far from the shack. She could have gone any direction. Maybe she's wandering in circles."

"That could be for the best. I'd take my chances with coyotes and bears over that creep any day."

"Maybe Bryce isn't a problem anymore."

"How's that?"

She shrugs. "Just saying. If he was smart, he'd be long gone—before the law or someone else catches up with him. He's a murderer—molester. He's bound to get what he deserves."

"My money's on the mare. She probably headed back to the barn as soon as she smelled the storm coming." I take Mercedes hand and lead her to the driest spot I can find. "When this downpour is over, we'll head to the ranch and see if she's there."

Deputy Sheriff Baker

The storm's finally letting up, but the sun will be setting in a couple of hours. Four deputies are out there pounding a 400 square mile grid, and I still haven't found a K-9 team. Those men might as well be stumbling around in the dark. I slam my fist on the railing of Chandler's deck.

My dispatcher's voice crackles over the radio strapped on my shoulder.

I snap back, "Give me some good news."

"Best we can do right now is an air sniffer dog from an SAR volunteer crew. They don't track like bloodhounds, they just get whiffs of any human in the area."

"Yeah. Let's just hope Chandler is the only human out there. Do you have an ETA?"

"Should be there in under an hour."

"Roger that." I stretch my neck side to side. It pops.

Grimes breaks in over the radio.

"Go, Grimes."

"Boss, we're losing daylight."

"Tell me something I don't know."

"What do you want us to do?"

I pinch the bridge of my nose. "Give it another hour, then come on in. With any luck, we'll have an air sniffing dog by then."

"Sure hope there's something left for the dog to sniff after that squall washed everything clean."

Jacob

I hunker down under an old cedar a couple hundred feet from the ranch house and let the storm pass. This is the place the neighbor led me to a few nights ago. The yellow tape cordoning off the house and barn says it's a crime-scene. It's got to be the place Carl mentioned on the phone. I stay put, even when a rider-less horse gallops into the corral. About nightfall a dog barks in the distance. The way noise travels after sunset, it could be over a mile away.

Now and then, the moon appears through gaps in shape-shifting clouds as they crawl across the slate-black sky. Each time the moon exposes itself I freeze, hoping that if anyone's standing guard they'll take me for part of the landscape. When the moonlight ebbs, I creep towards the barn. I've never ridden a horse, and wouldn't be attempting it now if it wasn't for those damn tracking dogs on my scent.

RJ

Mercedes insists I tie the stallion to a tree up in the woods about a quarter mile from the ranch house—just in case the place is swarming with sheriff's deputies. We leave the crossbow with the horse, along with one of the shotguns, and slip down to a spot at the edge of the trees overlooking the corral.

After dark, as we're about to step out into the meadow, Mercedes grabs my arm and whispers, "Down." She ducks behind some bushes for cover.

I start to protest, but she covers my mouth with her hand. "Shh ...." Her eyes widen.

She raises up to study a solitary figure approaching the opposite side of the corral. She whispers, "Way too big to be Amy. It's gotta be a man."

I raise up to see for myself.

"Anyone you know?" she asks in hushed tones.

"Don't think so." I point to the corral. "The mare made it back."

"Yeah, but no sign of Amy."

We watch the stranger prop his shotgun against a fencepost and climb onto the top railing.

I gulp. "Is he planning on stealing the mare?"

Mercedes opens the breach of the shotgun she's been toting and digs into her pocket for a shell.

"What the ..." I mutter.

"Just in case," she whispers.

As she closes the breach, a pair of headlights rounds the curve in the dirt road coming up from the highway. The solitary stranger jumps off the fence, scoops up his weapon, and takes off into the woods above the barn.

Mercedes ducks down. "Company."

I roll onto my back.

She glances between the bushes and whispers, "Sheriff's cruiser."

As the cruiser stops in back of the ranch house, sensors activate the flood lights. A lone deputy steps out of the vehicle, armed with a flashlight, and slips past the yellow tape into the house. We track his movements from room to room by following the flashlight's glow. When he finishes inside, he proceeds to the barn.

It's not long before the cruiser's speeding back down the dirt road, kicking up a cloud of dust. We stake out the ranch house for another half-hour, waiting for the stranger to return. When he doesn't, Mercedes says, "We don't need to search for Amy down there. The deputy would have hauled her out, if she was anywhere to be found."

I nod. "We should at least get the mare."

Jacob

Two figures creep down from the woods on the other side of the corral. My pulse quickens. By the way they're moving, one is clearly a boy; the other could be a girl. Not the girl from across the lake, though. This one has grace and confidence. God, could it be Celine? My heart races.

I watch and wait for the flood lights to come on so I can get a better view of them—more than just their silhouettes. When the boy climbs onto the fence, the area lights up. He drops down into the corral and sidles up to the horse, collecting its reins. The horse follows him out through a gate and lets him mount without resistance. The boy rides over to his companion and pulls her up in the saddle behind him.

Shadows obscure the girl's face, but I have an impulse to call out to them anyway. Then more images of Celine flash through my mind. It's not her. After a couple of minutes, they disappear, and I venture down to the house, to find out what happened here that night of chaos.

At the backdoor, a horrible stench draws stomach acid up into my throat. I pull out a bandana from my jacket pocket and cover my nose and mouth before going inside. The odor is dense, almost unbearable.

In the back bedroom, I take off my pack to retrieve a flashlight. Caked-on slime and blood stains cover the carpet. The sight reminds me of Jesse lying with Celine's mother in a pool of blood.

The stabbing pain starts again, just behind the ear, arcing to the top of my head. I grab my pack and stumble to the hallway—bracing myself against the doorpost. After a couple minutes, the throbbing goes away.

Amy

The moon peeks out from the clouds then hides. My clothes are soaked. I shiver, ache all over. Curl up in a ball, teeth chattering.

Where am I? Who am I? Names pop into my head. Some I think I know. None stick. My heart's beating fast, my throat's too tight to swallow.

My left arm throbs. When I try to sit up, pain sucks my breath away. Head's spinning, stomach gurgles. I'm burning with fever.

I'm freezing again. I roll to the side and prop up on my good elbow. There are trees nearby. I push up off the ground, but stay on my knees 'til the fog clears from my head. The wind kicks up. I stand and touch a sore spot behind my ear. It's tacky. When the moon comes out again, I study the smudge on my fingers. Blood.

I hobble over to the trees—a line of bush pine and live oak. A big pine's low-hanging branches reach out to me like hands. I crawl under it and hunch up. Hang my head. Shut my eyes to keep tears from pouring out. They come anyway. My shoulders shake.

Please, let someone be coming for me.

A dog barks in the distance. I snap my head up. My heart pounds. Coyotes? Don't let them eat me. Bryce says they eat girls. A crazy girl all by herself will die out here.

Who's crazy? Who's Bryce?

Tess

I slide onto a barstool next to a lean, clean-cut cowboy type. He smiles. I return the favor.

The bartender eyes me. "What can I get you?"

"A beer."

The cowboy raises his empty mug and winks. "Make it two—on me."

I swivel and touch his wrist, letting my hand linger as I search his face. He's eager. "Thanks," I say.

The tug of loose cotton on my nipples sends tingles through my body and turns up the heat between my thighs. Back when I was twenty-something, stalking the corporate jungle, sex landed me in a mother lode of trouble. Sex also landed me Bryce when I needed help getting what was due me. It worked on Eric, too. Tonight I need to score a meal ticket—or two. I shove the images of mangled faces as far back in my memory as they'll go.

The cowboy's hand finds mine. "Not a problem. I hate to see a pretty woman pay for her own drinks."

"They say a woman can't live on beer alone."

He calls the bartender. "The lady needs a menu—for starters."

As the barkeeper steps away, the cowboy introduces himself. "I'm Roy."

"Tess." I guide his hand onto my knee. Hold it there.

"So, what's a nice girl ...."

I throw back my head and laugh.

He copies my laughter. "Seriously, you're not a regular."

I slip my hand off his. "No. I'm just passing through. Been staying at a dive of a motel off the highway."

Roy sips his beer. "Where you headed?"

"Haven't figured that part out yet. Just away."

"From what?"

"Trouble, I suppose." My finger traces the rim of my glass.

"What kind of trouble?"

"My old man died. Left me broke ... and alone."

"My condolences."

"No biggie. Guess that gives me a clean slate, huh?"

Roy picks up his glass and tips it toward me. "Every cloud's got a silver lining."

My glass clinks his. "Here's to fresh starts."

We chug our beers and Roy signals for another round.

"Where you from?" he asks.

"Up on the mountain."

"So, you're local."

"Imagine you could say that. But never get to town much. Always think of town as—I don't know—another world."

He laughs. "You don't get out much."

"No, I don't."

"How long you lived around here?"

"About ten years—more or less."

"And before that?"

"Drifted with my old man and girl for a couple of years."

"Thought you were all alone."

"Am now. She split."

"Out of the nest pretty early?"

"More like flew the coop. Ran off. The old man was tough on her."

"Does she know he's dead?"

"Doubt it. She's not in touch."

"She still around?"

"I'm hoping she didn't go far." I check the view in the mirror behind the bar.

Roy signals for another round. "Maybe if you tracked her down you could get a fresh start together."

"I'd like that, but we don't have anywhere to stay."

"You could crash at my place 'til you get on your feet."

I gaze into his deep brown eyes. "Me and the girl?"

"While we're searching, it can be your base camp."

"You sure about that?"

"Got any better offers?"

I lay my hand on his knee. "That 'we' sounds like you're offering to help me find her."

His face brightens. "Barkeep." He motions for the check.

I slide off the barstool. "Excuse me while I visit the powder room."

"Take as long as you need."

When I rejoin him, he's got a local newspaper in his hands, reading intently. I lean into him, pretending that I'm interested. He slaps the newspaper with the back of his hand. "Getting to be as bad as the city."

The headline reads *Ex-Financial Tycoon Charged in Local Murders.* I stare at the picture below the headline.

Amy

An owl hoots. Shivers run down my spine. Bryce's hot breath, Tess's shrill voice—I'll take anything over this cold, damp freedom. Two other names, RJ and Mercedes. Are they searching for me, or are they like parents who never come to take a girl home?

That growling noise—? I scan the shadows for wild animals. Have to keep watch. Can't close my eyes. Sleep's no friend tonight. It's the enemy. My head droops, eyelids flutter.

Something rustles the bushes. I jerk up, shake off the fog in my head, and peer into the night. Can't let them eat me. I feel around for some kind of weapon. Come up empty-handed. Bryce—he's the one who pounces on me in the night. Nothing I can do to stop him.

I wait for the next sound. Nothing. The pounding in my ears stops. I say out loud, "It's not Bryce. I'm free."

Mercedes—the girl who learned to survive. I remember her saying, only be afraid of what's real ... if it's not real, it can't hurt you ... and just because something was real once, that doesn't mean it still is.

I've survived Bryce's touching. Closed my eyes and shut my mind, pretended it wasn't real. That's the secret. If he's not here, he's not real. I only have to be afraid of what's real.

It can be done. Alone doesn't have to be scary.

Chapter Twelve

Tess

The morning sun streams through Roy's floor-to-ceiling bedroom windows. I roll over and gaze at his tanned, taut body—it begs for my lips and tongue to slip-and-slide all over it. I'm coming up in the world so fast it makes me giddy. Satin sheets, king-size bed. Probably not as nice as the cabin across the lake, but a palace compared to the shack Bryce had us squatting in. This guy has something Bryce never did—class. Whoa, I would have settled for anybody who offered a meal ticket and an extra hand in finding the little bitch. I sure lucked out with this cowboy.

I ease my hand under the sheet and reach for his joystick. After all the years of Bryce's bullying I haven't forgotten how to enjoy a real man. Last night none of the orgasms were faked. Too bad I'll have to use him and lose him.

Before his eyes open, a smile unfolds on his face and the muscle in my hand stiffens. He stretches as if offering me every inch of his hard body. I nuzzle up to him, bringing my hand up to his chest and caress him.

I whisper in his ear, "I've been thinking."

His sleepy smile broadens into a grin. His eyes are still closed as if he's savoring an erotic dream.

"Will you help me find my girl?"

He turns to face me with his eyes open wide. "Huh?"

I lean over, glide my tongue across my lips, and repeat, "Will you help me find my daughter?"

"Oh that."

I brush my hand down his chest and stop just below his navel. "Well?"

"Anything you want."

I lean into him and cover his mouth with mine, giving him my tongue. After a long, delicious kiss, I sit up. "Last night you said you're a lawyer. That true?"

"Yeah—that doesn't disqualify me from a second helping does it?" His hand finds my bare ass.

The corners of my mouth curl upward. "Maybe it can earn you dessert." I reach down and caress his groin.

His abs tighten. "Tell me more."

"Last night—the thing in the paper—the tycoon."

"What about him?"

"I had no idea he was anywhere near here."

His muscle goes limp. He sits up. "So, what's your connection to this guy?"

I pull the sheet up around me. "Jacob Chandler's my girl's grandfather."

Roy sits up on the edge of the bed. "The girl they say he's searching for?"

"No. That's a different girl … he claims another grandkid went missing years ago, but I hate to think what the truth is. All I know is, he's hunting for me and my girl to make sure we don't make a claim against his estate. And he's serious. Like the paper said, he's already killed two people."

"But the paper said the victims were involved in his granddaughter's kidnapping. She was kidnapped, right?"

I draw my knees up to my chest and wrap my arms around them. "Like I said, that was my brother's child—the legitimate one. But who's to say what really happened to her? The kidnapping story could be made up. He's not exactly famous for telling the truth about anything. My daughter and I got the boot years ago—said he'd never acknowledge a bastard grandchild. As far as he was concerned, she was dead. Maybe he plans to leave both girls out of his will."

"Who would inherit his estate?"

"He's never given a shit about family. I imagine he thinks he can buy some kind of immortality. I wouldn't put it past him to dump it all into cryogenics ... keep himself frozen until they find a cure for death or something ... he wouldn't want heirs around to turn off the damn freezer."

"So how can I help?"

It's been a long time since I used the pleading puppy dog eyes, but it's worth a try. "Could you draw up some kind of legal document that gives me and my daughter what we deserve? When the cops find him—and we find Mercedes— maybe the DA can make it part of a plea bargain for the murders. And make it so that if he's convicted—which is a pretty sure bet—we will be taken care of while he's in prison. I only want what's due us."

"How much money are we talking about?"

"Billions."

"Billions?"

I nod. "And since his cronies can't be trusted, I ought to be the trustee of the estate while he's locked away."

"Why don't I draw up a codicil that leaves the entire estate to you? No reason your daughter can't wait for her inheritance."

Jacob

The morning sun breaking through the trees means I better get moving, and if the sheriff's crew got an early start, I've lost some of my time advantage. Aching bones, headache, and hunger aren't a prescription for a good day, nor are they excuses to slow down.

Another bad omen raises its ugly head when I stand and brush off—a small tear in my weatherproof jacket. I must have snagged it on something along the way. Good thing the sky's clear. Otherwise, weather would be high on my list of complaints.

Complaints? What the Hell. I'm starting to sound like a mid-level manager, more concerned about covering my ass than getting somewhere.

I'm barely two miles from the lake—that's only 30-40 minutes ahead of the manhunt. My best bet is to get deeper into the chaparral, force the sheriff to widen the search grid, add manpower. With any luck, the girl is still out there somewhere, and they'll be forced to sweep wide enough to flush her out, bring her home safe. I just have to point them in the right direction. When they find her, hopefully, she can lead Baker to the real killer. Then, I'll be able to turn myself in.

Mercedes

I stand over RJ as he's curled up on his side, lying on my pine needle mattress. I've been up since the first rays of sunlight streaked through cracks in the plywood siding. The last few cold beans from the bottom of the can are what's left of my breakfast.

I nudge him with my foot. He grunts. When that doesn't work, I plant my shoe in the small of his back and shove. He rolls over.

"Get up, lazy."

He props up on his elbows and shakes the cobwebs out of his head.

I glare down at him. "Cold beans or cold soup? Cans are in one of the sacks we brought over from the ranch."

"Huh?"

I scoop out the last spoonful of beans. "We've got to get a move on."

RJ rubs his eyes. "What time is it?"

"Who needs a clock?" I toss my empty can in the tub I use for washing. "It's daylight. Get a move on."

He gets up and stumbles over to the plastic sack of supplies we collected from Uncle Eric's. "Cold soup? Why don't we make a fire?"

"Not going to waste the wood or time. Got to find Amy as quick as we can, or we may never …. Horse might've thrown her. She could be lying unconscious somewhere."

"Okay. Okay. I'm on it." RJ digs a box of crackers out of a sack and tears it open.

He races to the door, stuffing another handful of crackers into his mouth.

"Coming with me?" he asks with his mouth full.

When he's saddled the two horses, he offers me the mare's reins.

I step back and hold out my hands to my side. "What do you want me to do with those?"

He grins. "Climb on board."

"You're crazy. I don't know how to ride."

He mounts the stallion and tosses the mare's reins at me. "Time for you to start pulling your weight."

I catch the leather straps. "Real funny."

RJ nudges the stallion with the heel of his boot.

"Wait, damn it!" I call after him.

He coaxes his horse to speed up.

"Damn it," I mutter as I stick my foot in the mare's stirrup and clutch the saddle horn, pulling myself up.

About twenty yards away, RJ pulls the stallion to a stop and looks over his shoulder.

"Good job," he says.

I stick out my tongue.

He turns his horse back and guides it up to me. "Now, if you want her to turn to the right, just lay the reins over the left side of her neck like so. Want her to turn the left, do the opposite. To make her stop, pull back gently on the reins and say 'whoa'. Goose her in the side with your heels to make her go. Goose her again to make her go faster. If she gets out of control, keep your head down and hang on. I'll come after you."

I grimace.

"We'll start out slow."

"Okay. I think we should go back to where we lost Amy's trail. We should have kept going in that direction last night, instead of heading back to the ranch."

"Fine," he says.

He urges the stallion forward and watches over his shoulder. I try to keep up.

So far, so good.

Deputy Sheriff Baker

Chandler's palace deck wouldn't be a half-bad spot for your regular cup of morning Joe, if you weren't waiting for a search party to get things in gear. And if you weren't having to settle for a sniffer dog instead of real bloodhounds. We have to find Chandler's trail now, not next week. A cooperative dog handler would be nice, too.

This lady dog handler says Edgar, her dog, doesn't follow a specific person's track on the ground; it just picks up any human scent or scents in the vicinity. She tells me you get much better results when the air isn't packed with moisture. The rain squall was her reason for not staying out much past sunset last night. This morning her excuse is patches of early morning condensation trapped in a few low spots. That has cost us at least a couple hours.

As I'm cramming a stale donut down my throat, the dispatcher's voice crackles over my radio. "Yeah, Baker here," I grumble.

"State Attorney General's office has a special team headed up to the Lamb ranch this morning to do extra forensic work."

"Do you have an ETA?"

"About an hour from now. They started out from Sacramento first thing this morning."

After signing off, I stride over to Deputy Grimes. "I'm heading over to Eric Lamb's place. Let me know if this sniffer dog comes up with anything."

Jacob

A dog barking spikes my adrenaline. The search party must be closing in. I have to come up with some kind of a diversion, something to confuse the dog, frustrate the sheriff into calling in reinforcements and expanding the search grid. The ammonia vials—they'll do the trick. Dogs hate the odor.

Just ahead, I spot a granite outcrop, half buried in the base of a cliff. The bluff is more than a story above ground level. The top must be the starting point of a new, perpendicular ridgeline. A sturdy young pine, standing about six inches out from the sheerest portion of the rock face, is just the right height for a makeshift ladder.

I cut a low branch from another tree—far enough away to be unnoticeable—and sweep away my footprints from around the young pine. I empty the vials in an arc at the base of my 'ladder' and chest-high on the granite face. I shinny up the sapling, carrying my makeshift broom to dispose of up above. On top I take a moment to survey the surrounding landscape from my new vantage.

Amy

The bright yellow sun's almost halfway up in the sky ... it's late morning. Tess would've rousted me hours ago, and Bryce would be having a conniption.

I rub sleep from my eyes. My stomach growls. Alone's no good, but being back with Bryce and Tess would be worse. RJ and Mercedes are the best option I have. Maybe they'll come now that it's daylight. Should I try to find them, or sit and let them come to me?

My stomach growls again. I stand. Everything's still damp and chilly under the trees, but the sun has already begun to dry out the meadow grasses. Did Mercedes live off grass and animal food 'til she made a home for herself in the old hut? The hut has to be fairly close. The mare didn't bring me that far. I start out across the meadow, toward dense woods on the other side.

The wind picks up. Clouds get thicker, blacker. I follow a path across the meadow, into the trees. Dark shadows overtake everything ... even the littler shadows that were there a couple minutes ago. Like Bryce's shadow when he stands over me. I have to keep thinking, Bryce isn't here.

The trail's flat for a while, but soon starts uphill. When I stop to catch my breath at a level spot, it goes straight up ... about as high as the neighbor's cabin. How am I going to do that? Don't remember Mercedes' hut being so high up. Is this the mountain where people eat each other? I fall to my knees. Tears run down my cheeks. My whole body quivers. Can't keep going. Bryce can have his way with me, if that's what it takes to get out of this.

There's more barking ... sounds far off. If coyotes come, let them eat me. Bryce is right. He's always right. Should never have let Mercedes set me free. A cool breeze whips up, and goose bumps spread over my arms and neck. Smells like rain. Storms scare me ... Bryce scares me. I slump down and sit on the hard ground. Lean back against an old log. Pull my knees up to my chest and hug them.

RJ

Mercedes insists we go back to the meadow where we lost the mare's tracks in the storm the day before. We find fresh human tracks, about the size of Mercedes' shoes, leading down to the meadow from nearby woods.

Mercedes frowns. "If she headed out across that field, we may never find her tracks again."

I point to the meadow. "If we're lucky, it'll be swampy in places."

She stares at the horizon. It's growing blacker by the second. "Storm coming."

A sliver of lightning is barely noticeable in the heart of the darkest clouds. I scrunch up my face. "Looks mean."

She points to the other side of the meadow. "Let's hope she headed straight across. We don't have time to sweep the whole field."

"But straight across won't take her back to your place."

"No, she'll need to angle a bit to her left. The trail cuts through some pretty thick woods and leads all the way to the ridge top. If she keeps on it she'll miss the hut altogether."

We mount our horses and ride to the other side where we find more tracks leading up into the woods. I coax the stallion ahead. Mercedes follows on the mare. As the storm closes in, shadows you could see when we entered the tree canopy are lost in growing darkness. Amy's tracks get tougher to follow, but as far as we can tell, she stayed with the beaten path.

Deputy Sheriff Baker

This lady dog handler insists we've lost the trail. I clutch the back of my neck. "So you mean he just vanished in thin air?"

She looks away. "That seems to be our situation."

"Does this happen often?"

"Enough to be frustrating."

The granite out-cropping makes me wonder. "It just stops here?"

She shrugs.

"What makes you think he didn't scale those rocks?"

She shakes her head. "Edgar, here, would be trying to paw his way up the rock face after him. He doesn't show any interest. Keeps sniffing everywhere else."

I turn to Grimes. "Heard anything of the status of those bloodhounds?"

"Not yet."

"Damn." I kick at the dirt.

"Sir—maybe if we widen the grid?"

I massage my temples. "Sure. Have someone call the surrounding jurisdictions to see what kind of manpower they can round up."

Grimes turns to leave, then stops. "By the way, how'd that forensic team do at Lamb's place?"

I purse my lips before answering. "They found a couple pieces of trace evidence we apparently missed. At least that's their story. Suppose they had to come up with something to justify their existence."

Tess

Roy turns off the highway onto the road that goes past Eric's ranch. My heart beats faster. "Where are we going?"

"Just up the road a ways."

How am I going to tell him I'm not going back to that place? Still can't shake the sight of Eric's mangled face. I stared at it the whole time Bryce was chasing after the girls. And when he came back for me, he glared at me with those coal, black eyes of his. His jaw was set, and he was spooky quiet like the eye of a storm, until he snarled, "Let's get outta here—somebody might come snoopin' around to see what all the ruckus was all about." When I said we should bury the body, Bryce shook his head and said, "Let 'em rot." Can't believe that monster didn't say another word ... until we got close to the shack. And then it was like ... he was just taking back what belonged to him.

I hold my breath as Roy drives on past the entrance to Eric's place. A few hundred yards farther, he parks.

"Why are we stopping here?"

"There's an abandoned hut tucked up in the woods a couple of miles from here. I noticed it when I was scouting the area for deer last fall. Looked like someone's set up housekeeping there."

"Do you think my girl could be holed up there?"

Roy takes his deer rifle off the rack mounted on the rear window. "Maybe, but if not, whoever's using it might have seen her."

An hour later, we crouch behind a granite outcrop on the ridge above the hut. Roy pulls out his binoculars and zooms in. He leans into me. "Let's go down and see if anyone's home."

I nod. As we stand, Roy slips an ammo clip into his pump action 30.06, chambers a round, and clicks off the safety. He signals for me to keep quiet and follow him.

Jacob

I rap on the door of a rundown hut near the bottom of the ridge. No one answers. I stand to one side, my shotgun poised, and nudge the door open. "Hello, anyone home?"

No answer. I push the door open wider. I stoop down, pick up a pebble, and toss it in. Still no response. I hold my breath and step inside to check the place out.

It looks empty, but lived in. A box full of books in the corner is one of several clues. I recognize most of the titles—a couple that I pick up have my nameplate inside. The last time I saw them, they were lined up on shelves in my library. In fact, there's a lot of stuff here that belongs to me, but all of it vanished long before the girl from across the lake went missing. So, she's not the thief. I take the only chair in the place and sit facing the door, the Beretta across my lap. Can't wait to see who shows up.

A few minutes later the latch starts to move. As the door opens slowly, someone pokes a rifle barrel through the opening. When the door swings open all the way, I yell, "Freeze!" Staring at the twin barrels of my shotgun pointed straight at him is a wiry cowboy. His rifle is angled away from me. I stand slowly, keeping my shotgun aimed at his chest, and demand. "Lay it on the floor and step to the side."

The cowboy puts his gun down and raises his hands in front him. "Sorry. The name's Roy. We didn't know anyone lived here. We're out searching for a missing girl."

"So am I. You're not alone?"

Roy glances over his shoulder. "Uh—no. I mean, there are others searching, but no one's here—with me—now."

"Step all the way in and close the door."

He follows my instruction. I tell him to take off his belt and hand it over. I point to the chair. "Now sit and tie your laces together."

As the cowboy loops the boot straps into a single knot, I lean my weapon against the wall and step behind him.

"Been camped out here for long?" he asks.

I don't answer—pull his arms behind the back of the chair and loop the belt around one of his wrists.

"If you're afraid of me blowing your secret, you've got nothing to worry about. I'm helping a friend search for a teenage girl. Have you seen anything of her?"

I wrap the belt around his other wrist and start to tie it off.

Roy lifts his legs a few inches and stamps his feet on the floor, launching himself out of the chair. He yells, "Tess!"

Someone swings the door open and barges in.

While I'm struggling to regain control, the cowboy nods at the rifle on the floor. "My gun!"

I lunge for my shotgun, but before I reach it, a woman grabs the cowboy's rifle and yells, "Stop. Right there."

I shrink back against the wall.

"*You*?" she shouts.

"Teresa?"

The cowboy unstraps himself. "Is this him?"

I stammer. "She used to—she—."

She glares at me. "Shut up, you."

Roy repeats, "Is it?"

"Yeah. And he killed my old man, too—just like the newspaper said—burned us out of our home."

"I wish I knew if it *was* me who killed him."

She stiffens. "What kind of scam are you cooking up?"

"All I remember is standing on my deck, some guy pointing a shotgun at me and misfiring. Next thing, I'm standing outside the shack across the lake, watching it go up in flames. The sheriff's deputy picks up a shovel that's laying at my feet and starts asking questions. I don't remember a thing that happened in between."

Roy runs his hands through his hair. "Tess, you didn't say one of the murder victims was your old man. What's this about?"

"Teresa, what are you doing around here, anyway? I thought you ...."

She keeps her eyes fixed on me. "He's been bullying us—trying to take our home away from us. Made up some cock-and-bull story that we were abusing the girls. Killed my old man over it."

Roy steps back from Tess. "What are you talking about? I thought...."

"Shut up, I said."

"I thought this was about your daughter's inheritance."

Tess swings the rifle around and points it at him—her face taut. "I'm not gonna say it again. Shut up."

I make a move for the door, but stumble.

Roy grabs for the barrel of the rifle.

The rifle's boom sends shock waves through the hut.

He drops to his knees.

I bolt out the door, glancing over my shoulder. I catch a glimpse of Teresa taking aim. My back tightens, anticipating the bullet's impact.

There's a click, but nothing else. She forgot to reload.

The snap from Teresa pumping a round into the chamber tells me I'm out of time.

I sprint as fast as my aging legs will go. I'm just a few feet from the tree line when I hear the crack of the rifle. A searing pain pierces my arm. I stumble several steps, dive behind some Manzanita bushes, and crawl over to a large live oak. As I lean against the tree trunk, I press the heel of my hand into the wound and take slow, deep breaths. I probe the wound; blood's flowing at a steady rate. It's an exit wound. At least the bullet isn't lodged inside. My face warms and my breathing accelerates. Beads of sweat collect along my lips and brow. I breathe deep, try to relax to slow my heart rate.

Soon a chill settles over me, a sure sign I'm going into shock. I grow weaker, struggling to remove my belt. By the time I have it off I'm exhausted, shivering. Again, I try to regulate my breathing as I loop the belt around my arm above the wound. I grit my teeth and cinch it tight. Losing more blood could kill me.

I fight to stay awake, but my eyelids grow heavy. Everything around me dims until I'm free falling down a dark, endless shaft.

Tess

Damn, I missed the bastard altogether. Wanted to wound him, stop him from getting away. I need him alive. Now, what am I going to do? Oh, hell … Roy. Didn't mean to shoot him. It was an accident. Can't lose him, too—who's going to help me find the girl … and track down Chandler? I turn back to the hut.

When I push the door open, I gasp. A shotgun's pointed straight at my forehead. Behind it, coal black eyes. I gasp. "Jeezus! You're supposed to be dead."

Bryce laughs. "Yeah, surprised ya, huh?"

"But how …?"

He nods at Roy, lying on the floor moaning, pressing his hand into his stomach to keep blood from gushing out. "First, who's this?"

"A guy I picked up."

"Shit." He spits on the floor. "You fuckin' whore."

"He was just helping me out. Seriously. Okay, I turned on the charm to get what I needed out of him, but nothing else happened. I promise."

"What was he doin' for you that I couldn't?"

I reach under my bra and pull out a folded sheet of paper. "The key to Chandler's fortune."

He squints. "Whaddaya mean?"

I toy with a button on my shirt. "Before we go there, how is it you're still alive?"

He grins. "Wasn't me you pulled the trigger on that night."

"Who ...?"

He shrugs. "Some homeless guy from Folsom. Picked him up after I got rid of those bloodied clothes. Told him I'd pay him a grand if he rode up with me to the shack and offed you."

"Why didn't you just do it yourself?"

"I'd planned to kill him after he'd done you in—then burn down the place. When the law figured out the dead guy wasn't me, I'd be long gone. Besides, after the way the sheriff talked when he came to check us out, they'd probably've gone after that squatter across the lake." His grin fades. "But that girl screwed things up."

"Girl?"

"Yeah. Can't be sure. Could've been your Mercedes. Too dark to say for sure. I stayed in the pickup while the bum went up to the door. Then she comes out of the woods, creeping toward him, shotgun leveled at his head. The door opens—kapow. He crumbles in a heap. She kneels and starts puking. I can barely make out your silhouette lying inside the shack, and flames spreading from the broken lantern on the floor. About the time I decide I just can't let her walk, you come running out, screaming. I slip out of the truck—hide in the woods. You take off in the pickup like a bat outta hell. Figured you were going to the cops. When I look around for the girl, she's gone. No idea which way she headed.

"It dawns on me that I can still go through with part of my plan—burn the place down with the bum inside. So I drag his carcass all the way in the shack and fix it so nobody can recognize him—bash in his face with the shovel he'd carried to the door to use on you. To be sure the fire takes hold and burns the place down, I grab the can of kerosene we use to fill the lantern and empty in on the floor."

"Why are you still hanging around? You could be in Mexico by now."

His eyes lock onto mine. "Been hunting those two girls. Before I can split, I've got to eliminate anybody who can tie me to this place."

"Including me?"

He points the shotgun at Roy's face. "For starters ... the cowboy."

A shotgun blast rocks the hut.

Cool and calm, Bryce takes a rag and wipes the shotgun clean of prints. "Guessin' this is our neighbor's fancy piece," he says. "Saw him tearin' out of here ... you takin' a bead on him."

I shiver. "Yeah. He was camped out here when we came on this place. Our neighbor for the past two years is none other than that little shit Amy's grandfather, Jacob Chandler."

"No shit? What's he doin' around here?"

"Don't have a clue."

"When were you plannin' on tellin' me?"

"Just found out the other night. Saw the headline in a newspaper—*Tycoon Charged with Murder.*"

"Shit. Let's get outta here. Bet the law's hot on his tail."

He lays the shotgun on the floor and grabs my arm, yanks me outside. We've only gone a few yards when a bright light flashes around us, and what sounds like a cannon goes off. A tree explodes up ahead.

Bryce yells, "Move it, before this whole place goes up in flames." We run up the ridge.

Amy

Gunfire. I sit up straight. Eyes wide open. Wait and listen. Another shot sends me scrambling to my feet. It came from down below. I stare up the trail. Too steep. I spin around … downhill … a small trail to the right … leads into some bushy pines, but that's where the shots came from. I head the other way … Manzanita almost as far as you can see. I keep the ridgeline in site as I wade through the scrub. Don't wanna drift too low. Maybe there'll be a spot where it's not too steep to climb to the top.

Another blast. That's three shots. Could it be Bryce on a rampage? Are Mercedes and RJ okay? Is he coming after me? A clap of thunder. Rain pours down.

Mercedes

As we ride into a small clearing, RJ pulls the stallion to a halt and turns in his saddle. "Did you hear those gunshots?"

The mare plods up next to him and stops. "Yeah— sounds like they came from near the hut."

"Could be poachers."

"Doubt it. Most poaching around here is done at night. Too easy to get caught in broad daylight."

"Somebody getting target practice?"

I shrug. "Maybe ... but, we better be careful just the same. The first shots sounded like a deer rifle. Those rounds can carry for over a mile."

A clap of thunder close by startles the horses. We look up. Sky's black, thick with clouds.

RJ leans over in his saddle and grabs the mare's halter. "Easy, girl," he murmurs.

I grab the saddle horn.

He prods the stallion forward. "Let's get to some cover." The mare follows. Moments later as we watch from back under the tree canopy, rain is coming down in sheets. We have to shout to hear each other.

"Been meaning to ask," RJ yells. "What were you doing out wandering around in the woods the other night ... after Bryce's rampage?"

I holler back. "Who says I was?"

"How'd you come up with the shotgun I lost?"

I shrug.

He sits straight up in his saddle like a rodeo champion waiting for his trophy. "You came looking for me, didn't you?"

"Not everything in life is about you."

He slouches, his ego deflated like a burst balloon. Takes out his pocket knife—checks to see if it's still sharp. As if it would get dull folded up in his pocket. "Let's just say I had a score to settle."

Neither of us says anything more until the storm passes.

Deputy Sheriff Baker

The sniffer dog strains against his leash. "Deputy," the handler calls out. "I think he's onto something."

A loud crack echoes from down below.

I turn to Grimes. "Was that gunfire?"

"Sounded like a deer rifle."

I point. "It came from over there."

The dog handler calls out, "Deputy."

I look back.

She points toward the crest. "Edgar wants to take us that way."

I wave her off. "Keep him here. We're going to check this out, first."

A fat raindrop splats onto my forehead. A clap of thunder follows. We head in the direction of the gunfire, traversing the ridge we've been climbing.

A short time later another loud bang stops us in our tracks. Grimes points straight ahead. "That's close."

I wrinkle my nose. "Was that a shotgun?"

We continue toward the sounds, pausing for a moment when a flash of lightning is followed by an explosion that rocks the hillside. I look at Grimes. "That's no gunfire."

The rain pours down in sheets, soaking us to the core. In time, we spot a tiny hut at the base of the ridge. We kneel beside a boulder and scope it out. Smoke near the ridgeline confirms what I feared from the explosion we just heard—lightning strike. I signal for Grimes to circle behind the hut. We spring from our crouched positions and scurry down the ridge. With weapons drawn, we converge at the door from opposite directions. As I push the door open, Grimes yells, "Police! Get down!"

I motion him in and follow. We pan the room with our sidearms.

Grimes stops short and mutters, "Not another one."

We stare down at a body lying on its back in a pool of blood, a crater where his face should be. A few feet away is a very expensive shotgun, which only one person in this part of the county can afford. I point to it. "Looks like Chandler's missing Beretta."

Grimes slips on latex gloves and picks up the shotgun.

"How the hell did we miss that?" I ask.

He shrugs. "He must've hidden it pretty good."

"Meaning he was planning to use it, *again*." I palm the back of my neck.

It doesn't escape me that all three victims have been about the same build as Chandler's neighbor. And all three got their faces destroyed by a point-blank shotgun blast.

This Chandler guy is more twisted than your average revenge killer.

Just as the rain stops, a second pine bursts into flames near the ridgeline. My eyes lock onto a cluster of parched live oak a few yards away. "If those go, this place is toast." I shake my head. "Grimes, radio command. Have them call in the lightning strike. Put all reservists on standby—prepare for an evacuation. And call for volunteers to help spread the word. The way the wind's blowing, any fire's going to take off and follow that ridge toward Chandler's place. If we're lucky, it won't jump the highway."

"What about Chandler?"

"If we're real lucky, the fire'll do us a favor and save the county the expense of a trial. But just in case he tries to use the evacuation as cover to slip away, order up a few dozen handbills to pass around. Give strict orders—do not approach—consider him armed and dangerous. If anyone spots him, they're to call it in."

"And the dog lady?"

"Radio her for their location and tell her to stay put. I'll call for an evacuation helicopter. Until the chopper gets here, you photograph the place with our cell phone and bag all the evidence you can—especially Chandler's shotgun. I'll get the body ready for transport."

Chapter Thirteen

Jacob

How long was I out? I'm woozy. Soaked. Must have missed a downpour.

I raise up on my knees and peer back at the hut. Fresh shivers ripple down my already chilled spine. Smoke is rising from a stand of pines near the top of the ridge, and flames are licking the boughs of nearby live oaks.

The rain has stopped, but dark grey clouds are still racing across the sky, broken up by wide patches of blue sky. Guess the storm hung around long enough to set this tinderbox on fire. That means the two sheriff deputies standing in front of that hut are the least of my worries. My legs wobble as I struggle to my feet. Another wave of lightheadedness strikes. My shotgun. I look around. Damn. Left it back in the hut. Teresa must have used it to finish off the dying cowboy, figuring he was on to her scam. Probably wiped her fingerprints and left it behind to put the blame on me. Baker will want me for a third homicide.

I kneel and grab a long stick lying at my feet. Need to put distance between me and what's about to become an inferno. I draw an imaginary line straight through the rugged terrain back to the lake and the underground bunker. It's probably my only chance. If I don't bleed out first.

Tess

Bryce marches me in drenching rain to the top of the ridge and along crest. When the downpour slackens he stops and backs me up against a tree—holds me there by my throat. I meet his stare. "Plan on killing me?"

"Depends on whether I can still trust you."

"What do you want from me?"

"For starters, you help me get rid of both girls and that boy from the ranch house. Do that, and I'll let you live."

I give him my sexiest smile. "I'd like to sweeten the deal."

He releases his grip and takes a step back. "You've got bigger balls than any man."

"I want to be sure they pin the body count on Chandler."

"Sure. My best bet for getting out of this mess is for the kids to disappear and for him to take the rap for all three bodies I've racked up so far."

"Why not make it a trifecta?"

"Whaddaya mean?"

"As we're getting rid of the girls and pinning the rap on Chandler, why don't we shake him down for a couple of those millions he won't have any use for behind bars?"

His eyes get big.

I touch my hand to my breast. "What I've got tucked away here is a legal document. The fellow you killed back at that hut was a lawyer. I got him to draft it. All we have to do is make Chandler sign it. What do you say?"

"You expect me to believe you didn't trade any favors to get that outta him?"

"All I did was make a promise I never planned to keep. You know you're the only one for me." I undo the top button on my blouse, peek up at him and pout, lean forward, and trace my lips with my tongue.

He leans toward me. I jerk back.

He clutches my shoulders. "What?"

"You smell smoke?"

We both sniff the air—look around for signs of fire.

I point back toward the hut. "That lightning strike must have set the whole ridge burning."

He grabs my arm and yanks me. "Let's get to the other side of the ridge. If we're lucky … the updraft from that side will keep it from crossing over."

I pull back, dig in my heels. "But what about Chandler?"

"We'll deal with that when we get clear of this fire."

Mercedes

After the rain squall passes, RJ nudges his stallion and mutters, "We need to get moving."

As our horses trudge along, I stare almost trance-like at his back, wondering what's going through his head. When I want him he doesn't let me get close, but when I'm distant he pulls one of his moods. Funny, books I've swiped from that fancy cabin say girls are hard to figure out. It's RJ who's the real puzzle. We both keep silent—interrupted only by his grunts when he reins in the stallion and leans down to study the ground for Amy's tracks.

After about half an hour, tiny white flakes snap me back to the here and now. No way it's snow, not in the heat of summer. I sniff the air. My head runs through all the possibilities. "There's a fire somewhere."

RJ jerks back on his reins and turns in his saddle. What started as a few cinders fluttering down is now light flurry. He holds out his hand to catch a sample of the ash and nods in the direction of the hut. "Must be coming from over there."

I turn the mare downhill toward home.

RJ grabs her halter and yanks us back. "Where the hell do you think you're going?"

"To the hut. To grab as much stuff as I can before the fire—."

"If a fire breaks loose with all this dry fuel lying around, we won't have a prayer unless we get out now. The last thing you wanna do in a forest fire is try to escape downhill. Fires tend to burn upslope, which means you'll be heading right into it. You're dead unless you win the lottery, and a strong wind moves it in a different direction. But the odds are against you, big time … sorry."

"Then we'd better keep after Amy. No way can she outrun a fire on foot. We've got to find her." I jerk the mare's reins out of his hands and dig my heels into her sides. RJ freezes in his saddle, his mouth wide open. The mare bolts past him and breaks into a full gallop. I scream, "Shit … not so fast," and hang on for dear life.

I take a quick peek at RJ and see him turn his stallion to come after me. Just as I get straightened around, a low hanging branch smacks me in the face. When I open my eyes I spot a tree down across the trail. The mare plants her feet. I fly out of the saddle and crash to the ground. Pain shoots through my shoulder, my neck, and arm. Flat on my back, I can't catch my breath.

Next thing I know I'm shivering. RJ's kneeling next to me, his hand is on my forehead, his shirt draped over me like a blanket. My feet are propped up on a saddle. Ash is falling around us. He says to stay still.

I mumble, "Wouldn't think of moving."

"We'll have to get going again soon. But first, we have to be sure you're not going into shock."

Amy

I push harder through the scrub. Brush is getting thicker. High branches scratch my face, low ones snag my ankles. I stumble ... catch my breath. Check the ridgeline. It's getting farther away.

I slant uphill ... press against the Manzanita branches. White flakes are falling ... ashes. Like when we burn garbage, and sparks shoot up ... and float away. Maybe they're coming from Mercedes' stove. My throat's scratchy. The brush keeps getting thicker. Now it doesn't give way at all. I turn straight uphill ... one step is as far as I get. Maybe going to the top isn't a good idea.

Downhill is easier ... just have to worry about loose rocks. Or ... what if I step on one of those killer snakes? I breathe fast. Try to swallow ... can't. Eyes sting ... lungs burn. Smoke everywhere ... ash is getting thicker. Summertime snowflakes swirl around ... tiny red candy wrappers, too. They turn black before they hit the ground. Bryce says you have to be careful burning garbage. Sparks can fly off, catch dry needles on fire … maybe grass, too. If sparks land up in the trees, the whole forest will burn down. Somebody didn't listen. They weren't careful.

My heart beats faster. My chest is gonna explode. Reach in my pocket … no candy wrapper. Fall to my knees, sobbing. Cry 'til there's no tears left. Stand and look downhill. The Manzanita peters out at the bottom. There's a flat clearing about as big as the lake. Way off to the right side … grass is on fire. Flames reaching for the low hanging branches. To the left it's clear. I race through the Manzanita to the bottom … go hard to the left … hot, dry air burns my throat, lungs. Have to get away from this fire.

Mercedes

RJ helps me back onto the mare, but this time he ties a lead to her bridle and cinches it to his saddle horn. I don't have to steer any more … just hang on. He nudges the stallion into a walk and we head uphill. I keep an eye out for Amy's tracks, but my throbbing neck and shoulder paralyze my brain. Can't really say when I zoned out.

At the top of the ridge, RJ says he hopes she's following the crest 'til she spots the lake down below. If she misses it, she'll wind up on a bluff that overlooks the highway.

I wince from a stabbing pain in the pit of my stomach. "But, what if she's headed the other direction … right into the fire?"

"They'll find three charred bodies if we follow her. We just have to hope she made the right choice."

I squeeze my eyes shut to hold back tears. A short time later, a wave of nausea hits. I hunch forward and let out a weak, "Hold up—please."

RJ halts his stallion, and the mare stops, too. He jumps down and rushes over to catch me as I lean to the side. When my feet hit the ground he braces me and helps me down the backside of the ridge—about a hundred feet. I slide down and rest my back against a tree stump ... hold back a surge of vomit working its way up my throat.

He pulls off his shirt and tucks it under my head. "Here. Lie down ... point your feet uphill. You're going into shock from the pain."

My teeth chatter.

He leaps up, sprints to the top of the ridge, and leads the horses back down to where I'm shivering to death. He ties them up, unsaddles the mare, and drapes her blanket over me. I close my eyes, hoping sleep will carry me off this mountain.

I wake up, moaning, drenched in sweat, my face clammy. My shoulder throbs. Someone—not RJ—says, "So sleeping beauty's decided to wake up?"

I know the voice. But it can't be. He's dead. I saw it with my own eyes. A woman laughs. Is that Tess? I try to prop myself up. Pain shoots down my arm. "Where am I? RJ?"

The man and the woman laugh again. Hard, cold metal presses against my temple. I eye the barrel of a rifle, follow it up to a bony hand clutching the narrow part of the stock, an index finger resting along the trigger guard. I look up at his face and gulp. It is him. How the hell ...? He's wearing the same creepy smile that used to turn my stomach when the bastard came up to the loft for his "special treat."

Someone moans a few feet away. I call out, "RJ!" Another moan.

The woman laughs again. It *is* Tess. My heart sinks.

Bryce pokes at my head with the rifle. "Tess, what do you say we just finish these two right here and now?"

Tess's shrill voice sends a chill down my spine. "No. We need the girl, she's the key to Chandler's millions."

"Then how 'bout the boy? He's just dead weight."

"Good point. Only thing he can do is cause trouble. Just leave him tied up here. If the fire doesn't get him, he'll make a good meal for some hungry coyote or mountain lion. And nobody can trace him back to us."

My eyes dart back and forth between Bryce and Tess. Neck's too stiff—can't turn far enough to get a glimpse of RJ.

I blurt out the best argument I can think of. "That stallion—it's a one rider horse. You'll need RJ—or you'll have to hoof it all the way to wherever you're planning to take me."

Bryce grunts. "We'll do the riding. You can do the hoofing."

"But I can't—the pain—that's why we stopped."

Tess mutters, "Put her on the mare. Shoo the stallion back home."

My heart pounds in my ears. "Our best chance of out running the fire is all of us on horseback. To do that we'll need the horses... and RJ."

Bryce swings the rifle barrel away from my face. "She'll do the walking. Now, let's get a move on. Don't like how that ash is blowin' over to this side of the ridge. Only takes one spark in the wrong place to set the whole place ablaze."

"And the boy?" Tess asks.

Bryce swats the stallion's hindquarter. "Git ou...."

The horse bolts and gallops away.

Amy

Watching ash fall as I run. Embers catching in the grass ... burning small patches then dying out. Up ahead, something on the ground ... a bundle ... or .... I slow to a walk. A body. I step closer. It moves. I freeze.

A man ... he gets up on his knees ... his head drooping ... shoulders sag. One arm dangling limp ... an ugly red and purple splotch above his elbow. I tiptoe close to him ... bend down for a close look at the bloody arm. He turns his face ... looks up at me. God, it's the man from the huge cabin.

He takes my hand. His voice is weak. "Help me up."

I pull him to his feet.

He staggers ... leans into me ... drapes his good arm over my neck. Almost whispering, he says, "Have to keep going. Fire's coming our way. It'll pick up speed. Got to get to my bunker."

He takes a step. I stay with him ... look up at his face. The frown tells me he's worn out from the pain ... probably lost lots of blood. But that doesn't slow him ... each step's a little quicker than the last. His breathing gets faster, too— and louder. Sometimes he coughs ... then winces. When he stumbles ... his face gets all screwed up ... and he mumbles things I can't understand.

Ash and embers are getting thicker. I keep peeking over my shoulder ... smoke spreading along the ridge ... no Bryce in sight. Once in a while, I tell him to stop and rest. He shakes his head ... points straight ahead.

Not much farther we find a pasture ... most of the grass is eaten or worn away. Across it ... a barn and ranch house ... the one where RJ and his uncle lived. The neighbor man sees it, he walks faster ... grunts with every step. As we come around to the front of the barn my heart jumps up into my throat. RJ's stallion is waiting at the barn door.

RJ's uncle, his butchered face, the pool of blood—it all flashes through my head. I slump over ... my knees wobble. The neighbor grabs my arm with his good hand and holds me up.

His voice is raspy. "Let's go inside."

I glance over my shoulder. No Bryce. We head for the kitchen door.

In the kitchen, I help the man into a chair. He rests his head on the table ... his good arm for a pillow ... bloody arm dangling by his side. I get a mug full of water—he raises his head—I lift the mug to his lips. When he finishes drinking he whispers, "Booze?"

"Huh?"

He winces. "Got to be some around. See what you can find."

Search the whole house. At the doorway to Uncle Eric's room ... flies ... like the ones swarming his body ... sucking his blood. I study the dark stained carpet. Puke pushes up into my throat ... hold it back. Close my eyes for a second. Try to think what everything would look like through crinkly, red candy wrappers.

Find booze in the cabinet next to the bed. When I set the bottle on the table next to the man, he whispers, "Towel." I hand him one. He douses it with whiskey and starts dabbing the wound. Then he pours booze right on the bloody hole in his arm.

I walk over to the cupboard, holding my breath as I peek out the backdoor. Still no Bryce. Good.

The shelves are almost empty. Only a few things got left when Mr. Miller, Uncle Eric's neighbor, interrupted us.

There's a jar of honey. I take it and pull up a chair next to the man ... slather the honey over his wound. He wrinkles his nose ... frowns.

I say, "Kills germs. Helps it heal. Bryce taught us that."

"So ... what are you doing out here ... all alone?"

"Kinda got lost."

He nods. "Me, too. Where do you live?"

I screw the top back on the honey ... take it to the cupboard.

"You look a lot like the kid who lives across the lake from me."

Point to the booze. "You gonna drink any of that?"

Shakes his head. "My name's Jacob ... you can call me Jake. What's yours?"

Put the top on and start back to Uncle Eric's bedroom. I stop ... look back. "Amy."

"Thanks, Amy ... for saving my life."

"It's nothing."

He wheezes. "Since it's my life, I should be the judge of what it's worth."

I walk back ... set the booze on the table ... sit down. "Your granddaughter."

His eyes get big. "What about her?"

"She's lucky ..." my voice breaks like I'm gonna cry.

Hangs his head. "I lost her ...."

"That's right ... you said somebody ... took her."

He wrinkles his forehead. "*I* told you? When?"

"You gave me a ride. I was walking up the mountain. I lied. Told you I didn't live across the lake."

He rubs the back of his neck. "Guess I forgot ...."

I stare down at my hands folded in my lap.

"Amy, I'd like to return the favor."

"What favor?"

"Saving my life."

"It's not saved yet."

He grins. "When we get out of this mess …. "

I shrug.

"Do you like candy?" he asks.

"Sure …."

He digs into his pocket. "I always carry these. Just in case I find her again. They're her favorite."

When he opens his hand, I smile big. Cinnamon candy … in a shiny red, crinkly wrapper.

He stands. "We better get going if we're going to outrun this fire to my bunker. Real medicine there … and food."

When we step outside … big orange flames and smoke up on the ridge. A loud, groaning noise.

"Choppers," he says. "Could be good news, could be bad." He points ahead. "This fire break will take us home. Let's just stay to the far side, away from those flames—and try to keep under cover so the helicopters don't spot us."

I look over my shoulder for Bryce. Maybe he's not coming, after all.

Mercedes

Bryce and Tess ride double on the mare. With my wrists lashed together at one end of a rope—the other end tied to the saddle horn—I trot behind, gyrating to stay on my feet. Pain shoots through my shoulder every time the rope goes taut and jerks me forward.

The rocky ground would make it tough enough to keep my balance with arms free. Tied up, it's only a matter of time before I do a face-plant. My stomach's drawn tight as a crossbow. We left RJ lying back there on the ground. By now, the fire's got to be closing in on him. I fight back tears—stumble—twist one way then the next—barely able to stay upright. Another surge of pain.

Bryce calls back to Tess, "We're lucky that fire isn't moving any faster. Won't be long before it starts making its own wind—blows the flames along the ridgeline and over to our side. We better get to the lake fast or we're toast."

Tess scolds him, "Careful. She's got to be in one piece when we find Chandler. He's not going to pay for damaged goods."

My foot catches a root. Twist to my good side ... lose my footing. My ribcage slams against the ground. Rocks rip my shirt, pants ... skin. Bryce pulls the mare to a stop. I get up on my knees ... struggle to breathe.

Bryce shouts at Tess, "Not my fault that bitch can't run without falling."

Tess slaps the side of his head. "Don't go so damned fast."

They're arguing—this could be my only chance. I peek around for an escape route.

Bryce grumbles, "Hey. It's not me. It's this damn nag."

Tess smacks him again. "Shut up. I'm tired of doing everything your way. You've done nothing but screw up my life since we met. From now on, I'll be calling the shots."

"The hell you are. You're living on borrowed time as it is."

Tess laughs.

He turns in the saddle. "What's so funny?"

"You. You're what's funny. Think you're some hotshot. No, you're a wannabe. Just a worthless, weasel wannabe.

You've got this all backwards. We don't need you. Not anymore. And I'm tired of being your surrogate mommy—somebody you can cling to, who won't leave you all alone, staring out a window, worrying whether she'll ever come home. No. Go ahead and stand by that damn window if you want. But get it straight. This 'mommy's' never coming home to you again. Never. If anybody around here's living on borrowed time, it's you."

Bryce turns away from her. "What makes you think you can handle Chandler on your own?"

"I've got the leverage of three murder raps—on top of *two* granddaughters." She mutters, "Once we find the other little bitch."

I grit my teeth and stand up. "What are you talking about, 'two granddaughters?' And what murders?"

She glares at Bryce. "First of all, the sheriff thinks Chandler killed that bum at the shack the night it burned down—we all thought the poor schlep was Bryce. They also want him for Eric's murder. In addition to those two murders, Bryce just set him up to take the fall for killing a local lawyer named Roy."

Bryce murmurs, "Amy's his granddaughter, and so are you."

First, I'm Tess's daughter? Now I'm some rich dude's granddaughter? Makes no sense. But it keeps me alive ... whatever. I narrow my eyes. "Since I'm worth a million bucks to you, seems like you should be treating me with kid gloves."

Tess sneers. "Stay out of this. Chandler doesn't know about you—and until I give him proof, he'll just think we're trying to scam him. But the proof's right here." She pats her breast.

Bryce clutches the stock of the rifle that's hanging by a leather strap next to his knee. "She's bluffing. Let's get a move on before that fire catches up with us."

Tess reaches in front of Bryce and starts untying the end of the rope that's tied to the saddle horn. Bryce grips her hands. "Don't get so grabby. I'll say when I want to be touched."

"Sorry. I didn't mean what I said. Just thought it would be safer if I hold the rope. She's less likely to fall and break her neck."

Bryce lets go of her hands. "Fine, and while you're at it, you can start worrying about what I'm liable to do, once ...."

In a blink, she draws the rope tight around his throat, pulling harder and harder. "Say good night—for good, you ugly bastard."

Bryce clutches the rope, gasps for breath. Tess cinches the rope tighter. He jerks from one side to the next—reaches back for her hands. She yanks down on the rope, pulling his head against her chest. He tries to turn in the saddle, his arms fall to his sides. His head droops. His body goes limp. Tess loosens the rope from around his neck—shoves him to the ground. I study his lifeless body. Always thought I'd dance at the sight of him dead, but instead, I'm frozen in disbelief.

She climbs down and unties my wrists. "Cooperate and you get to live...." Her cold, hard eyes start to twinkle. "And in grand style, I might add."

My shoulders slump, my mind is numb. A question comes out of me—don't even know how or why. "How you going to prove I'm his granddaughter?"

"Trust me, I've got it handled. But cross me, and you're dead."

I nod.

"Now, get up in the saddle. That fire's not going to stand still for us."

From on top of the mare, I glance down once more at Bryce's corpse.

Tess prods the horse. "Only room for the two of us—good riddance."

Chapter Fourteen

Deputy Sheriff Baker

My feet are propped up on my desk as Grimes walks into the substation and reports that he's faxed the handbills to all the evacuation centers.

I sit up in my chair. "It's just a waiting game at this point. Forest Service says the fire's burning slowly—staying on the ridge—moving toward Chandler's place. But if the wind picks up, it'll charge through like a thoroughbred down the backstretch at Santa Anita."

"Hope they give us plenty of time to alert folks if there's an evacuation order."

"I'm sure they'll do their best."

Grimes turns to walk away then looks back. "Oh, the dog lady is on her way back home. Told her we wouldn't be needing her anymore."

"Yeah, that was a bust."

"Think we'll get another shot at bringing in Chandler? Hate to think he'll get away."

"Don't worry, Grimes. Justice will be served—one way or the other."

The phone rings. Grimes turns and waits.

"Sheriff's substation, Deputy Baker speaking."

The caller reports, "Weather Service says the wind's shifting to westerly at ten miles per hour—building to twenty—expect gusts to forty ...."

When I hang up, I look at Grimes. "This thing is bearing down on Chandler's place, and it'll have quite a head of steam by the time it gets there. Of course as the fire gets hotter, it'll create its own wind ... and higher wind speeds. They might have to ground the choppers at some point."

His eyes widen. "It'll be a disaster if the flames jump the highway, or if the wind shifts and blows the fire into town. So what's their plan?"

"They're building a firebreak along the highway. Airborne assets are spreading retardant in the fire's path. Controlled burns to check the fire's progress are 'under consideration' at this point."

"They'd better make a decision soon, while the winds are still down."

"They've got their jobs ... we've got ours. Let's get do it."

RJ

My head throbs. The butt of Bryce's rifle left a nasty gash. Pain shoots through my neck, too. I squirm, work my hands into the back pocket where I keep the pocket knife Uncle Eric gave me—the one with the church key for those times you come across a bottle of beer that needs opening. Good thing that Bryce creep didn't pat me down before he tied me up. I pull out the pocket knife. Feel for the edge of the blade—pinch it between the tips of two fingers—open it.

Damn. Slips out of my hand. I roll on my side fishing behind me for the knife. A helicopter's drone on the other side of the ridge gets louder. It's not just ash falling. Embers, too.

Found it. Push the blade up between my wrists—grip the knife as tight as I can with the tips of my fingers and thumbs—roll on my back—use the ground to help hold it—slide the blade back and forth across the rope—keep working it. It takes a few minutes, but I cut through. Turn to my side and wriggle my hands free. Sit up and untie the knot at my ankles. Scramble to my feet. Look around to get my bearings.

It's only a matter of time before the fire breaks over the crest and starts scarfing down the fuel on this side. Not a safe escape route anymore. But if I cross the ridge and head straight down, I should find myself pretty close to Uncle Eric's ranch—and with any luck, the stallion will be waiting at the barn door.

As I get close to the top, the air burns my throat and lungs. A flash of heat on the crest sucks the wind out of me—every bit of moisture sapped from my eyes. I drop to one knee. An explosion off to my right is followed by trees thundering to the ground. Can't stay here. Don't dare go over the top. Have to outrun it. Stay just below the crest until it's safe to cross over. But the heat's too much to stand up. Have to crawl.

The ground gets hotter by the second. Can't stop. Have to keep moving. Another explosion ... right overhead. Limbs come crashing down. I look up. A large flaming branch—headed right at me. I scramble ....

Mercedes

The reins tempt me. Tess can't see my hands gripping the saddle horn—she's behind me in the saddle. I see hers real good, though. She's got a loose hold on the reins. I could just grab them. 'Course, the pain in my shoulder reminds me of why I hate horses. But I gotta get back to RJ—what other chance does he have? I glance over my shoulder at her. "So you never answered my question back there."

"What question?"

"How you going to prove I'm this rich dude's granddaughter? I thought *you're* supposed to be my mother. How does that work?"

"Don't get sassy with me ... I told you ... I've got it handled."

"No ... seriously." I force a laugh. "Are you his bastard daughter, an oops from some drunken one-night-stand he forgot ever happened?"

She lets go of the reins in her right hand and slaps me hard on the side of the head.

I yank the reins out of her left hand and plant my elbow hard in her gut.

She hammers both fists into my bad shoulder. "You little bitch ...."

Pain shoots through my neck and arm. I slump forward, face buried in the horse's mane. My hand goes numb.

She grabs the reins and pulls the mare to a stop. Pushes me off.

I collapse to my knees.

She jumps down and stands over me. "I need to deliver you to Chandler in one piece—but, that doesn't mean you're going to be a pretty sight. Now up on your feet."

I stand slowly, hunched over, holding my throbbing shoulder.

Tess takes rope and binds up my wrists. As she boosts me up, I slump over the saddle horn ... slip in and out of consciousness, catching glimpses of RJ's freckled face racing in and out of my mind.

Bryce

This damn ground's hard. My head's all fogged up. What the hell happened? Grab my throat —neck burns like I scraped myself shaving, big time. Throat's sore—almost swollen shut. Can't swallow. Can't breathe.

A crack—an explosion—somewhere close. What the hell's going on? I prop myself up. Open my eyes. Right eye's sore—like I got poked with a damn finger. Blurry. Everything's flat white, colorless—except for tiny gray spots floating in front of me. My head starts spinning. A ringing in my ears. I lie down. Got a headache—a bad one, worse than any hangover. Close my eyes. My heart's pumping in overdrive.

That damn whore! She tried to kill me. I grabbed for the rope—choking. Strong bitch. Never fought me so hard. She yanked the rope tighter. Popped a damn blood vessel in my eye. Sore as hell. I remember thinking, *this is it—meet your maker*. Broads have dumped me before—even my fuckin' mother—but shit, none of them tried to kill me.

It's getting warmer. Air tastes hot, dry. Throat stings.

There's laughing inside my head. Not my maker laughing. Her. The bitch is trash talkin' me—"Go straight to hell. Don't pass Go. Don't collect squat. Go right to the biggest, meanest whore of all. Now let's see how you like being tortured." I laugh that same sadistic laugh. What the hell?

Another explosion. It's getting closer. I jump into a crouch, look all around. Remember where I am. The damn forest's on fire. This isn't Hell. Gotta get outta here. Get to the damn lake. Get away from these exploding trees. And when I catch up with that stupid Tess—she's dead meat. And so are those girls.

Amy

Jake's arm's draped over my shoulder—he gets heavier with every step. Groans when he breathes. Says his arm is mostly numb—only a dull pain—his lungs hurt more. He's lightheaded.

Smoke's getting thicker. I'm coughing as bad as him. Eyes sting. Ask him about his granddaughter. Catches his breath, almost between every word. "Lots of ... spunk. Sweet. Cute ... as a ... button. Should've .... " He leans, points to the ground. We sit so he can rest.

I say, "Did people try to find her?"

He nods. "Lots of people. I keep looking."

"How long?"

"Twelve years. I'm still looking for her."

"Wish people came for me."

He sits up straight. Takes my hand. "Amy ... they are ... I'm sure."

We don't talk for a while. His chest rattles when he takes a breath—like Bryce when he got really sick ... was burning up with fever. I fed him broth Mercedes made from birds she killed. I put cold rags on his forehead for days. Jake motions for us to get up and walk some more.

At the end of the firebreak there's a heap of charred, broken-up boards. Jake says, "It's all that's left of where you used to live." He looks at me. "Were you ... here ... when it happened?"

"No."

"You ran away before?"

"Didn't run. Tess took me."

"Where's she now?"

"Dunno ... I got away."

"Good."

I point at where our shack used to be. "It's not real anymore."

We walk on. A loud roar comes from the lake—gets louder. Trees shake like there's a big wind. Cover my ears. I wrap my arms around Jake.

He hugs me close. "More helicopters," he says, barely loud enough for me to hear.

When the noise isn't so loud, Jake tells me the helicopter is scooping water out of the lake to dump on the fire. He points to the gravel road that leads to his cabin. We walk slowly, stopping a couple of times ... once at the stump by the little trail down to the cove. The stump's too small for both of us, so I let him sit—catch his breath.

I rub the top of his head. Smooth. Wet from sweat. Hot from the sun ... the fire. From fever? I say, "Wait. Be right back." Run down the trail to the cove, dip the bottom of my shirt in cool water. Come back and wipe his face, the top of his almost hairless head.

We don't stop again until we reach the cabin. When we go inside he points down a hall ... nods at the last doorway. Books cover shelves that reach from floor to ceiling on two of the walls. He shuffles behind a desk, reaches between some of the books. Two bookshelves swing out toward us like thick, heavy doors.

Footsteps out in the hallway, hurrying. We turn. Before I can blink ... Mercedes is standing in the doorway. Behind her, Tess with a rifle. The barrel is pushed up under Mercedes' chin.

She nods at Jake. "Mr. Chandler, I have some unfinished business I'd like to wrap up ... if you don't mind."

Jake shoves me toward the opening in the wall—shields me from Tess.

Tess yells, "Everyone where I can see them. And put your hands up."

I step out so she can see me. Jake raises both hands in the air; his bad arm comes up slowly. He yelps and tumbles into a chair ... his face twists up in pain. He slumps over ... his arms stretched out across the desk ... head buried in a stack of papers. He groans.

I bend over him ... put my hand on his forehead ... look back at Tess. "We have to get him in there. He's sick ... bleeding ... needs medicine."

She glares at Jake. "It's what I need right now that matters."

I squint up at her. "What good's he going to be to you dead?"

Tess motions for us to go through the secret opening, the rifle barrel still shoved up under Mercedes' chin. I help Jake up from the chair ... he leans on me ... we stumble into the secret hiding place. Once all four of us are through the opening, Jake touches the wall. The big bookshelf doors slam shut, lights come on like magic. A humming sound starts up. Can't tell where it's coming from. Cool air gives me goose bumps.

Deputy Sheriff Baker

I hang up the receiver on my desk phone and look at Grimes. "A couple of chopper pilots are reporting civilians in the fire's path. One's trying to get down off the ridge about halfway between Eric Lamb's place and Chandler's cabin. The fire's moving in on him fast. Two others appear to be headed toward the lake."

"Okay, Boss. I'll head up in the Blazer and intercept the two by the lake. They're probably headed out to the highway. We'll have to send a chopper for the other one. He's on borrowed time."

"I'm coming with. We'll radio for the chopper on the way." I grab my hat and we head for the door.

Half way up the mountain, we get our first kick in the teeth—choppers are grounded due to wind turbulence. The civilian up on the ridge is on his own for now, and the fire's closing in fast. Just hope the two headed for the lake make it into the water before the fire gets them.

Grimes looks at me. "Boss, there's gotta be something we can do. The poor bastard doesn't have a chance without help."

"And what do you suggest—getting ourselves barbequed along with him?"

"No. Just saying ...."

There's not another word between us the rest of the way to Chandler's place. I'm busting my brain to figure out how to help—can practically smell Grimes's brain overheating, as well.

When we pull into Chandler's drive, his Jeep is parked where it's been since he went off the grid. That means he's likely still in the area, unless someone helped him get away.

Grimes points to the kitchen French doors. One side is standing wide open. We draw our weapons as we step out of the Blazer.

I point to the cabin. "This takes priority."

Grimes covers. I go in first, shouting, "Sheriff's Department. Get down!"

We alternate covering for each other as we move through the place, clearing each room. In the library, I point to some papers smeared with fresh blood. "What do you make of this?"

Grimes shrugs. "Chandler's struck again?"

"Yeah, but where's the body?"

"I'll check the perimeter. You give this place a second going over."

Outside, I scan the ground for footprints and find two sets—the first set doesn't surprise me. Two people almost in lockstep, headed toward the cabin. One small, the other clearly an adult male—neither with a normal gait. The smaller one's leaning away from the other. Prints are leading to the cabin. The other set—two people also. About equal weight—possibly females. I don't find any exit tracks for either party.

Something's not right. We cleared every room. Checked the closets, under the beds. I backtrack both sets of prints. The man and his companion came down the gravel road from the neighbor's burned-out shack. The others came from the woods along the side of the lake. Their trail leads me to a horse tied to a tree about a hundred yards from Chandler's cabin.

After untying the horse, I lead it back to Chandler's place where Grimes is waiting on the deck.

He laughs. "Tell me that's not the source of the blood."

"No, it's your ride—might come in handy if we wind up rescuing our subject up on the ridge. I'll drive the Blazer. There's a firebreak behind that burned-out shack across the lake. Let's meet there and proceed along the base of the ridge. Maybe we'll get lucky."

He steps down off the deck and takes the reins. "Where'd you find her?"

I point toward the woods. "A set of tracks coming from over there."

He climbs up on the mare. "Anything else interesting?"

"Yeah, there's another set coming from the road. But, no tracks leaving the cabin."

"That's weird."

"Tell me about it."

Amy

Tess pushes Mercedes and me into a corner. Jake flops into a chair by a table near us. She waves the rifle around—tells us to keep quiet. She killed Bryce and some bum he hired to off her. She shot a lawyer too. And she wounded Jake.

Mercedes says, "She and Bryce tied up RJ and left him to die up on the ridge."

"No!" I scream. I hold back tears.

Mercedes hugs me.

Tess orders. "Quiet, everyone."

One of the walls lights up. Tess mutters something about 'closed circuit TV.' Bright pictures of rooms ... Jake's car ... his dock ... the lake ... other places outdoors. Two cops ... walking around. I glance at Tess. She's watching one go outside. Tess tracks him from one picture to the next.

We watch the men in the pictures for a long time. One gets in a car and drives away. The other gets on the mare and heads into the woods along the lake.

Tess looks down at Jake. "Now for our unfinished business."

He groans.

She points the rifle at Mercedes. "Meet your granddaughter."

Jake sits up straight. "Celine?"

I glance at Mercedes.

No way she's the little girl in the picture ... her hair's not black ... like Mercedes ... like Tess.

Tess laughs. "Not Celine—Mercedes. My daughter, your granddaughter."

"What kind of game are you playing?"

"That's no way to greet your own flesh and blood."

"Are you saying—you seduced Jesse and she's his?"

"No. I'm your daughter." She glances at Mercedes. "And I'm not going to be denied anymore."

Jake breathes like he's sucking air. "*Daughter*? What the hell are you talking about?"

"Mom said you wouldn't remember."

He coughs a weak cough. "Who? Who's your mother?"

Her face tightens. "What? Were there so many you couldn't keep track?"

"I'm sorry ... uh ... if I had known ...." He wheezes.

"Doesn't matter now. Water under the bridge. Besides, she died a while back—heartbroken. She never got over you—always loved you."

"I don't have the slightest idea ...."

"Stop. You're just digging a deeper hole for yourself. She deserved a hell of a lot better than you."

"So what do you want from me?"

She raises her chin. "I want what's due us ... our share."

He sputters. "Your share ...?"

"Our inheritance."

He gasps for air. "Guess I got it wrong."

"How's that?"

"My will gives each of my two grandchildren half of everything."

Tess lowers the rifle. "It what?"

"Yes ...." He nods at Mercedes. "I hired a detective to follow the two of you. Thought you were having an affair. When he reported you were pregnant and things had cooled off between you, I had the detective keep tabs on you. Just in case you made trouble. I had the baby figured for Jesse's."

"No affair—not with me, at least. He was happy as hell to have a sister—said he couldn't wait to break the news to you. Almost got up the nerve to tell you, but I got pregnant—one of your brokers. He dumped me as soon as I said I wanted to keep the baby. Once I had Mercedes, I begged Jesse to get you to accept us as family. He laughed. Said his wife was pregnant and no bastard was going to horn in on their child's inheritance. Next thing I know, I'm blackballed, out of a job."

He winces. "After Ellen died, I woke up to what an asshole I'd been. I changed my will to include your daughter. Now, if you don't let me take care of the hole you left in my arm, you'll have to prove your case in court. Somehow, I don't think you want to go that route."

"I've got all the proof I need right here." She reaches under her shirt ... pulls a paper out of her bra.

"Let's patch me up then I'll check out your 'proof.'"

She points the rifle at Jake's head. "You've forgotten who's in charge. Besides, how do I know you're telling the truth about your will?"

He slumps in the chair.

I start towards him. Tess waves me off.

"All right," he says. "Have it your way. I'll just sit here and die ... and a judge can tell you what's in my will."

She stares at him. "You're no good to me alive, anyway."

"So, what do I have to gain? Either way, I'm a dead man."

She nods towards me ... sighs. "Tell her what you need."

He reaches out to me. "Here, give me a hand. I'll have to show you."

Jake wobbles as he stands.

I grab him ... help him stay on his feet ... walk him over to a cabinet. He opens it. Points.

I take things out—bottles of medicine ... a needle ... bandages ... alcohol ... scissors. When we're done, we move to another cabinet.

He opens the top drawer, his back to Tess ... reaches in ... opens a small box ... touches the pistol inside. He winks at me.

I gulp.

He opens a folder ... pulls out some papers ... lays them on the pistol ... looks at me. "I'll let you know when I'm ready for them."

Tess calls over to us, "What's going on over there?"

"Just showing her things I might need."

She sneers. "Hurry it up."

He staggers over to the table. "Gotta lie down."

His words echo in my head. *Ready for them*.

Jake lies down on the table ... points to shelves full of water in bottles. "Water ...."

I rush over ... grab a couple bottles ... carry them to the table. While he guzzles them down, I put the medicine ... needle thing ... bandages ... scissors ... alcohol ... on the table. Reach into my pocket ... feel for the crinkly red wrapper—the cinnamon candy he gave me back at the ranch. Still there.

Tess yells, "Keep those hands where I can see them."

I show her my hands are empty.

Mercedes—still crouched in the corner—offers to give me a hand.

Tess points the rifle at Mercedes. "Stay right where you are."

"You really think you should trust her with that needle? If she screws up, she could kill him. Maybe he's bluffing about that will."

"Why should I trust you?"

Mercedes stands. "It's my inheritance we're talking about."

I keep my head down ... dabbing alcohol on Jake's wound.

Tess nods in our direction. "Then get over there and keep an eye on things."

Jake coughs. "So what's in this for you, Teresa? Somehow I doubt this is about a mother protecting her daughter's future."

"Don't worry. I've got it all figured out. But we're just going to take things one step at a time. Like you used to say back when you were teaching us how to squeeze the last nickel out of every deal."

I wrap his arm in clean bandages.

Mercedes tears off strips of tape ... smiles at me as she sticks them on the bandage. "You still like cinnamon candy?" she asks. I think she wants to remind me of when she used to give me some of her candies on the nights Bryce would beat us, send us to bed hungry—back when we were little, and I'd cry myself to sleep, cradled in her arms. She stopped holding me when the touching started.

Jake sighs. "Either of you girls given a shot before?"

We shake our heads.

"Not that hard," he says. "Hand me that vial." He points to the little medicine bottle.

I hand it to him.

"Now the needle."

Mercedes gives it to him.

"Antibiotic—kills the germs," he says. He turns the needle point into his bad arm ... his thumb presses down on the stick end of the needle. Drops the needle and vial ... breathes deep ... closes his eyes.

Tess mutters, "Her name was Francesca."

Chapter Fifteen

Deputy Sheriff Baker

Red dye covers every square inch of landscape starting a half-mile into the firebreak. Trees, scrub, rocks—everything's red. I'm bouncing along under twenty miles-an-hour, searching the tree-line, hoping our subject stands out, although he's likely coated with fire retardant as well.

Grimes rides about twenty yards out in front of me, becoming hazier as we close in on the fire. The green bandana he soaked in the lake to cover his nose and mouth is now a shade of purple. Another quarter mile in flames are leaping out of the smoke near the ridgeline. The wind's pretty calm down here, but up there it's blowing hard—reported at thirty knots with gusts to fifty.

I glance over at Grimes. He's pulled the mare to a halt and is pointing at something up on the ridge in a large patch of blackened hillside that escaped the aerial dump of fire retardant. I stop, shift the Blazer into park, and step out. Below what was once woods—now an array of charcoal spikes sticking out of reddened earth—is a charred, smoldering lump, about the size of a man.

Grimes digs his heels into the mare and charges uphill. When he reaches what appears to be human remains, he wipes his forehead and leans over, lowering his forehead to listen for signs of life. While Grimes is still bent over, a patch of wheat-colored grass between us bursts into flames. The mare bolts away in full gallop. He straightens, stares down at the smoldering corpse, and extends his hands toward me as if begging for help.

I jump in the Blazer and spin up a cloud of dust in a desperate effort to reach Grimes before he's trapped behind the flames. When I get to him, I jump out and nudge the body with my boot. Not a sound, not a twitch. Remnants of clothing turned to soot stick to the toe of my boot. I drop to my knees and reach for the victim's wrist to feel for a pulse. Roasted flesh comes off in my hand. I jerk away.

Grimes retrieves a fire retardant blanket from the Blazer that we use to wrap the body, and we lift it into the back of the Blazer. As we get into the vehicle, patches of unburnt grass below us explode into flames.

I gun the engine and we bound over bumps and ruts, dodging flames as we race to safety. Once we reach the gravel road, a voice crackles over the radio, "Central to Baker. We have an emergency response requested. Chandler residence."

I grab the radio mic. "Baker here. Are you sure about that location?"

"Roger, Boss."

I turn to Grimes. "What the hell's going on here? We cleared this place."

He wipes his mouth. "Yeah, that was over an hour ago."

I unholster my service revolver. "Let's go."

After making another sweep of the cabin, I look at Grimes. "What are we missing?"

As we walk out to the Blazer I radio dispatch. "Baker here. Who called in that emergency from the Chandler place?"

"Came from one of those home security companies. Said they had a distress signal from inside the residence."

I gaze out over the lake. Smoke covers the whole ridge; flames are erupting out of the trees along the opposite shore. "Grimes, let's go. Stat. It's coming right at us."

We jump in the Blazer and head out to the highway. As we turn down toward town, I tell Grimes, "It's going to jump the road."

Amy

Tess points to the bright pictures up on the wall. "Shit ...."

Mercedes nudges me.

I look up. Lake's on fire.

I shake Jake—his eyes are still closed. Lean over—put my ear to his mouth. He's barely breathing. I look back at the bright pictures. Some of the rooms ... filled with smoke. Dock and deck on fire ... bright orange flames ... black smoke ... water falling out of the sky. Grab Mercedes' arm ... "We're gonna die."

She hugs me and whispers, "No, we're not ... and we're sticking together... I promise."

On the wall ... bright pictures flicker ... turn black. Everything turns black. Humming goes away. I reach for Jake, lying on the table ... find his face ... hot ... fever.

Tess screams, "Where's the damn lights?"

The lights come back on ... like they're listening to her. Not bright like they were. There's that humming again. I start over to the shelf for more water.

Tess yells, "Stop! Where the hell do you think you're going?"

I hold up my hands. "Just going for more water." Point at Jake. "Fever."

She nods, "Okay, just don't move so fast."

Grab two bottles. Open one as I walk back to the table. Pour water over his forehead. Prop up his head. Press the open bottle to his lips—let water trickle out. Some goes in his mouth. He coughs, chokes. Twitches, moans.

Tess walks over to the table. Reaches under her shirt ... pulls out the paper again. She smirks. "Here, Mr. Chandler. You should always read the fine print before you sign."

I help him sit up. He takes the paper. Squints. Reads it. When he's done he lays back, drops paper to the floor.

Mercedes stoops to pick it up.

Jake points, motions me to the drawer. "Teresa, you should read my will ...."

Tess huffs. "I don't care what it says. What the lawyer gave me is all we need." She looks at me. "Come back here."

Jake rasps. "Bring me the will."

As I walk to the drawer my back stiffens, like when Bryce is about to stick his thing into me. I reach in the drawer, lay my hand on the pistol. Lights go out again. No more humming. I clutch the gun and wait.

Tess yells, "Everybody over here."

The lights don't come back on.

Pad ... pad ... footsteps on the hard floor. Someone's moving.

I stay put.

Pad ... pad ... pad. Footsteps moving away.

"Stop." Tess's voice. "Stay close so I can see you."

Pad ... pad ... pad ... pad. Farther away.

Jake moans.

Tess says, "You awake over there, Chandler?"

He moans again.

I slip off my shoes, tiptoe to the table. Feel for Jake's hand, brush the pistol over it.

He groans.

I turn his palm up. He balls up his hand in a fist. I press the gun against his knuckles. He won't open his hand. Why won't he take the gun?

Tess calls out, her voice scratchy, like when she's spooked. "Amy, Mercedes—sound off so I know where you are."

Good she can't see us.

Pad ... pad ... pad. That's got to be Mercedes. She's getting close to Tess.

Tess calls out, "Mercedes! Amy!"

Neither of us answers.

Pad ... pad ... pad.

Tess yells, "Who's that? Speak up."

Pad ... pad.

Tess grunts.

Feet shuffle. Someone groans, gasps.

"You—you—evil bitch." That's Mercedes' voice.

An explosion a few feet in front of me—the noise almost makes me deaf. A thud—the bullet hitting the wall? Someone hits the floor. A gasp. A sigh. I hold out the pistol. Point into the dark.

Chapter Sixteen

Deputy Sheriff Baker

Back at my desk, I check with the 911 operator who took the call from Chandler's home security outfit, who gives me the company's contact info. The security consultant I connect with balks at giving me details about the installation design. Wants me to produce a search warrant. I tell him lives might be at stake. He asks for a call back number. I transfer him to Central Dispatch so they can transfer him back to me.

When he's back on the line he tells me what I hoped to hear. Whoever we tracked into the cabin didn't just disappear. There's an underground bunker with a hidden entry. I grab Grimes and we head to Chandler's. On the way, I call Dispatch, requesting backup and SWAT. They say it'll take at least forty minutes for help to arrive.

About halfway up the mountain, Forest Service has the road blocked. The fire jumped the highway above— Chandler's place is toast. A ranger tells us the ground's still too hot to let us through. I bang the steering wheel with my fist. "Dispatch got an emergency call from an underground bunker at the Chandler place."

The ranger replies, "In that case, they survived the flames and are out of danger."

My heart's pounding in my ears. "Not if they're severely injured. Fires aren't the only dangers up here."

"I'll call the captain and see what he says."

The command vehicle is in view just up the road. I sigh and nod. "Thank you."

A few minutes later a couple of fully equipped firefighters approach our cruiser. They're followed by a couple of others who are carrying armloads of protective gear. We're directed to pull over and park on the shoulder. The firefighters will take care of us. I tell the ranger, "Expect a SWAT unit about a half-hour from now. We'll need them, so be sure they get clearance to pass."

She nods and radios the message on to Command.

Amy

There's the pad ... pad ... pad, again. It's over there.

Point the gun at the noise. It stops.

Or was it over there? Wave the pistol in front of me ... right to left ... left to right.

"Amy, it's Mercedes. I'm okay. We're okay. She can't bother us anymore."

"How do I know?" I point the gun at the sound of her voice.

"Believe me. I took care of her."

Poke the gun into the dark in front of me. "Don't know I can trust you."

"She just been using us to get to at his money, and she threatened to kill me if I didn't cooperate."

Pad ... pad.

I yell, "Stop. I'll shoot."

"Okay—okay. You don't have to be afraid anymore. They're gone. Both of them. I watched her kill Bryce up on the ridge." Her voice cracks. "She was going to kill us both when she got what she was after."

"But she was your mother. You killed your own mother. How could you?"

"Maybe she birthed me, or not—whichever—she was no mother. She knew what Bryce was doing to us. She just let him keep doing it." Mercedes chokes ... sobbing. "A mother's supposed to protect her kids."

I swallow a lump in my throat. "But, RJ ... you left him out there to die. You were jealous."

She blubbers through her tears. "I tried to go back—honest. I tried to go back for him. It didn't matter to me that she said she was going to make me rich. My shoulder ... she ... she ... the pain was just too much. I couldn't fight her off. She overpowered me."

She's not sobbing anymore.

Pad ... pad.

"I said stop."

"I'm putting down the rifle. If we're gonna get out of here and get him to a doctor, we have to work together. You *have* to trust me."

"Just don't move. I'm thinking."

Jake groans.

I lean over and feel for his face. It's even hotter ... sweatier.

Pad, pad, pad, pad, pad.

I look up … trembling … grip the gun tighter … an explosion rips my ears … the gun jumps out of my hand … glass shatters across the room. I shriek.

Pad, pad, pad. Mercedes wraps me in her arms and whispers, "Shh … everything's gonna to be okay. No one's gonna ever hurt you again, I promise."

My sobbing won't stop. "I … I thought …."

"You weren't pointing that thing anywhere near me." Mercedes lets out a nervous laugh. "Guess it's a good thing I've learned to get around in the dark. In this country, you have to adapt to survive."

Feet shuffling just a few feet away. A rifle booms … nearly splits my ears.

A voice croaks. "Yeah, but never forget the rules—finish what you start and don't let your guard down."

Tess! How?

I hug Mercedes like she's all I have to keep me from tumbling off a cliff. "I thought …."

Mercedes holds me tight. "It's going to be okay."

Tess rasps. "You two are right about one thing—he's got to be alert enough to sign my papers."

Mercedes mutters, "I'd rather take my chances with what's in his will."

Tess laughs. "Always the little smart ass. To set the record straight, I did save you from Bryce. Who the hell do you think fixed it so you could escape?"

Mercedes sneers. "Yeah, but he beat me for years, and he raped me for weeks before I got away."

"I did what I had to for both of us to survive—and I took the first chance I got to get you out of there."

"But what about her? You let him go on abusing her for two more years. You did nothing to save her."

Tess grunts. "She's the reason we're in this mess in the first place. And you've picked the wrong side. So here's the new deal—we get out of here alive with my papers signed and I give you a twenty-four hour head start to disappear and never be heard from again. Cross me, and you die on the spot. I only need one of you to get what's due me." She clears her throat. "I know Amy, here, won't put up a fight. She never does."

Mercedes pulls away from me. Nudges me aside. "Guess that leaves me without much choice. So we better start saving him. We need to get him more water and see what kind of nourishment there is around here. His body's got to start building back its blood supply. Gotta fight off infections."

Tess laughs. "What? All of a sudden you're a doctor?"

"When you spend two years alone in the wilderness with boxes of books and magazines, something's bound to stick."

I touch Mercedes elbow. "I'll get some water. You can use those night eyes to see what he's got around here in the way of food."

After feeling my way to the cabinet, I bring back as many bottles of water as I can carry. Trickle some on his forehead ... try to cool his fever.

A beam of light flashes on across the room. Mercedes calls over, "Found a flashlight."

Tess spits out, "Good. Now I can keep an eye on you."

A couple minutes later, Mercedes is back with me at Jake's side. She hands me a bottle ... the bright blue liquid sparkles in the beam of the flashlight. The label says 'Energy Drink.' She unscrews the top, props up Jake's head, and tries to get him to take some.

Mercedes shines the light on Tess.

Tess yells at her, "Put that thing down—jeez. Don't shine lights in people's eyes."

"Sorry."

"Not funny," Tess screams.

Mercedes shines the light on the cabinets across the way. "We need to give him more medicine—fight off infection."

"All right," says Tess.

When Mercedes comes back, she nudges me. I watch her fill the needle just like Jake did. She hands it to me.

I look up at her ... scrunch up my nose.

She whispers, "When I give the word," she gives a quick nod over her shoulder, "stick the needle in Tess's arm and push this thing all the way down so the medicine gets in her veins."

I glance over at Tess.

Mercedes spins around and shines the flashlight in Tess's eyes. "Now," she says.

I turn ... lunge at Tess ... grab her arm ... jab it with the needle ... push the medicine into her.

Tess yelps ... jerks away ... slams the butt of the rifle into my shoulder. I drop to my knees. A few seconds later, the rifle crashes to the floor ... a loud thud ... Tess is on the floor, too, reaching for the rifle.

I scream. "Mercedes!"

Tess collapses.

Mercedes crouches down and grabs the rifle ... puts a hand on my knee. "You okay?"

I stare at Tess's limp body.

Mercedes sighs. "I recognized a word on the medicine bottle—'anesthesia.' Remembered it from one of the books

I scarffed off—uh—I guess it's okay to call him 'grandpa.' Anyway, it's a drug that makes people go to sleep so doctors can cut them open."

I lean into her, and she stokes my hair while I cry.

Deputy Sheriff Baker

Shades of grey—from ash to charcoal—nature's new palate for a landscape that used to be greens and browns. What was once a tangle of Manzanita looks more like bundles of twisted rebar. Blackened spikes—the remnants of tall pines—stick up out of the smoldering landscape. All that's left of this multi-million dollar cabin—save a crumpled, blistered metal roof and heaps of charred timbers—are blue-grey steel doors and thick concrete walls protecting the bunker entrance.

I tell the SWAT commander, "No idea who or what's in there, but somebody gave the security company operator the impression they were in trouble."

He looks at me sideways, "No shit. They were trapped in an inferno."

I furrow my brow. "A place that solid—they could have waited for the fire to burn over them. No, they wanted out of there for some other reason—just when it was supposed to be the safest place around."

"We're going to have to blast it open."

"You're the experts. Besides, I don't see any other options."

"We'll get it set up. Keep your people back until we give you the all clear."

"Will do." I motion to Grimes and the others to back up to the gravel road where two EMT trucks are standing by.

The SWAT team forms behind portable barriers as the demolition guys rig their explosives. The second they hear the blast, they'll charge forward, carrying the barriers in front, then fan out inside.

Amy

After I feed Jake more of the blue liquid, Mercedes shines the flashlight on the medicine bottle—the one Jake used on himself. She carries the empty bottle to the cabinet and searches, then she goes over and feels along the wall next to the big metal doors. When she comes back she shows me the medicine bottle and says, "This is the one."

I hold the flashlight while she fills the needle. Shine it on to Jake's arm so she can see what she's doing when she sticks it in.

She looks up at me. "Couldn't find any way to open the doors. Guess we'll have to wait for him to wake up or hope someone comes looking for him."

We sit on the floor and wait. Mercedes insists we turn off the flashlight to save batteries—except now and then, she shines it on Tess's limp body to be sure she's still asleep. She could be dead for all I care.

The air tastes stale—like we're breathing it for the umpteenth time. My cheeks burn the way they do on a hot day. Mercedes coughs. Jake groans. He mumbles something that makes no sense.

We jump up at the same time. Mercedes switches on the flashlight. I touch his forehead—clammy, cool. He turns his head away from my hand.

"Jake," I whisper.

He blinks. "Uhh ...."

Mercedes grabs the blue liquid. Props up his head. "Here, drink some."

He opens his mouth—lets her dribble some of it in. Coughs, sputters. He lifts his hand to his face, wipes his mouth, whispers, "More."

Mercedes helps him drink until the bottle's empty, then lays his head back on the table. He sighs.

"Can you hear us?" I say.

He lifts his hand off the table ... whispers something ... opens his eyes. "'S dark."

"Lights went out," I say. "The humming stopped."

He coughs. "Generator ... must've blown."

Mercedes and I shrug.

He takes a deep breath. "How long?"

"A while," Mercedes says.

He moves his head a little, side to side. Twists his body, tries to prop himself up on his elbow. "Gotta get up."

Mercedes blurts, "No. You need to rest. You lost lots of blood." She rolls him onto his back.

A sound like thunder from the big metal doors—stomping feet—men yelling, "Police! Police! Everyone down! Down on the floor!" Bright lights shining in our eyes.

"Down now! On the floor! Everybody!"

I drop to the floor and cover my head with my hands ... peek to the side ... Mercedes feet ... she's still standing by the table.

She yells at the men, "He's hurt—needs help—get a doctor in here."

A man shouts again, "Down! Everybody on the floor! You too, ma'am."

Someone shoves her to the floor. I'm too afraid to move.

I turn my head to see Jake. One of the men is standing at the table. He shouts, "I've got a pulse. Get the medics in here—stat."

Another yells, "Got another one over here. Unresponsive. Gonna need a bus for this one, too."

A hand reaches down ... someone helps me up. They're helping Mercedes, too.

A man says, "Come this way."

I peek over my shoulder as I'm pushed along. People are standing over Jake ... hooking up tubes. Others are kneeling next to Tess punching buttons on their machines.

Mercedes turns to me. "Everything's going to be okay."

Chapter Seventeen

Deputy Sheriff Baker

This is one of those times I've had to call on every ounce of professionalism and every minute of training I've accumulated over my career. The dark-haired girl sitting at the interrogation table just told us a story that makes me want to take off my badge and dispense some form of primal justice directed at the Tess woman we already have in custody, not to mention the Bryce character who's still at large. The female deputy from Central and the CPS caseworker don't appear any happier.

"Okay," I say. "Do you mind going over this one more time—just to be sure I've got things straight?"

She nods.

"You're about seventeen?"

"Yes, sir."

"And you used to live in the shack across the lake from that bunker where we found you?"

"That's right. 'Til about two years ago when I ran away."

"And that was because this guy Bryce was—uh—he was raping you?"

She lowers her head and mumbles.

"Sorry, can speak up so I'm sure of what you say?"

"Yeah," she says.

"This woman, Tess—she's your mother?"

"That's what she says."

"And Bryce? Is he your father?"

"No ... at least not to me."

"She knew what Bryce was doing?"

The girl looks straight at me. "Oh yeah, she knew."

I don't know whether to smash a fist through that two-way mirror or cry. If I do nothing else the rest of my life, I'm going to nail this Bryce creep and make sure the ADA has everything she needs to put Teresa Armato away for a good long time. I take a deep breath. "Since you ran away, you've been living in an abandoned hut?"

"Over an hour hike from the lake ... on the other side of Uncle Eric's ranch."

"But he's not your uncle?"

"No. He's RJ's."

"RJ's your friend. He helped you get the other girl free from Bryce and Tess. But, they left him up on the ridge, tied up, so he'd die in the fire?"

Her eyes mist up. "Did you find him? I mean, his body."

I swallow a lump in my throat. "We found a body. Not able to identify it, yet."

"He has red hair."

"Sorry, we couldn't ...."

She turns away—starts to cry—looks back at me. "Hope you make Tess fry for what she did ... and Bryce, too, if you catch up with him."

"You said Bryce probably died in the fire."

"Maybe. Tess strangled him with a rope—he seemed to be dead."

"Okay. Now the man in the bunker. We know him as Jacob Chandler."

"Amy called him Jake. Tess always said Mr. Chandler."

"Now, you say he's your grandfather?"

"That's Tess's story. But she might have made that up—just to get his money."

"You also said Tess claims to be his daughter."

"She claims—but she lies a lot."

"We have ways of telling if people are related. There are tests we can do. We'd need a sample—a swab from your mouth. Would that be okay?"

She shrugs. "Sure."

"Before we do that, I have a few more questions—do you mind?"

She folds her arms across her chest. "Shoot."

"The other girl ... Amy."

"What about her?"

"Is she your sister, a cousin—or what?"

"No. When I was about five, she and Bryce came to live with me and Tess—if you can call what we did living."

"Where'd they come from?"

"Don't know."

"Did Bryce or Tess ever say anything about where Amy came from—anything at all?"

"No."

"No? Never?"

"No."

I close the file. "There is one other thing—you talked about the night when you helped Amy. RJ's uncle was shot."

"I guess it was Bryce who shot him. He's the only one who was there except me and RJ and Amy. He had a shotgun. He was shooting it off—shot at Amy and me, but missed."

"Where was Tess?"

She purses her lips. "Getting it on with Uncle Eric. That's why Bryce shot him."

"Are you sure it was Bryce who was in the ranch house?"

"Yeah. He came storming out of the ranch house—into the barn, yelling for Amy and me. As much as I wanted to forget the sound of his voice ...." She points to her head, her eyes wide and wild. "I can't get him out of here."

"And later that night—you said you went to the lake—waited for Bryce to show up. When he did—at least you thought it was him—you walked up behind him with a shotgun pointed at the back of his head."

"Actually, it was more like I was coming from the side than from the back—and all I could think was that I was going to rid the world of that scum."

"But it wasn't him."

"I didn't know that at the time. Not until Bryce and Tess ambushed RJ and me on the ridge."

"Did you pull the trigger?"

Her head droops. "The door opened just as he reached for the latch. A shotgun went off ... he flew backwards ... dropped in a heap." She looks up at me. "Don't remember pulling the trigger. Can't remember the recoil."

I scratch my chin. Study her face for the slightest tic, but all I see are pleading eyes. I clear my throat. "He was shot in the face—and there wasn't any buckshot on his backside. That's what the forensics report says. So if you weren't standing in front of him, there's no way you're the one who shot him."

"Wish I could remember. Everything after the sound of that shotgun going off is a blur."

"Thank you, Mercedes. You've been a big help."

When we step out of the interview room, the case worker escorts Mercedes to meet her foster parents. A young couple has taken in both girls while CPS figures out what to do with them.

A couple of weeks later, Grimes is waiting for me.

"What do you have for me, Grimes?"

He hands me a folder. "Ballistics report, Boss."

I scan it. "So in addition to having his face blown apart with Chandler's pricey shotgun, our attorney friend, Roy Peterson, had a slug in him from his own hunting rifle."

"Yeah, it's the same weapon we found in Chandler's bunker."

"It was covered with Tess's fingerprints—and it appears Chandler never touched it."

"That's what it says, and forensics says Tess's DNA is all over Peterson's house and inside his truck. But, it doesn't look like the hunting rifle killed Peterson. The murder weapon was Chandler's shotgun."

I close the folder. "And there's an unidentified set of prints on it—matching some we found at Eric Lamb's ranch, likely belonging to this missing Bryce character."

"Yeah. The same set was all over items we collected outside the shack by the lake, the one we thought Chandler burned down to cover Bryce's murder."

"Looks like I had Chandler all wrong."

"I guess, but how do you explain the victim's blood on Chandler's shovel?"

"You said there were several sets of prints?"

"Yeah—in addition to Chandler's, one of the girls, and the unidentified person who fired Chandler's shotgun, killing Peterson."

"So it's either Mercedes smashing in the bum's face in the aftershock of Tess shooting him, or Bryce trying to plant evidence to point us to Chandler. In any event, Chandler's off the hook. Extend our apologies and let the hospital know that he's no longer in custody."

Jacob

Baker leaves it to one of his lackeys to break the news that I'm not a killer. Seems like Teresa and Bryce were the ones he should have been chasing after. I have to admit it. With those black holes in my memory, there were time even I thought I might have....

Carl picks me up at the hospital, and I insist we get lunch at the Sutter Street Grill in Folsom. Doctors say I need to build up my blood supply. I ignore their dietary suggestions—order up a big plate of biscuits and gravy that the diner's famous for, plus a side of crisp bacon, a large orange juice, and coffee.

He looks at me across his plate of chorizo and eggs. "So what's next?"

"Find Celine."

"And the cabin."

"Guess we box up the stuff in the bunker and store it somewhere. Clean up the lot and rebuild."

He takes a sip of coffee. "What about the girls?"

"I suppose part of that's up to them. They're both almost eighteen. But as far as I'm concerned, anything they need, they get. And I hope that includes spending a lot of time with an adopted grandfather."

He reaches into his valise and flashes a grin. "I have some copies of DNA reports I've been dying to show you. I just wanted to feel out your reaction first."

"I don't need DNA. I'll know Celine when I see her."

"Okay, but remember the DNA evidence they cited at your arraignment? It linked Celine to that shack."

"Sure, and if Teresa is telling the truth about her mother and me, that DNA could belong to Mercedes, right?"

He holds the file in front of my face. "Amy is the girl who lived in the shack with those two monsters—her DNA is an exact match to Celine's profile in the missing children's database."

"How can that be? I'd know my own granddaughter."

"Jake, it's been twelve years. As Ellen said—you were just a shell—"

"Of a husband and father—and I guess a shell of a grandfather, too." A lump forms in my throat. I fight back tears. My lips tremble. "The nightmare's finally over."

"I've talked with the social worker assigned to both girls. They're running a paternity test to determine if Teresa Armato is the other girl's mother. But here's the kicker—from the DNA samples they collected from the girls, it appears that they're related."

"Does that mean Teresa is telling the truth about being my—my daughter? And about Mercedes?"

"It's certainly possible."

"How soon can we know?"

"A few days."

I snatch up the check and pull out my wallet.

"Hey, what are you doing?"

"Paying—we've got to get the girls."

"Whoa—don't get ahead of yourself. Maybe—"

I hold up both hands. "Maybe what?"

"Maybe Mercedes' DNA will come back negative."

"So?"

"So, are you sure you want to get any more involved with her before you know for sure?"

"Listen, Carl. I have a granddaughter, maybe two! Sure, I've been an asshole. That doesn't mean I have to stay one. Those girls need me. And as far as Mercedes is concerned, if she's not my real granddaughter, there's no law that says you have to be related by blood to—to be family."

"It's not just up to you. CPS will decide."

"Even if I'm next of kin?"

"We don't know that yet ... and even if that's the case, it won't be automatic. They'll check you out—and Mercedes will be interviewed. Maybe she's better off somewhere else. Both those girls have been through a lot. You might not be the best—"

"I'm Celine's grandfather—and as for Mercedes, I'll adopt her. I can do that can't I?"

"Let the system work it out. If we don't like what they come up with—if the girls want to live with you—we'll appeal and let a judge sort things out."

I slump back down in my seat. "I want to see the girls as soon as possible. They need to know I'm here for them."

"Okay. I'll see what we can work out. But for all your sakes, don't make any commitments you can't keep."

"I'm not about to hurt those poor girls."

"There's one big question you haven't said a thing about."

"What's that?"

"Teresa."

"What about her?"

"What if she's your daughter?"

"And she's a kidnapper, a murderer, an extortionist ...."

"The DA'll have her DNA."

I shrug.

Amy

Mercedes told the social worker not to split us up. I agreed. So we're staying with these people in town. Bryce brought me to this house one time ... late at night ... said folks who have foster kids expect things to go missing. If I was quiet, nobody would notice. I was, and nothing bad happened.

It's different here, now ... don't know what to think. I'm scared ... but not sure what of. At least nobody makes us do chores ... they even cook for us ... and nobody comes at night and hurts us. Mercedes swiped a knife from the kitchen ... sleeps in a bed next to mine ... hides it under her mattress just in case. She keeps saying everything will be okay. I ask her how she feels about being Jake's granddaughter. She's not sure ... says being rich would be nice ... as long as I could come with her.

The social worker brings another lady with her who sticks a 'swab' in my mouth. Does the same to Mercedes. Says they're checking to see if our families are looking for us. I tell her mine never came. Mercedes asks about RJ. The woman says they don't know anything. I ask if the swab will help them find him. She says "No."

A couple of weeks later, I wake up screaming. Everything's black.

Mercedes holds me ... stroking my hair. Sweaty ... hot. I was dreaming ... grandpa standing by a lake ... a man holding my hand, tight. Grandpa always gave me cinnamon candy ... wrapped in crinkly, red see-through papers. Grandpa's cell phone rings. The man pulls my arm. I throw myself on the ground, screaming like Mommy told me. The man picks me up ... puts his hand over my mouth ... I try to bite it. He carries me off ... running. Grandpa yells ... I reach out for him. He's gone. A door clunks shut ... someone covers my head ... everything's black ... the car races off.

Mercedes tells me it's not real anymore ... just then the foster lady comes into our room. Mercedes says, "She just had a bad dream. She's okay now."

The lady asks, "Can I get you some hot cocoa?"

"No, thanks," I say.

"We'll be fine," Mercedes says.

"All right," the lady tells her. "I'm just down the hall. Let me know if you want anything."

I slip my hand under the pillow ... feel for the crinkly red wrapper from the candy Jake gave me. Clutch it in my hand ... whisper to Mercedes, "Want RJ back."

"Shh ...." She lies down and holds me 'til I fall asleep.

A few days later the social worker is back. Still doesn't know about RJ. My heart sinks. Everything I see is gray.

The lady says Jake asked if we want to see him.

Mercedes' face lights up. "Sure ... when?"

I nod. "If he wants to."

Chapter Eighteen

Mercedes

The sign on the door says *Sutter Street Grill*. There's a lot of people inside. More people are waiting on the sidewalk out front. The social worker opens the door.

I peer inside, searching for Jake's half bald head. He's sitting in back at a corner table with a couple of men. One is a big guy—even bigger than Jake—with thick silver hair. The other one, about Jake's size, has just as much hair as the big guy—only black. A tall woman in an apron is standing by their table, talking and laughing.

Jake jumps out of his chair when he sees us.

I break out into a big grin—my eyes so wide the skin on my face stretches.

When the social worker says, "Go on," I run right up to him. He catches me in his arms and hugs me tight.

"I've been dying to see you two," he whispers in my ear.

I look back at Amy. She's staring at the floor, still standing with the social worker at the door.

I wave her over. "Come on, Amy."

She shuffles toward us—her head still hanging—and stops a couple feet away.

Jake holds out an arm to Amy as he clings on to me with the other. "Come on. I owe you a big thanks. You saved my life."

Amy takes a couple of steps and leans into me—avoiding his touch. He rests his hand on her shoulder, anyway, and tells us he has some news.

As we sit down, Jake introduces Tim with the silver hair and Carl. The tall lady is Lorna. She owns the business.

I look at Jake, waiting for his news, but he hands us menus and says Lorna will take our orders first.

I ask for a big stack of pancakes and sausage.

Amy's eyes get big when she sees the humongous cinnamon rolls.

Tim says, "We saved one just for you."

She smiles for the first time in days.

Jake starts to say something, but he chokes. His eyes are misty. When he finally speaks, his voice is hoarse. "The past twelve years—for me—have been hell."

Carl says, "Take your time."

I look over at Tim, whose eyes are red.

Jake takes a deep breath. "I've searched twelve years for a granddaughter I hardly knew—I'd wasted my whole life chasing the next big deal. I had a family, but in my self-absorbed view of things they were only trophies. It wasn't until I lost the most precious part of my life that I realized I'd never taken time to know any of them—my wife, son, daughter-in-law, granddaughter. That's when I started losing my grip, could barely function. The firm I'd invested my whole life in kicked me out the door. So there I was—alone."

He reaches across the table and squeezes my hand. "Now I have a granddaughter I only suspected I had—never gave much thought to her, never looked for her." His lips tremble. He struggles to get the rest out.

Carl clears his throat. "Mercedes, your DNA tests prove that you're Jake's granddaughter—for certain."

I pull my hand away from Jake's. "Does that mean Tess is really my mother?"

Jake shakes his head. "We don't have to go there unless you want to."

Carl adds, "It's not something you have to think about until you want to, and even if she is, it doesn't have to change anything."

I turn to Jake. "Change what?"

Jake sips his coffee. "I want you to know—if it's all right with you—I want to be the best grandfather in the world. And I'm planning to rebuild the cabin with two extra bedrooms.

I glance at Amy. Her eyes are red, misty with tears.

"Does that mean Amy can live with us?"

Jake nods, his mouth quivers. "That's ... that's ...." He covers his mouth and closes his eyes.

Tim rests his hand on Jake's shoulder.

Carl sighs. "What Jake is having a hard time saying—not because he's sad, but because he never imagined being this happy—is that Amy's DNA is identical to Celine's—the granddaughter he's been searching for these past twelve years."

Jake's shoulders shake, tears roll down his face.

Amy jerks up out of her slouch, her mouth wide open.

Carl adds with a grin, "That makes you cousins."

I jump out of my chair, pull Amy out of her seat, and

throw a bear-hug on her, start jumping up and down, squealing.

Amy jerks back and runs to the door. Before taking off outside, she turns for a moment and stares at us. Tears are rolling down her cheeks. I take a couple steps toward her, and she bolts out the door.

When I catch up with her, I try to hold her, but she pushes me away. I grab her by the shoulders and shake her. "What's wrong? Didn't you hear what he said?"

She screams, "You're the granddaughter he never looked for. You have a mother, even if she is a bitch. Where is my mother ... my daddy? Why didn't they come looking for me?"

Jacob

It's the second time I've been inside the county jail. This time I'm not the one in chains, thank God.

The glassed-in cubicle where the deputy is sitting reminds me of a ticket booth at a cinema. He directs me to station #26. I sit in a stackable chair, facing a monitor that displays the image of an empty concrete-block wall. I rest my elbows on a narrow desk between me and the monitor, massage my temples, and dredge up faint memories of the bright, rising star in my old firm, Teresa Armato.

She takes a seat, and her face fills the screen. I study her for the first time, recognizing her nose and mouth as being my own. The hair, complexion, eyes—all belong to someone else. I could study her for hours and never get a clear picture of who her mother was.

"Hello, Teresa."

She laughs. "No one's called me that for ages."

"Are they treating you okay?"

She shrugs.

"I read over the paper you wanted me to sign. Don't think it's appropriate—under the circumstances."

She sneers.

"I have to be honest. I don't remember your mother."

"She said you wouldn't—or at least wouldn't want to."

"She knew me a lot better than I knew myself."

Teresa looks down. All I see is the top of her head.

"How did you get mixed up with this Bryce guy?"

"Mom never wanted me to know who my father was. By the time I graduated from the University of Chicago, she'd died of cancer. I went there on a full ride—graduated cum laude. I used what little inheritance she left to hire a private detective to help me find you.

"First, he discovered Mom had been an admin for one of the executives at a large trust in Frisco. That led him to Bryce, who worked for the trust as head of maintenance. Bryce told him he knew my Mom pretty well, and was aware she'd had an affair with the CEO at an investment firm that handled the trust's money. When the detective dug deeper, he figured out you were the CEO—and per your MO, the affair was short lived.

"I applied for a job with your firm so I could figure out whether I wanted to meet you—had no trouble getting hired. Kept my nose clean, worked hard, got introduced to Jesse. He set me up with one of the senior brokers who insisted I sleep with him to 'accelerate my career.' I was stupid—fell for his line and wound up pregnant. Of course, he dumped me. But that wasn't the worst rejection.

"When I told Jesse who I was, he was excited about having a sister, but wanted to hold off telling you—until the time was right. Then my baby bump started showing, and his wife had just learned she was expecting, too. She wasn't about to have her child share the Chandler legacy with the bastard of a bastard. He didn't have the balls to stand up to her.

"Before Mercedes was even born, I got canned. Work was hard to find—learned I'd been black-balled. Kept being told I was overqualified for minimum wage jobs, and daycare ate up almost every dime I made. Besides, I deserved better; I deserved to be accepted by my own flesh and blood. It wasn't my mother's fault she fell in love. Wasn't my fault either.

"I struggled for a couple of years, living hand-to-mouth, before reaching out to Bryce. He came up with a plan to kidnap Jesse's daughter and use her as leverage to force you to acknowledge Mercedes and me. We took the girl, but Bryce got greedy, demanded a ransom, and you refused to deal. I crumbled, spiraled into depression. The only bright spot I could hang onto was believing that Jesse was suffering just as bad as me. When the trust cut back and Bryce got laid off, he moved us out to a shack at the lake—it was on the trust's surplus property list. No one ever used it.

"After he brought us out here, he changed—everything had to be on his terms. He got more and more controlling. I was afraid of what he'd do if we didn't play his game. Besides, where would we go? Certainly not to the cops. They'd throw me in prison and things would be worse, not better.

"He didn't touch the girls in the beginning—not until they started to develop. By then I was in too deep. I tried to make myself believe it wasn't happening. After a couple of months of him abusing Mercedes, I got her out of there."

"I'm sorry Jesse didn't tell me about you."

She looks up, her jaw set. "Would it have made any difference?"

"You've got a point. Guess I was a real ass back then."

"How's now any different?"

I tap my chest. "Twelve years of heartbreak."

She nods. "Want to hear what thirty years was like?"

"I'm truly sorry."

Her voice is icy. "Too little—too late."

"The DNA tests prove you're my daughter—and Mercedes is yours."

"So?"

"So, Mercedes is taken care of for the rest of her life, exactly the same as her cousin, Celine—that is Amy."

Her chin quivers. "Then from where I sit, it was all worth it."

"Worth it?" I slam my fists on the narrow desk. "How the hell can you say what you put those girls through was worth it?"

"I said, I got Mercedes out of there the first chance I had."

"What about Celine? You stood by ...."

She hangs her head. "She was the cause of all my problems."

I sit back in my chair. Stare at the top of her head. "No. She was just an innocent child. She never did anything to hurt you. I'm the selfish bastard you should have come after in the first place. I used your mother and didn't give her a second thought. She tried to contact me after our fling. I just laughed it off. Told the receptionist to park her on hold until she went away. Eventually, your mother quit calling. I was a colossal ass in those days."

She looks up, tears welling up in her eyes. "All I could see back then was getting revenge on Jesse for rejecting his own sister. I took away the thing that caused him to turn his back on his own sister. I didn't give you or your wife a second thought, except as a way of getting what was due me. As you used to say back at the firm when we stepped on a few little guys to squeeze the last ounce of profit out of a juicy deal—you were 'collateral damage.'"

"But think about what you've done to yourself. You were the brightest, could have been the best. Now you're never going to see the light of day—kidnapping—child abuse—murder." A lump forms in my throat. "You don't know how much I regret not showing your mother the respect she deserved."

She rubs her eyes. "I know it now. Wish I'd known it a long time ago. You'll take good care of the girls?"

"The best."

"Does Mercedes know about the DNA? I mean proof that I'm ... or does she hate me too much to care?"

"She's confused."

Teresa combs her fingers through her hair. "Can I ask you a question?"

"Sure."

"Why didn't you pay the ransom? You could have saved us all a lot of grief."

My chest tightens. "Back then I thought I was God. There was nothing I couldn't control. I had the stupid idea Celine's ransom was negotiable, just like any other deal I'd squeezed the last dime out of. I don't know—I was like a shark when it smells blood. I showed up at that lake with my silver tongue, thinking I could pull off a bluff. All I got was a glimpse of her. My cell phone rang. I checked the caller ID. What can I say; it was just force of habit. She screamed. I looked up. She was gone. "

I swallow a lump in my throat. "Years of nightmares and a tidal wave of broken hearts later, here I am. Jesse said it in his suicide note, 'I gambled with her life and lost.' Every time I hear sirens or see emergency lights, my shame doubles. My mind reels with a constant loop of instant replays of that day—FBI agents and police swarming to the scene on learning the kidnappers had fled with Celine, me botching their plan."

Teresa screws up her face. "Being part of a family is all I ever wanted. Mom's loneliness taught me that."

"I'm sorry. I wish I'd shown your mother the respect she deserved. Sounds like she was a special woman."

Teresa brushes away tears. "She was … the best."

"Tell me about her."

"What do you want to know?"

"Everything. Was she a good mother?"

"She was beautiful, funny, the smartest person I ever knew—my best friend. Always there for me, telling me I was beautiful, I could do anything I set my mind to, boosting me up when life got overwhelming. But deep down, she was sad. She'd cry at night after I went to bed. Some mornings her eyes would be red and swollen. I asked her why she never married—she didn't even date. She told me she was in love once, and it didn't work out. I could tell there was more to it than she would let on. When I learned about you, I knew for sure you were the reason she was so miserable."

I sit up straight. "I know I can't undo the past, but I'd like to do right by her. Do what she'd do if she was still around. Stand with you through what lies ahead. Will you let me help? I can line up the best criminal attorneys—"

"That's not right. I did terrible things. I need to face up to what's due me."

I lean forward in my chair. "Teresa, they don't have Bryce's body. For all we know, he's still alive. At worst, killing Roy was an accident—he might have lived if it hadn't been for that bastard Bryce. And as for that homeless guy who Bryce sent up to the shack to kill you—the cops weren't able to lift any fingerprints off the shotgun. It was too charred."

She looks up at me, her eyes red, etched with pain. "That's not the point. I'm fully responsible for my actions. You may deserve for me to loathe you, but those poor girls didn't deserve what I let happen to them ... what I did to them."

I massage my temples, trying to stifle a headache that's growing more intense. "If there's any way I can help .... This time I'm not leaving my only daughter out there twisting in the wind."

"Hearing you acknowledge I'm your daughter means the world to me. That's something no jury can take away."

Celine

It's been a couple weeks since I found out my real name is Celine, and my family did come for me after all. Only, by the time he got there, Grandpa Jake was all that was left. I get sad, wondering what it would be like to have a mom and dad, a grandma. It's not that I don't love Grandpa Jake. It's just that .... Anyway, the counselor he's been taking me helps. And the nightmares that wouldn't go away aren't as bad as they used to be, and they don't come as often. I don't have to hide behind candy wrappers, either.

Grandpa has taken Mercedes and me up to the lake to show us his plans for our new home. I'm not crazy about coming back to the lake, especially the idea of living here, but he says we don't get stronger by running away from our pain. We have to become bigger than our fears. I don't know. Whenever I think of Bryce, I want to crawl in a hole.

We stand on the foundation and look across at where Bryce and Tess's shack used to be. Without the trees blocking it, the spot where it stood is in plain sight.

I take Jake's hand, then Mercedes'. "Do they know what happened to RJ, yet?"

Jake rubs his forehead. "I guess there's no good time for bad news. The body they found up on the ridge was his. I'm afraid RJ didn't make it out."

Me and Mercedes wrap our arms around Jake and start bawling. He cradles my head and holds me close to his chest. I hear his heart beating—slow as if telling us about RJ has made him tired.

"I'm so sorry," he says.

I pull away. "Does missing people you love always hurt this bad?"

He brushes a tear from his cheek. "The hurt's always there … but eventually it gets easier to bear. At least we have each other to lean on, to help us be strong."

Mercedes still clutches on to him. "Do we know what happened to Bryce?"

My heart races. All the colors are brighter for a second … then everything turns grey. "Oh God! He's coming back … I know it."

Grandpa Jake grabs my shoulders and pulls me close. "If he comes back on my watch—it'll be the biggest mistake of his miserable life."

He digs into his pocket and hands each of us a cinnamon candy, wrapped in bright red, crinkly wrappers.

Mercedes whispers, "Even if he's dead, he'll be with us—forever."

Grandpa puts an arm around each of us and kisses the tops of our heads. "We have to move ahead, not backward. Sure, we've got some horrible memories, but together we'll build new ones—good ones. When bad memories sneak up on us, we'll remind each other the difference between what's real in the present and what's only in the past. To know what to let go of and what to hold onto. None of us can handle the future alone. We're in this together—so don't be ashamed to ask for help."

I lean back and look up at him. "Maybe we can have a funeral for RJ. In the end, we're the only real family he had."

Jake nods. "I'll talk to the sheriff and see what we can do about that."

Afterward

Hello, again! It's me, Annmarie.

Are you wondering what will become of Amy, Mercedes, and Jacob? Even Tess? It's likely their difficulties have only begun.

After struggling with Post Traumatic Stress (PTSD) for more than 30 years as a result of childhood trauma, I found a way out and have enjoyed a 100% symptom free life for almost a decade. It wasn't easy and it took building a team to help me achieve it, but healing from PTSD is possible. It doesn't have to be a life sentence. Please enjoy a personal message from me and learn more about my story in a preview of *PTSD Self Help: Transforming Survival into a Life Worth Living* located at the end of this message.

That's why I wrote *PTSD Self Help: Transforming Survival into a Life Worth Living* - to give survivors a step-by-step guide for wrapping their mind around the commitment to healing, recruiting a team of 7 key individuals for support and engaging in low/no cost activities that bring off-the-couch, therapeutic results. I show survivors and their families:

- Workable, empowering tools
- How to hire a counselor
- Easy-to-follow suggestions
- Practical activities for healing
- An Emergency Plan of Action
- How to create a Healing Team
- Low/no cost DIY alternatives
- And so much more!

When trauma happens, all of the person is present—mind, body & spirit. This is why PTSD can be so difficult to unravel. Traditional on-the-couch therapy addresses mind and behavior. Western medicine addresses physical symptoms. People are left on their own to reconcile their deeper spiritual connection to what happened.

Add to this the disabling experience of being so overwhelmed by symptoms, and survivors are sometimes unable to focus long enough to read or make sense of words, which creates huge barriers to accessing traditional resources. Certainly, it's one thing to read a book, but it's something else to *experience* a book. What if there was a place PTSD survivors could go to experience the transformation talked about in PTSD Self Help?

Originating in 250 acres of evergreen rich environment found in the Pacific Northwest, The Center for Hope & Renewal could be just such a place. The only organization of its kind exclusively offering PTSD workshops and Healing Intensives to survivors and their families in an experiential learning environment, The Center for Hope & Renewal would exist to achieve the following three goals:

- To facilitate PTSD education and recovery plan development for individuals, families and industries

- To provide alternative wellness services in conjunction with traditional, trauma-focused psychotherapy for individuals diagnosed with PTSD
- To develop nationwide collaborative partnerships with agencies, healthcare/wellness providers, universities, and PTSD programs to collect and report statistics related to the study of alternative PTSD treatments

Everyone who visits The Center for Hope & Renewal for help would begin their journey with an orientation that explains the dynamics of PTSD and prepares them to develop a recovery plan —in the case of family members of survivors, a support strategy—based on the PTSD Self Help method. Most importantly, orientation participants will be guided in the formation of a Healing Team. Through partnerships with professionals who understand PTSD and how it impacts their clients (as a result of the PTSD Self Help training and certification program) The Center will offer participants high-quality, holistic Healing Team referrals to practitioners in their local area.

What Would I Learn?

You already know the damage it has caused; now learn exactly how PTSD keeps tripping you up and how to begin the healing process. The Center's PTSD Orientation will offer a two-hour opportunity open to anyone who suspects they might be struggling with PTSD, has been diagnosed with PTSD, or cares about someone with PTSD. You'll discover:

- How PTSD consistently interferes with life
- Practical ways to help healing begin
- How partnering can accelerate healing

This orientation will be a solid foundation upon which to begin creating your recovery plan, and a first step and pre-requisite for future participation in all workshops, programs, studies and intensives offered by The Center for Hope & Renewal. You can be confident of understanding exactly what to expect from the healing journey and what to do to ensure healing success!

What Are Healing Intensives?

The only thing intense about this program is the relief you'll feel! Designed to plug you into resources that will help you feel better fast, the Healing Intensives are experiential learning immersions. You'll enjoy an extended stay in The Center's lush retreat environment, consume the highest quality organic foods harvested locally and prepared by expert chefs, explore your senses in the serenity of the Ayurvedic spa, and cocoon in the luxurious comfort of individual mini-suites, where you'll surrender to deep, restful sleep in our renowned Heavenly Beds. Healing never felt so good!

By day, as you live out the Healing Plan developed during the PTSD Orientation, you will be:

- Actively doing. Experience practical collaborative healing activities and alternative wellness therapies in an environment created to accelerate your healing process.

- Actively learning. Gain an education from respected professionals who provide services that alleviate PTSD symptoms.

- Actively connecting. Journey along with other survivors who are dedicated to achieving not only a life free from PTSD, but also a life of triumph!

Thanks to you, the dream of creating The Center for Hope & Renewal is already underway. A portion of the revenue from the purchase of PTSD Self Help: Transforming Survival into a Life Worth Living goes toward building not only this amazing facility, but also an interactive, virtual reality version of it at www.PTSDSelfHelp.com. But healing won't stop there! With plans to open regional facilities and programs across the United States, hopefully one day there will be a Center for Hope & Renewal near you!

Thank you for cheering on our Ripples heroines, Amy and Mercedes. Now, a personal message from me and more about my story in a first-pages preview of *PTSD Self Help: Transforming Survival into a Life Worth* Living. Enjoy!

AE Huppert

Excerpt - PTSD Self Help

Transforming Survival into a Life Worth Living

A.E. Huppert

AUTHOR'S MESSAGE TO THE READER

Many PTSD survivors suffer years of disappointment in traditional on-the-couch psychotherapy; three months' worth of twice weekly visits was enough for me. Because of my negative experience, I didn't return to the PTSD healing journey for ten years. However, I eventually found a holistic approach to healing to be the most beneficial. Through this, I finally started listening to my intuition and began integrating other activities that weren't focused solely on my mind, as I couldn't stand having my brain picked at anymore! Surprise—these other activities opened a back door to healing my mind.

Before I learned how helpful a holistic approach to healing PTSD could be, the body symptoms were excruciating, wearing me down physically and emotionally—never mind the mental symptoms. I was so distracted by the pain I was suffering and how miserable I felt that I didn't make any connection between the intrusive thoughts, unwelcome memories, and what had happened to me during my lifetime.

Does your life sound like this (or some version of it)?

Here's some of what I was dealing with: not wanting to go anywhere without knowing where the nearest bathroom was; intense jaw pain and tension (affecting not only the ability to eat but also the ability to hear); migraines that began with a slow darkening of vision, resulting in an entire day spent in an unlit room, nursing an implosion of the brain that would make me puke until I passed out; grinding my teeth during those rare nights of sleep; loss of hair; limited mobility and chronic aching of the shoulders; a weakened immune system, resulting in susceptibility to viruses and colds; frequent episodes of tachycardia (an excessively rapid heartbeat), sweating and an unexplained sense of impending doom; digestive disorders, including heartburn, acid reflux, a burning stomach, hiatal hernia, diarrhea, hemorrhoids, and feeling like my guts were literally going to drop into the toilet bowl; unexplained nerve pain, making areas of the skin painfully hyper-sensitive to touch; a really screwed-up menstrual cycle, beginning every twenty days with severe cramping, clotting, and an abnormal amount of blood loss—often lasting for ten days, leading to anemia (or having all the nasty symptoms with no bleeding at all); unexplained "eruptions" of staph infections on my fingers and toes.

Yeah. Fun times—and that was just the physical part. After my first visit to the emergency room for a mental breakdown (when I was twenty-five years old), I did my best to bury what was coming up in my mind. As a result, the effect of the crimes committed against me erupted in my body. That got my attention. Unfortunately, I didn't yet understand the dynamics of unhealed trauma, so I traveled down more than a few rabbit trails before confronting PTSD head-on at the age of thirty-eight.

Giving up my career as a felony trial paralegal with the prosecuting attorney's special assault unit was part of the fallout from the physical onslaught. Leaving was bittersweet; it was there I'd discovered I was a crime victim. One day, I added up all the possible charges that could have been filed against sexual predator number two (there were four in my life) based on the memories I still had of the incident. A quick tally of the hash marks revealed thirty-two counts, ranging from indecent liberties with a minor to rape. That ranked up there with some of the most heinous crimes I helped prosecute. Thirty-two. That number never left my mind. My transformation had begun, and there was no stopping it.

Always the optimist, I chose to take a different view of why, only five years in, I needed to leave a career I had studied so long and hard to enjoy. The truth was that PTSD was killing me. Oh sure, to my husband and anyone else with whom I closely worked, it was obvious that my ailments were stress-induced. I was the only paralegal to nine attorneys and was working on one of the most high-profile death-penalty cases our county had seen in a long time. Without a doubt, stress was killing me slowly. However, it wasn't just the huge caseload that was the cause of my stress: what neither the people around me nor I realized was that I was still suffering from trauma related to a series of events that began when I was seven years old and continued until the year I turned forty (I'm grateful that it ended. For some, I know it never ends).

In those early years after leaving my career, I told myself that I just needed a break. Owning my own business seemed like a good way to be able to set my own schedule, and since I'm a fan of working smarter, not harder, I capitalized on my talent for guiding people in a practical way, and started a life coaching business. In the late '90s, life coaching had not yet become popular, and the term "coach" was just starting to catch on in the business world.

But I didn't want to plug in to the professional world; I wanted to reach the stay-at-home mom with a four-year degree who was living in the shadow of her husband. You know the one: she's given up everything to raise a family and support a husband, only to wake up one morning to realize she doesn't remember who she is. I brought a few other women on board and trained them to focus on their natural, relational abilities, supplemented their experience with solid, factual understanding, and connected with our lost clientele to deliver quick, three-month transformative experiences. We did well. We helped a lot of people. We felt good about ourselves and the impact we were having in our community. However, we weren't making money.

It would take a couple of business name changes and redefining our focus over a period of seven years for me to admit two things: One, I suck at the small things of business; two, my ideas are ahead of their time. But I'm great at marketing! Out of this world at innovation and visioneering (usually five to seven years ahead of the curve)! Spectacular at delivering value! Yet I stink at the minutiae that a growing business needs in order to flourish. Plus, our nation was on the verge of near financial collapse, and I could sense it coming.

I closed down Character Development Coaching (turned Life Navigation Concierges) just in time to avoid financial disaster. By now, I had multiple degrees and certifications, and had experienced a number of life-changing programs, ranging from The Pacific Institute to Landmark Education (a descendent of Est) to SGR (an off-shoot of The Secret) and ten years of dedication to the Christian church. I was ravenous for knowledge; my personal library of more than 500 self-help books, all of them read cover to cover, is proof of this. Deep within myself, I was trying to unravel the mystery of how and why the early events of my life were haunting me. If I could understand how and why, maybe I could break free of the effects. Why not help a few folks out along the way?

It seemed selfish to keep all that knowledge to myself, especially since I was finding answers. I spent a lot of time in front of audiences as a motivational speaker, in classes as an instructor, and in groups as a facilitator, although it took a number of years to break away from being asked to share my abusive history. Whenever I shared what had happened to me, I always followed it up by delivering practical steps for alleviating the pain and suffering I had known. I had thousands of letters, notes and messages from people who were thankful for the advice and found success of their own. Still, I felt inauthentic; the shadow of PTSD was still following me, and I still had unanswered questions. By this time (the early 2000s), my second marriage was falling apart, I was rapidly approaching a second nervous breakdown, and my church had abandoned me. After my life blew up for the second time, I learned that most of my physical symptoms were directly related to how anxiety shows up in my body. PTSD, being an anxiety disorder, was the root cause; however, it was a little-known program called Attacking Anxiety and Depression from a small organization in the Midwest that was instrumental in setting me on the path that would save my life. The practical advice given in the fifteen-week, home-study, recovery program gave me the relief I needed to begin making pivotal decisions toward healing—the most important of which was finding a mental health professional.

I wasn't hung up on degrees or titles when it came to resourcing myself with whatever I needed to make sense of the chaotic world my life had become. To me, normal was what worked. Period. If it didn't work, it or he or she was outta there! Fired! People didn't like that very much. As a result of having been abandoned to the ravages of men for most of my life, I was used to starting over, breaking bonds, and unfortunately, being disappointed. So, after three close encounters with suicide, walking away from relationships that were toxic (either because of the nature of the relationship or because certain individuals didn't agree with the recovery methods I embraced) was easy. My heart became hardened toward people who wanted me to be someone they thought I should be. I still have no tolerance for it, even if my heart is softer.

The look on a person's face when you say, "I've found belly dancing to be really helpful in healing childhood sexual abuse," is priceless. It's true. I've tried a lot of unorthodox activities. When a person's life is on the line, they have permission to do just about anything they see fit in order to reclaim their life. Belly dancing, along with karate, equine-assisted psychotherapy (EAP), and afternoon "play" dates are just some of the out-of-the-box activities that circumvented my intellect to bring me the healing I so desperately needed.

Child sexual abuse inflicts a unique kind of trauma in that it not only annihilates a person's sense of security and trust, but also rapes their very soul. Karate, my first experience in anything even remotely connected to self-defense, was key in teaching me that I could choose to no longer be a victim. Beyond giving me confidence that I could defend myself should someone sneak up behind me in a dark alley, my body taught me, through karate, that another's malevolent intentions can be diverted to my benefit. Similarly, belly dancing was also an effective tool. By using slight, intricate movements limited to specific parts of my body, I learned that there were whole regions of my body that I had ignored to the degree that those areas were numb. Pilates and yoga taught me how to control the chemical surge brought on by adrenaline; through their unique breathing techniques and a devotion to building strength in the core muscles, these practices helped my mind let go of its panic-stricken reactions. I began to experience balance and flexibility in my body, resulting in the belief that I could find inner balance and flexibility in my daily life, too.

Sometimes you have to do something practical and active in the natural realm to see change happen in the mental, emotional and spiritual realm. One hundred percent of the time, the change I saw was a shift in my perspective, how I was thinking about symptoms, and the story I was telling myself about how child sexual abuse was limiting me. Consequently, with PTSD safely eight years behind me, I now believe that choosing to fully engage in the healing process can be the doorway to the most profound personal transformation you'll ever experience. That's what happened for me. I know it will happen for you. I'll show you how.

INTRODUCTION
THE TREE OF LIFE

The self-help method I developed and advocate for in this book finds its foundation in two metaphors. Carl Jung, a student of Freud and himself a famous psychologist, introduces us to the first. He used a metaphor of a growing tree to describe an actively healing client. When a tree, naturally growing taller and fuller while its roots spread out wider and deeper into the ground, encounters a large stone or other obstacle, does it try to shove the stone away or demolish it? No. The roots just continue growing, embracing the obstacle and moving on.

The stone may have postponed or delayed the tree's growth for a while, but no stone, no matter how large, can stop the tree from growing. Stones in the way of tree roots symbolize obstacles to personal growth—things like an internal emotional conflict (such as loving and hating the same person) or an external stressor (such as a traumatic experience). Certain emotional conflicts are never eliminated; they are outgrown. Metaphorically speaking, pushing away or cracking stones encountered by the tree's roots is a deeply-entrenched and ineffective approach to mental illness that is shared not only by society, but also by many mental health practitioners.

Just as stones surrounded by tree roots become part of the tree, people can integrate and grow beyond their trauma, with their roots moving far past the stones in their path into new territory. A person can redirect the powerful energy generated by the trauma to their benefit, using it to pursue goals of their own choosing. Trauma, the core component in developing Post Traumatic Stress Disorder

(PTSD), can become a vital part of a person's life, just as the stones support and strengthen the root structure of the tree.

The second metaphor is my own interpretation of the healing journey. It has been said we are sojourners, travelers in this world and when it comes to walking the pathway toward transformational healing, it is one that is personally challenging in every way. Let's imagine together.

The place where you've been living has become a desolate wasteland. Out of desperation, you decide to set out on the pathway others before you have taken—never to return. Beginning this journey is filled with uncertainty and fear. Others have sent back reports of the beauty and richness of reaching a place of healing, cheering you on to freedom; however, instinct tells you the trip will not be easy. You wonder if you'll have what it takes to make it to the other side alive. You've loaded your backpack with supplies to sustain you and keep you on course. You know the general direction in which you will travel and have seen images of your abundant destination, but each step along the path is an unraveling mystery, a sometimes treacherous stumble or breath taking relief. At times, darkness reduces your visibility to only the few feet revealed by the light you shine at your feet. Other times, clear vision reveals hopeful vistas and motivating sights. One thing is certain, the journey requires all of your abilities—physical, mental, emotional and spiritual—in order to make it safely to your destination.

The all-at-once treacherous and breath taking pathway is your own transformational healing journey; a journey you set out on as a last resort to escape the pain of past trauma. You are free to detour from the path as you wish in order to gain personal insights, but decide there is wisdom in continuing along the path's general direction. Just as you would be sure to head out on a hike with a good pair of boots and a map, this book becomes the "boots" that will carry you and the map that will guide you to your destination. The solutions introduced here are supplies and tools you'll use in concert with your brain—the backpack in which you carry every single meaning you've given to events in your life. Before you know it, you are using not just your brain but all of who you are to travel this amazing path and find yourself whole, complete and restored at the journey's end. You will carry with you always the skills you learn and abilities you've honed on this healing journey. Whereas desperation thrust you upon this initial pathway, before long, you are climbing mountains of your own choosing.

By now, you've been struggling with the debilitating effects of PTSD for a while. You understand the havoc it can wreak in your professional life, your relationships, and your own peace of mind. There's no need to convince you that getting rid of PTSD for good would be a miracle! A Godsend! A huge relief! So, in this book, you won't find a rehash of depressing symptoms designed to convince you to help yourself. You and I are focused on one thing only: moving ahead toward healing your PTSD.

Is This Book For You?

Strengths-based mental health professionals who are Post-Traumatic-Stress-Disorder-savvy are hard to find—not impossible, but for someone in the throes of full-blown PTSD symptoms, it can be extremely difficult. Combine this with the overwhelming number of people being diagnosed, limited professional resources and the challenging financial circumstances of our times, and we have a recipe for an epidemic of biblical proportions.

With demand high and resources low, self-help methods are one way to get started on your healing journey. You're probably looking for self-help alternatives because you:

1. Can't afford traditional therapy
2. Don't have adequate medical insurance
3. Have had a bad experience with an agency, therapist or counselor
4. Are having to wait a long time to see a professional

The fact that you're interested in self-help methods is a good sign that you're on your way toward healing. Did you know one hundred percent of survivors with PTSD feel victimized by the original traumatic experience? Heck— that's the nature of PTSD! Because the traumatic incident was out of your control, it feels like someone or something acted upon you. This sensation can keep you paralyzed and is a key element in a PTSD diagnosis. The idea that you are ready to help yourself (even in small ways) is the beginning of a paradigm shift that will grow into a strength that will heal you.

In PTSD Self Help: Transforming Survival into a Life Worth Living, I reveal step-by-step details of how I overcame more than half a lifetime of living under the burden of Post-Traumatic Stress Disorder (PTSD). We'll take the journey together, starting at the very beginning. First, you'll wrap your mind around the possibility of healing. Then, you'll begin to develop a Healing Plan and a Healing Team. Along with easy activities and lifestyle changes, you'll start feeling better fast! Next, I'll introduce you to ways you can enjoy your new life, never to return to the fear-driven existence you endured while in the grip of PTSD. Finally, you and others reading this book, will join together in a PTSD Self Help group on Twitter, Facebook or Instagram, where you can share your experience, ask questions, or encourage one another.

Caution!

However, there's one more thing. PTSD Self Help comes with a warning label. There are two cautions:

- Self-help methods must be used in collaboration with a high-quality mental health professional . . . eventually.
- Beware of individuals who claim to have PTSD expertise—do your homework.

The nature of PTSD drives survivors into secrecy and isolation. This is a dangerous place to reside. As much as you might like to ignore PTSD's symptoms in the hope that they will go away, they won't. Although you will gain much-needed relief from implementing lifestyle changes, there comes a time when self-help isn't enough.

Unlike a cold that can be remedied with rest and fluids, PTSD requires the assistance of a very unique professional, someone I call a PTSD-informed, strengths-based mental health professional (MHP). In the chapter Season of Renewal: Recruiting Your Healing Team, I'll define this professional's qualifications, teach you how to form a healthy collaboration, and show you how to find a professional in your area. At last, you can know with confidence what to expect! With PTSD Self Help in your back pocket, you can design your own plan for overcoming

PTSD. Best of all, you can heal at your own pace, beginning whenever you are ready. Transforming survival into a life worth living is as easy as going on a journey—all it takes is commitment, planning and action. Once you're underway, moving smoothly from point A to point B is not how healing from PTSD works; it is not a linear process. However, there are clear seasons you can expect to move in and out of, or occasionally return to, over the course of your journey. Much like the growth of a tree, you'll revisit each of the four seasons many times over the course of your entire PTSD healing journey. No two traumatic incidents are alike, and neither are the survivors who experience them, so the details of each season will be different for every survivor. Generally, if you actively participate in PTSD Self Help, you can expect the following:

Season of Hope: Plan & Pack

In this first season, you're preparing for a journey. It's a mystery how long you'll be traveling this path, but you can be sure that any journey undertaken with planning and preparation will bring you to your destination quickly and safely. Season of Hope will show you what it takes to wrap your mind around walking away from PTSD forever, and introduce you to action steps as you begin preparing for the journey. But wait! Don't wave good-bye to the Season of Hope entirely. You may pass this way again to repack with new tools you've discovered along the way, and reorganize your plan to continue moving forward as you gain in confidence and healing.

Season of Renewal: Recruiting Your Healing Team

One of the biggest illusions PTSD presents is a feeling of separation—separation from your body, loved ones, helpful professionals and a normal human experience. This sense of separation is heightened if your country is barely functioning with a broken healthcare system, has a medical culture where specialists work independently instead of collaboratively, and where patients have limited access to their own medical records. During this important season, you'll interview and recruit seven key members of your Healing Team, and with their help, coordinate the team's efforts in moving yourself toward feeling better fast. Without realizing it, you'll be actively traveling the path toward healing while creating your Healing Team. Helpful questionnaires, exercises, guidelines and online resources to connect you with qualified professionals will bridge the gap between your past efforts at seeking help and this new, final push toward reclaiming a life worth living. One key task you'll complete is the creation of an Emergency Plan of Action (EPA), a step-by-step instruction guide for what to do during a healing crisis. Once again, don't wave good-bye to the Season of Renewal. You may find yourself adding additional members to your team after experiencing the next season, a Season of Transformation.

Season of Transformation: Let the Journey Begin!

By the time you reach this season, you've done the preparatory work of committing to the healing process, created an Emergency Plan of Action (EPA), developed a Healing Team, and adjusted your schedule to accommodate the difficult work you are now fully engaged in. On the other hand, maybe you've read the material about commitment, recruited professionals for your Healing Team, and have thoughts in mind for moving forward at some later time. Either way, during Season of Transformation, you'll really engage the PTSD Self Help method and continue to gather information, learn to act on your intuition, and follow through with advice from your Healing Team. Tools such as HomeWork, the InnerAction Journal, the Toy Box and Enlightenment will help you along your way. Since life never stops happening, Season of Transformation will become your constant companion; however, you'll notice times when actively engaging in healing activities will slow down to make room for other life events. Don't mistake the occasional subtlety of this season for inaction. Like plants in Autumn and Winter, there's a lot going on under the surface in preparation for Spring, but the growing never stops.

Season to Enjoy a Life Worth Living: Try on the New You!

Toward the end of your PTSD healing journey, physical symptoms and emotional roller-coaster rides are few and far between. However, something new presents a challenge: vulnerability. The heavy burden of PTSD symptoms has lifted, and a new strength emerges through knowing you can face and process the meaning of flashbacks or intrusive memories should they arise. The entire world seems new, beautiful, and even a bit intimidating. No longer driven by old ways of coping, survivors often struggle with re-entering their lives as a whole, feeling individual. This is the point of no return. You have a choice: retreat back into what is comfortable yet painful, or learn how to enjoy the vibrant life you've travelled so far to find. Season to Enjoy a Life Worth Living will help you adjust to living as a whole person through suggestions that can help you re-enter life without returning to unhealthy coping habits. Presenting lifestyle recommendations and ways to celebrate what you and your Healing Team have accomplished, this advanced season will introduce you to a new beginning and the life you were intended to live.

Are you ready to reclaim the life that was intended for you?

Copies of PTSD Self Help: Transforming Survival into a Life Worth Living are available at:

http://www.amazon.com/Ptsd-Self-Help-Transforming-Survival/dp/1460232291

You may contact the author at:

3110 Judson Street, PMB #21

Gig Harbor, WA 98335

(253) 228-9843

a.e.huppert@live.com

Acknowledgements

I am deeply grateful to my wife, Judi, for giving me space to do what brings me joy and satisfaction. Without her encouragement, none of my stories would ever come to life.

My editor, Cheryl Feeney, is another jewel. She makes me work hard, which she says builds character and characters. Her perspective never fails to make the story stronger. She also designed the book cover.

Annmarie Huppert is a key inspiration behind Ripples. Her insights into the emotions imprinted by trauma and the process of healing from those wounds have been invaluable. Her wife, Rebecca Cooper, also made key contributions, including the prism through which Amy views her world—crinkly, red candy wrappers.

Finally, with deepest respect, I thank my critique partners (all extraordinary writers) who don't let a single weak word, phrase, or idea make it into print; Michael Smith, Brett Gadbois, Barbara Winther, Jan Walker, Cheryl Feeney, and Richard Heller.

About the Author

Bestselling author DL Fowler gets inside people's heads and invites readers along for the ride. He spent much of his youth backpacking through the San Gorgonio Wilderness Area and Sierra Mountains, and earned a bachelor's degree in Humanities/English from the University of Southern California. His MBA studies at California State University-San Bernardino focused on human behavior. A career in financial counseling gave him ample opportunity to gain a deep understanding of how various people operate in stressful situations.

Made in the USA
Columbia, SC
29 October 2021